COLD CREEK
JUSTICE

R. Orin Vaughn

LIVE THE WILD WEST
R. ORIN VAUGHN
CODY, WY 2016

ISBN: 1499661819
ISBN-13: 978-1499661811

DEDICATION

Dedicated to the memory of the personalities, both men and women, who settled and helped to tame the American Southwest. Hope you enjoy.

Yours Truly,
R. ORIN VAUGHN

CONTENTS

Acknowledgments

Contents Continues

ACKNOWLEDGMENTS

Once again I wish to thank my Family and my good friend Mike Brose.

CHAPTER ONE
LAW OF COLD CREEK

I think it's about time somebody told the story of Cold Creek. My name is John Q. McCord and I was a lawman for many years. Twelve and a half of those years I spent as deputy to Marshal Emmett A. Cross in Cold Creek, Arizona Territory. Cold Creek is southeast of Tucson just over the mountains, not far from the San Pedro River. Emmett Cross, became my closest friend and we had many memorable experiences together. I remember the day I first met him; it's like it was yesterday—

My mother had traveled west to the Territory of Arizona in order to join her childhood sweetheart Quincy McCord. Quincy, my father, had come out west earlier to seek his fortune prospecting. He did well for a time, until a rockslide took his life. I wasn't quite a year old when he died. My mother took the money my father had and bought a boarding house down in Cold Creek.

Now, I've often heard tell about wild towns, such as Tombstone and Dodge City, but I'll tell you, Cold Creek could spawn many a tale of its own. I grew up in this Wild West town without a father.

When I was almost fifteen years old, some school chums dared me to steal some candy sticks from Cahill's General Store. Marshal Bob Coleman caught me red-handed. Marshal Bob, as a lot of folks called him, made me work cleaning and sweeping that store after school for a whole month.

Let me tell you, I never wanted to steal anything ever again. After that, Bob Coleman took me under his wing and we became constant companions. He told me I was a good young man, that I just needed a little push in the right direction. He said he would like to have me become his deputy someday. So, I learned all I could from Marshal Bob and looked forward to doing just that.

When I was nineteen years old, Marshal Bob told me he had recommended my appointment as his Deputy, and because I was honest and well-spoken of by the townsfolk they approved his recommendation. I was glad to accept the appointment; it was what I had been hoping for a long time.

I met Emmett Cross because of a terrible tragedy. Here is what happened-

One day, after I had been deputy for about six months, a fellow known as Wild Jack Pike rode into town from the foothills. He was a mountain man and about as ornery a varmint as you would ever want to meet. Wild Jack had murdered his wife up there where they lived in a little shack. He had stabbed her with a long bladed hunting knife. Those two were always fussing about something or other, but this time Jack had taken his skinning knife and done her in.

It was early afternoon when a local cowboy came in the Marshal's Office and told us that Wild Jack had been drinking all day long over at the Silver Stallion Saloon. He said Wild Jack was telling it around that he had, 'put his wife to rest forever and she weren't gonna nag him no more'.

There happened to be a couple of Army deserters locked up in the jail waiting to be transferred to Fort Bowie. So, Marshal Coleman wanted me to stay at the jail while he took care of the matter of Wild Jack.

The Marshal had been gone near a half-hour and I was starting to get concerned when a local dance hall girl, Sally Belle as she was known, rushed in the office crying frantically. "He's went and stabbed Marshal Bob," she said.

I jumped to my feet and said, "Wild Jack stabbed the Marshal?" I went to the gun rack on the wall.

"That's right" said Sally Belle. "With that Bowie knife of his. An' he's got a big pistol wavin' it around and shootin' it too."

I grabbed the double barrel 'Greener' shotgun from the rack, loaded it with buckshot and headed straight for the Silver Stallion Saloon. I left Sally Belle there as she was rambling on to herself.

I hurried down Main Street the two blocks to the entrance of the Silver Stallion. As I stepped up onto the boardwalk in front of the saloon I leveled the sawed off shotgun. Slowly I pushed through the double swinging doors. Right off, I saw Wild Jack leaning against the bar about half way down. He had the big skinning knife stuck in the top of the bar, still covered with blood, in one hand and a big Walker Colt in the other.

I looked to my right and saw Marshal Coleman slumped in a chair holding his stomach. He looked weak and pale. Casey March, a local gambler, was trying to help. "Doc's been sent for," he said when he caught sight of me. "I believe he's on the way."

I was young and inexperienced then, so I started for the Marshal, instead of taking care of Wild Jack right off. That was a big mistake on my part. I hadn't taken two steps when Jack raised his .44 and let go, hitting me high in the right shoulder. The force of the lead ball knocked me back and the shotgun went sliding across the floor as I fell hard on my back.

The next thing I knew when I opened my eyes and looked up, Wild Jack was standing over me with that big pistol pointed right in my face. It was like looking down the barrel of a cannon. Then the cold heartless eyes of Wild Jack looked down on me. He sneered and said, "Well kid, it just ain't you and that Marshal's day…is it?"

At the same moment that Jack cocked back the hammer on that big Walker Colt, a commanding voice from the doorway said, "It's time to end this."

"Yeah... Well... just who the hell says so?" said Wild Jack as he turned his attention toward the doorway.

"Emmett A. Cross says so," the voice said. "Now, put that smoke wagon down you big ugly jackass, or use it." The man doing the talking stepped through the batwing doors. He stood six feet or better, with rugged dark features, a long thick cavalry mustache, and being dressed in buckskins, he could have easily been mistaken for Wild Bill. This fella who had identified himself as Emmett A. Cross had his hand to a pearl handled, nickel-plated .45 Colt Army, holstered in cross draw fashion. His solid six-foot frame was topped off by a black, wide brimmed, Texas cowboy hat.

Jack grunted something and raised his pistol. Before he could get off a shot, Emmett pulled the Colt and from about seven feet away put a single shot to the center of Wild Jack's chest and then another. Wild Jack stumbled back about three steps. As Jack's knees went limp, he squeezed off a shot that went into the bar splintering a large hole in the mahogany, which is still there until this very day. Then he plunged face down into the floor, and there he lay.

No sooner had Wild Jack hit the floor than Doc Baker rushed in with Jim Hawkins right behind him. Hawk, as he was known, was the cowboy who had come down to the Marshal's Office and told us about Wild Jack in first place.

Doc Baker looked at Wild Jack on the floor as he passed by and said, "He's dead, not a thing I can do." Then he tended to the Marshal. "Better get him up-stairs boys," Doc said shaking his head. "This doesn't look a bit good."

Casey, the gambler, Hawkins and a cowboy, who was still there carried Marshal Coleman upstairs to a room.

Doc Baker came over and took a look at my shoulder. He said, "Have to get that bullet out of there, you know? It's not going to be a pleasant experience for you young man."

"Take...take care of Marshal Bob first," I said.

"Don't worry, I'm going to do just that son," said Doc. "Take him upstairs too, fellas." Emmett and Dan the bartender came over to help me. I felt extremely weak and that was the last I remembered for two days.

CHAPTER TWO
EMMETT

I woke up in my room at my mother's boarding house two days after the shootout at the Silver Stallion Saloon. As I awoke, I could barely make out my mother as she sat in the corner of the room mending something. I was trying to bring things into focus when she said, "It's about time you stirred. I've been terrible worried. How you feeling now, son?"

I started to sit up, but was so weak I couldn't. "I guess I'll do all right," I said, trying to assure myself that was so. "What's the Doc say about my arm?" I was concerned because my shoulder was bandaged and my arm was in a sling.

"Now John, don't you go worryin' yourself. The Doctor says to take it easy for a while. You were hurt pretty bad you know. You're gonna be a bit stiff for a time. Might have some stiffness in that shoulder from now on. We'll just have to wait and see. You're alive that's the main thing."

She went to the door of my room and said, "If you feel up to it, there's a fella been waitin' to see you."

She opened the door and Emmett poked his head in.

"How you doin', Deputy?" he said as he stepped inside.

"Hey, Ma," I said, "This is the stranger that saved me from getting my head blown off by that varmint, Jack Pike.

"What did you say your name was mister? Where'd you come from anyways? How long you gonna be in town?" I said excitedly as I tried to raise up again. I was just too weak, I dropped back down in the bed.

"Slow down there, Deputy," said the man as he grinned. "You'll have plenty of time to get all those questions answered."

"I'm gonna make you some broth son," said my mother, "It'll help you get your strength back."

"Yeah Ma, I'm terrible hungry," I said.

My mother left the room and Emmett pulled up the chair she had been sitting in. He reached over and shook my left hand.

"You're John McCord, Deputy Marshal here in Cold Creek," he stated. "My name is Emmett Cross. I've been doing some scouting for the Army out of Fort Bowie. I felt it was time to move on, do something else. Before I left, Lieutenant Carlson asked me if I would travel out here and pick up a couple of prisoners. Being a good friend, I told him I would. That's how I came to be at the saloon when that hombre was about to put you away with that hand cannon."

"Just a minute," I said. "I've only been thinkin' of myself here. How's Marshal Coleman?" I feared what the answer might be.

Emmett paused and looked away. Then he said reluctantly, "Sorry I have to be the one to tell you Deputy... he didn't make it. He died a few minutes after they took him upstairs."

"What? Marshal Bob dead?" I said. "No... He was one of the best. Hard to believe he's gone."

That was a very difficult thing for me to swallow. I looked up to Marshal Bob Coleman; he had been like a father to me.

"The prisoners back at the jail?" I said, "Who's takin' care of those deserters right now?"

"I got your Blacksmith watching them. He seemed to be a trustworthy sort. And some townsfolk said he had stood in as extra deputy before," Emmett said.

"Yeah, Ben Decker will do all right," I said. "It's just awful about Marshal Bob though." I wondered and asked, "Who's gonna take his place and be Marshal now?"

"I guess you will be in line for the job, Deputy," Emmett said.

I instantly protested saying, "O-h n-o, not me. I don't mind bein' the deputy around here, but I ain't never had any notions at all about bein' the Marshal. I just ain't ready for that."

Emmett leaned back in the chair and said, "Well, I'm sure they'll come up with somebody. Listen Deputy, now that I know you're gonna be all right, I'm gonna collect my prisoners and head back to Fort Bowie."

"Emmett," I said, "I sure wanna thank you for steppin' in and savin' my hide like you did."

"Glad I was there to step in Deputy," said Emmett. "You take care of yourself." Emmett got up and went to the door and turned. "Do what the Doc and your Ma tells you, son. Get yourself healed up. See you, Deputy," he said as he opened the door.

Emmett would be just the man to take Marshal

Coleman's place I thought to myself. "Hold on there, Emmett," I said. "Why don't you take the job as Marshal? You'd be just the right man for the job."

He quickly responded saying, "Naw... not me Deputy. I had my fill of wearing a badge back in Fort Worth. I'll be seeing ya around." Emmett turned back and slipped through the door. I figured that was the last I would be seeing of him.

I wasn't so sure I even wanted to be a Deputy Marshal anymore without someone like Marshal Coleman or Emmett. After all, it never got me anything but shot up. I thought about the townsfolk. They trusted and depended on me, they respected me even though I was young and somewhat inexperienced. I couldn't let them down.

In about a week I was up and around. Though I didn't have much use of my right arm I still made my rounds through the town. Fortunately, I was pretty handy with either hand. I could carry the 'Greener' shotgun with me and support it with my bad arm without too much trouble. The 'Greener' carried a lot of authority when it came to dealing with a crowd of drunken cowboys.

Since I had turned down the town Marshal's job, Mayor Potts told me he had sent a wire to recruit a new Marshal, but hadn't received an answer yet.

Things were quieter than usual around town since the incident with Wild Jack. That was good for me, it made my job a lot easier. Then a couple of days after I had talked to the Mayor, I saw Judge Bryant. He told me that they had just received a wire informing the town that a new Marshal had been recruited and would be arriving in a few days. I couldn't help but wonder what kind of man this new Marshal would be. Two days later I found out. It was about sundown and I was sitting down to some fried chicken my mother had sent over to the Marshal's Office for my supper. I planned to eat before making my evening rounds. There was a knock at the door; not many people would knock before coming in at the Marshal's Office, so I was curious as to who it could be.

"Come on," I said toward the door. In walked Emmett, boy was I surprised. "What the heck are YOU doin' here? Why, I didn't think I'd ever see your face around here again."

"Hello there Deputy," he said as he peeled back his buckskin jacket and revealed a tin marshals star pinned to his faded red flannels.

"You…You're gonna be the new Marshal?" I said. "I thought you didn't wanna be a lawman anymore."

"Ain't a fella got a right to change his mind once and a while?" said Emmitt.

"Why…Why, sure he does," I said. "But, don't just stand there in the door. Heck, this is your office, you are the Marshal you know."

With a bit of a smile on his face Emmett sat down and began to explain saying, "Well Deputy, I figured I ought to stay put for a while and this seemed like a good place to do it. I mean, it seems like a nice little town to settle in. Besides, it's steady income." He paused, then said, "That is, unless you want the job?"

"N-o sir, I ain't changed my mind," I said. "I'll be more than happy to let you do the Marshalin' around here. I'm glad to have you Emmett."

"Say Deputy," Emmett said as he looked the place over, "I'm ready to shed these buckskins for some more civilized clothes. And, I'll be needing a place to stay too. You reckon your Mother might have a room for me at the boarding house?"

"Sure Emmett," I said. "I mean, it's Marshal Cross now. Ma will be glad to give you a place. If you don't mind waitin', I'll finish my supper and then walk you over to the boardin' house as I'm makin' my evenin' rounds. Here, have a piece of Ma's fried chicken, it's mighty tasty."

Emmitt took note of the plate of home fried chicken as he placed the rifle he was looking at back in the gun rack. Emmett picked a drumstick and pointing with it he said, "I reckon we ought to put a lock on that gun rack." Emmitt bit off a mouthful of chicken and shook his head approvingly. Then he agreed to wait on me.

I told him he would have to wait until morning when Cahill's General Store opened to get some new clothes. After we finished eating and made a check around town, we went over to the boarding house and my mother got him settled in for the night.

The next morning when Emmett came in he was wearing a new pair of canvas pants and a new frontier shirt. However, he was still wearing that buckskin jacket over the shirt. The Texas cowboy hat was the same too, although it had been brushed and cleaned.

Over the next twelve and a half years, I learned a lot about what kind of stuff Emmett was made of, and some about his background.

He was born in Indianapolis, Indiana in the late forties. His father was a city constable there, and was a strong believer in law and order. He was a man who would not back down from a fight if it meant keeping the peace. Never heard much about his mother, though I realized Emmett had loved her very much. She had died not long after his sixteenth birthday of scarlet fever. He had an older sister and a brother who was two years older than him. His brother joined the Union Army right after their mother died, and Emmett did the same as soon as he turned seventeen. A cannon shot during the Civil War killed his brother, and Emmett himself was wounded twice before the war ended.

When he returned home from the war, Emmett and his father had a falling out over his running off and joining the army, and over land he thought he was entitled to since the death of his mother and brother. Emmett left embittered, never to return. Emmett then headed west to Texas and although he held a grudge against his Father, he still respected his strength of character and his principles of law and order.

Emmett wandered around Texas, doing a little bit of everything. He did some trail herding, rode stagecoach shotgun, even was a Deputy Sheriff in Fort Worth for a time before coming to Fort Bowie to scout for the Army. I heard tell that while Emmett was Deputy Sheriff he had stopped a gunfight one night between Bill Kelley, a notorious shootists, and a cowpuncher. He had done this by getting between the two men and standing nose to nose with Kelley. Then Emmett challenged Kelley to either make his play or just forget it for the night, telling Kelley it wasn't worth it.

After a brief staring match, Kelley said, "I got no fight with you. I'll finish it with the cowboy another time."

Emmitt said, "That's a good idea," and Kelley loosened up and left the saloon to drink elsewhere for the night. Emmett had probably saved the cowboy's life, for that night anyway. Bill Kelley was a seasoned man-killer and wouldn't have minded at all putting one more cowboy down, but Emmett stood firm and Kelley backed off that time.

It wasn't three days after Emmett arrived in our town that some fellow calling himself Clarence Pike rode in claiming to be Wild Jack's brother. Nobody even knew Wild Jack had a brother. This character started spreading it around town that the ones who were responsible for Wild Jack's death were claim jumpers, and had killed him to steal his claim and the gold Wild Jack supposedly had found. This was somewhat ridiculous, because no gold had ever been found around the Cold Creek area. Just the same, in and out of the saloons mostly, he got a few of the unscrupulous townsfolk stirred up, and they wanted an inquiry into Jack Pike's death.

Now, most of the citizens knew what kind of a man Wild Jack had been, and they believed he had got what he deserved. However, there had been enough of a stink raised by this troublemaker that

Mayor Potts had Judge Bryant open an inquiry as to just what took place that afternoon at the Silver Stallion Saloon. So about a week after this Clarence Pike fellow hit town, there was an inquiry held right there at the Silver Stallion Saloon where it had all happened. This was due to the fact that there had never been a Court House built in town, there had been talk about building one but nobody ever made any plans for one.

You see, Cold Creek wasn't what you would call a big town at the time, but it was slowly starting to grow. The town had the only source of water for a long way and being on the new railroad line the train stopped here to take on water for the steam engine and to drop off mail. Cold Creek was also an overnight stop for the stage line. It stopped to get fresh horses and to let the passenger's rest up, before heading out again for Benson and Tombstone. This kept the town going pretty good. Two cattle ranches just outside of town helped also, by keeping a constant flow of cowboys in and out. The cowboys came to the saloons for entertainment and gambling, so there came to be three saloons and no courthouse. The talk about building one really never came to anything. Gold had been discovered in the mountains in my father's day, but it seemed to peter out pretty quick although rich deposits of silver had made a boom town out of Tombstone. Now, there was only an occasional prospector in the hills.

The Chambers' Bar-C Ranch was north of town about three miles. It was a fair sized spread, with five or six hundred head of cattle. The Chambers' were very honest, hardworking ranchers and good people to know. They had a half dozen or so ranch hands around, mostly members of the family. Then there was the Rocking W, a questionable outfit to say the least. They would have maybe eight hundred to a thousand head on the open range at times. There were always fifteen to twenty cowboys, from most anywhere, hanging around at the ranch. Two brothers, Jesse and Terrance Wonderland ran the Rocking W.

Terrance Wonderland, the younger brother, loved coming to town and raising cane with the other cowpunchers from their ranch. Jesse was more reserved and kept to himself most of the time, but he was always there to bail his brother out of trouble. The Rocking-W was five miles southwest of town, and not too many people liked riding out that way.

There was this young lawyer in town by the name of Thomas Boone. He was fresh out of some famous law school back east. Being eager to build a reputation for himself and having just hung out his shingle, Boone readily took up Clarence Pike's cause at the inquiry.

The afternoon of the shootout at the Silver Stallion Saloon, there had been five witnesses besides Emmett and myself, who saw what happened with Wild Jack. First, there was Sally Belle, then Jim Hawkins and another cowboy from the Bar-C Ranch, Pat the bartender, and finally, Casey March, a gambler who made his living playing poker with the cowboys who came in town. Rumor had it Casey was pretty handy with a six gun. However, Casey always kept out of affairs that didn't involve him personally.

CHAPTER THREE
PIKE'S CONSPIRACY AND SALLY BELLE

Ben Decker, who owned the livery stables and was the town's blacksmith, served as bailiff whenever Court was held. Whenever there was a need he also would be appointed Special Deputy. The inquiry was all set up in the saloon and Ben called court to order, with the announcement, "No more drinks bein' served. Court's now in session, the honorable Judge, Francis Walter Bryant presiding. Everybody sit down," he said.

Judge Bryant entered from the back room of the saloon and sat down at a table that was set up in front of the bar. The judge was one who believed that carrying a gun was part of living in the West, where a lot of time the gun was the Law; probably the reason there was never a gun ordinance in Cold Creek. In fact, Judge Bryant carried a double-action Colt under his coat, one like Billy the Kid was known to carry. Judge Bryant was a tough old crow and he always took that pistol out and laid it on the table when holding Court.

One time, before I became Deputy, a man whose brother was being sentenced to hang for murder pulled a pistol, and Judge Bryant shot him dead where he stood. Everybody had respect for Judge Bryant's Court after that. The Judge was tough all right, but he was one of the fairest men I have ever known.

Judge Bryant told lawyer Boone to, "Get on with it. So, we can get this inquiry business over with."

Boone started pacing back and forth, telling the onlookers how he was going to prove there was a conspiracy to kill Jack Pike and steal his claim and the gold he had found. Judge Bryant interrupted, "Ah, hog wash, Boone," he said. "Settle yourself and call a witness."

"But, Judge...," said Boone. "I mean your honor." Boone tried to explain, but Judge Bryant just cut him off again, and told him to call a witness, or he was going to dismiss the inquiry for lack of evidence.

"All right your Honor," said Boone and he called out, "Then I call Clarence J. Pike to the stand."

The fellow that stepped forward was wearing buffalo skins and had at least a week's worth of whiskers on his face. A big chaw of tobacco bulged in his jaw and he pulled a dusty old cowhide hat off his head as he walked up to the table where Judge Bryant was. Ben swore Clarence Pike in and he sat in a chair beside the table.

Judge Bryant gave Pike a frosty look, leaned toward him and said, "Just what is this notion you got that somebody murdered that good-for-nothing brother of yours anyway?"

"JUDGE?" said Boone in protest. "I object, this is my witness."

"And this is my Inquiry. Look here Lawyer Boone," the Judge said, "This is an inquiry, not a damned trial. I aim to get to the truth, not play law-school games with you. This man has made serious accusations about some of the good citizens of this town, and I'm gonna get to the bottom of it quickly.

And, if you get in my way again, I'll have you arrested and thrown in the town lock-up for contempt of court. Do I make myself clear to you, young lawyer?"

"Yes sir, your Honor, I understand you," Boone said.

"Good," said the Judge. "Now sit down and shut up, and I'll let you know when you can make your speech."

Judge Bryant turned to Clarence Pike again and said, "Well, let's hear what it is you got to say about this so-called conspiracy, Pike. It better be good."

Pike looked for a place to spit his chaw, but there was no cuspidor close. He looked at Judge Bryant, who gave him an impatient hard look. So, Pike swallowed hard, choked a little, then started in with his sad tale as he leaned forward and fed the brim of his tattered hat through his hands.

"Well yar'onor, I waz'a getting' ready ta carry a load'a dynamite down ta Tombstone, with me mule team, fer da silva mines, yuh know. Dat's when I got da news dat my dear bruder, he'd been shot dade. Well yar'onor, I's so grief strickin', I couldn't hardly make da trip. After I dropped off dat dar dynamite, I got ta tinkin' 'bout dat claim my bruder had showed me. He went'n told me one night in Bisbee, when we were a drinkin', dat he knew dar were gold ta be found. So's when I comed up here, I waz'a nosin' round ol' Jack's cabin. Dat's when I found dat dar claim paper dey must'a killed him fer."

"Let me get this straight," said Judge Bryant, "You base this whole thing on a claim paper? I don't suppose you have those claim papers with you now, do you?"

"Sheer," Pike said, "I got'm, ri'cheer." Pike took some old wrinkled up, yellow papers out of his shirt. Judge Bryant snatched them out of Pike's hand and looked them over carefully.

"Why, this claim's been expired for well over a year now," said Judge Bryant. "Besides, I don't know of anyone in this town besides you and your brother who would think there's any gold where this claim is staked out."

The Judge called to Mort Cahill who, besides owning the general store, was the town assayer, and asked, "Jack Pike ever bring in any gold samples to you, Mort?"

Mort stood up and answered, "Nope Judge, never did see any gold from Wild Jack, only a few bear skins once in a while."

Lawyer Boone got up and cautiously moved toward Judge Bryant. "Excuse me Judge," he said. "May I bring something to your attention, please?"

"Yeah, go ahead," said the Judge. "Let's see where this thing is going."

"Judge Bryant," said Boone, "You see, just because the claim is expired does not mean Jack Pike was not murdered. If I could be allowed to call Sally Belle to the stand?"

"Now hold on there, Boone," said Judge Bryant. "Just what's Sally Belle got to do with this?" Boone was treading on some dangerous territory calling Sally Belle up to the witness chair. I mean, everybody in town knew Judge Bryant and her were sweet on one another.

"Now Judge, she was a witness to the killing," Boone said.

"All right Boone," said Judge Bryant, "but I'm warning you, my patience is wearing mighty thin with you. Go ahead, call her." You could see Judge Bryant was getting tired of all this, especially since Sally Belle was to be involved.

"Sally Belle, come on up here honey. Answer some questions for this greenhorn lawyer. Pike, you go on over yonder and sit a spell," said Judge Bryant, his tone was a lot calmer when he spoke to Sally Belle.

After Pike sat down, Ben swore Sally Belle in as a witness. Sally Belle was wearing an emerald green satin dress that matched her eyes and accented her full head of thick red hair. Her hair was pulled back in a bun and topped with a black plumed hat.

Sally Belle sat down in the witness chair proper, like a lady and Boone stepped up and started in, "Sally Bel-l-e?" he said. "Now.., that is an interesting name. Tell me, is that your real given name?"

Sally Belle looked over at Judge Bryant for help. "Judge?" she said softly.

"Sorry darlin'. You'll need to answer his questions truthfully. Go ahead and tell him your real name."

Sally Belle whined as she stomped her foot, then looked around the room and said, "It ain't that I don't love my Daddy. I just like Sally Belle, better'n the name he gave me, that's all."

"Yes...And, what is that name?" said Boone.

"Beulah May Salukis. NOW," Sally Belle said, "you happy, you...you pimple faced little jerk?"

Sally Belle stood up and took a swing at Boone. She missed however and fell back down in the chair crushing the bustle of her dress and knocking a long red curl of hair down in her eyes.

Everybody just hee-hawed, which really riled Judge Bryant. He grabbed his Colt and fired it in the air. "I'll have order in this court or I'll have the whole lot of you thrown in the lock-up and fined twenty dollars," he said. When Judge Bryant fired his pistol about half the towns-people there hit the floor, and everybody got straight-faced in a hurry.

After the smoke cleared, the ones on the floor got up slowly and sat back down cautiously.

Judge Bryant looked across the crowd, then at Boone. Through his teeth he said, "This is a Court of Law and it's gonna be held respectably. Boone, I'm telling you for the last time...go somewhere with this or they just might be trying me for murder, if you catch my point?"

"Yes sir, Judge," said Boone. "You will see, I am going to tie all this together, yes sir, I am."

"Then do it quick, or else I'll not be responsible for the consequences," said Judge Bryant.

"All right now, Sally Belle. Tell this Court how long have you lived in Cold Creek?" said Boone.

"Well, about a... little over a year, I'd guess," Sally Belle said. "What's that gotta do with anything?"

Boone walked slowly around the room then stopped beside the witness chair. Looking away with his chin in the air Boone said, "Where were

you before that, and what did you do for a living?"
It was clear Boone's actions were supposed to make
Sally Belle uncomfortable and it seemed to be
working. She, no doubt, wondered what his
question had to do with the inquiry. Most
everybody there was wondering the same thing.

Sally Belle answered his question with a
puzzled look on her face saying, "I come up from
Bisbee. I was a dancer on the chorus line at the Star
Light Palace Saloon. It caught fire one night and
burned out the inside so bad that it had to be torn
down. That's when I came up this way to work at
the Silver Stallion. There ain't nothin' wrong with
that now, is there?"

"No," said Boone. "Nothing wrong with that.
Tell me though, Miss Sally Belle. Don't you have
part ownership of this saloon, that is the Silver
Stallion Saloon that we're all present in right now;
and where Jack Pike was murdered?"

"I don't know about any murders here mister,"
said Sally Belle. "But I sure do have part ownership
of this saloon. And, let me tell you something too; I
saved a long while and did without things I would
like to have had for the money I had to invest. And
when an opportunity came to buy into a business, I
took it. Now, I don't know what that's got to do
with that no-good Wild Jack Pike a dyin', but that's
sure enough what I did."

"Well, tell me this then Miss Sally Belle," said
Boone. "Did you ever entertain cowboys at the
tables in the Star Light Palace Saloon?" Boone
turned quickly and looked her straight in the eyes.

Sally Belle didn't seem at all rattled by his

question, as it was obvious Boone thought she would be. She said, "Hells fire yes I did. That was part of the job after the show was over. The girls were supposed to go out and help the customers have a good time. We made'm feel good. I had a lotta good times and don't feel a bit guilty about it." The crowd smiled and chuckled at her answer.

Continuing Boone said, "Now Miss Sally Belle, you should think about this before you answer. Did you ever entertain Jack Pike and his brother Clarence at the Star Light Palace Saloon?"

Sally Belle sat back in the chair, crossed one leg over the other, and pushed the hair out of her face and answered saying, "Mister, I entertained a lotta drunk cowboys, and I would sure try an' forget those two real quick if I ever had anything to do with them in the first place, that is." Sally Belle smiled at the crowd, being pleased with her answer. Everybody got a little chuckle out of that too.

Accusingly, Boone raised his voice and said, "Here is the thing, Sally Belle. I think you remember all right. You entertained Jack and his brother Clarence." Boone pointed at Clarence. "You got them drinking heavy, and then you sweet-talked Jack Pike into telling you about his claim and the gold. Then, first chance you got, you came up here, conspired with the Marshal and that Cross fellow, who you knew from Bisbee. Yes, conspired." Boone looked at the crowd. "Conspired to kill Jack Pike, steal his claim and the gold he had found."

"You can damned well think what you want; NO, I ain't never done nothing like that in my whole life," said Sally Belle crying out as she stood up stiff with anger.

Judge Bryant had all he could stand and the townsfolk, except for a few no-counts, felt the same way. Everybody in town except probably Boone, knew that there wasn't a more honest man to be found than Marshal Bob Coleman.

Judge Bryant stood up and raising his voice he said, "BOONE, SIT DOWN. And, don't you say another damned word... cause if you do, I'll have you tarred and feathered, then run out of town on a rail. I'm takin' over this inquiry right now."

Judge Bryant pointed at Boone and said, "Emmett, if that darn fool even so much as breathes funny, I want you to take him out, hog tie and gag him."

Emmett who had been leaning against a door post observing quietly said, "Be my pleasure Judge, to do just that." Emmett gave Boone a harsh look.

Mayor Potts hadn't said a word through all of this. He and Judge Bryant had known each other for a lot of years and the mayor had pretty well always trusted his judgment. "Mayor," said the Judge, "I'm gonna conduct this inquiry from here on out, unless you got some objection to that." He sat Sally Belle back down in the witness chair.

"No, I have no objections at all Judge Bryant," Mayor Potts said. "In fact, I think it's about time you did."

The crowd mumbled among themselves as they shook their heads in agreement with Mayor Potts' decision. Judge Bryant looked into Sally Belle's eyes and said, "All right now Sally Belle, I just want you to tell us about the events that took place the day Marshal Bob Coleman and Jack Pike were killed. In your own words, what did you see and hear?"

"Judge, I don't never remember seein' Wild Jack, or his brother before I moved up here, honest," said Sally Belle. "I never ever got anybody drunk to steal from them."

"Alright darlin'," said the Judge, "I believe you, and I'm sure the good folks of this town do too. Just tell us what you saw and heard that day, that's all."

"Okay Judge. I think I'll be able to do that," Sally Belle said as she settled back in the witness chair.

"Wild Jack come in early that day, must'a been ten o'clock or so. I'd just come down to the bar as he walked in the door.

"Pat was behind the bar washin' glasses. Casey and two cowboys were playin' poker. You could tell Wild Jack had already been hittin' the whiskey pretty hard. He came over to the bar, bought a bottle and nursed it till early afternoon. All day long he mumbled to himself. Though nobody paid him much mind he mumbled to everybody that came in about how he'd shut her up, and she weren't gonna nag him no more. I just knew he was talking about something bad he'd done to his wife.

"Then Hawk.., excuse me, I mean Mr. Hawkins, asked him, how he was keepin' her from naggin' him. That's when he pulled out that big huntin' knife of his and stuck it into the bar and said, 'Never yuh mind how cowboy, I jest did and that's a fact. I jest did it all right'.' A few minutes later Hawk...I, Mr. Hawkins left."

Tears started to well up and roll down Sally Belle's cheek. Judge Bryant handed her his handkerchief and said, "Now, take your time darlin', I know it's hard but, we need to hear just what happened."

Sally Belle dried her tears with the handkerchief, then started in again saying, "Then Mr. Hawkins left, he must have went for the Marshal, cause about ten minutes later Marshal Bob come in and walked over to Jack. They had some words, and then...then, Wild Jack pulled his Bowie knife out of the bar and stabbed the Marshal. Marshal Bob tried to pull his pistol, but...but..." Sally Belle was sobbing so much that we couldn't quite understand her.

Judge Bryant put his hand on her shoulder to try and comfort her and said, "Now, just take it easy Sally Belle, go on when you can."

She wiped her eyes again and said, "It was just awful Judge. He pulled the knife out of the Marshal and stabbed him again. The Marshal stumbled back. Casey and the cowboy helped him to a chair. Pat grabbed for his ax handle that he kept under the bar, but before he could do anythin', Wild Jack pulled his pistol and stuck it in Pat's face. He told Pat that it wasn't a good idea. About that time, Mr. Hawkins stuck his head in the door and Wild Jack started to shoot at him, but I screamed and he missed. That's when I ran out of the saloon. As I was leavin' Casey said, 'Better get Doc Baker quick'." Sally Belle paused for a minute and asked for a drink of water.

29

Emmett went outside to the pump and brought a tin cup of water. After sipping the water Sally Belle continued saying, "Mr. Hawkins was on the porch ducked down. I told him to go get Doc Baker, and I'd be goin' for the Deputy Marshal. I didn't want to go back there, so after I told the Deputy what had happened and I stayed in the Marshal's Office. That's all I know Judge."

Judge Bryant looked at Jim Hawkins and the other cowboy who had been there at the Silver Stallion and said, "Hawk, that the way you boys seen it?"

"Yes sir Judge, we see'd it that way," Hawkins said.

The other cowboy agreed nodding his head and saying, "Yeah. That's the way it happened."

The Judge turned to Casey and said, "How about you Casey, anything to add?"

"Not a thing Judge," said Casey, "those would almost be my exact words if I were to tell it."

"Will you all swear to that under an oath?" said the Judge.

"Sure will," said Hawkins and the others in agreement.

"Then you all stand and raise your right hands," Judge Bryant said.

"Do you swear what was told was the truth so help you God? Say you do, if you do," Judge Bryant said and they all nodded their heads and said they did.

Judge Bryant told them to sit down and he said, "Pat, did you hear the conversation between Marshal Coleman and Jack Pike?"

"Heard every word said," Pat said.

"Ben, swear him in," said Judge Bryant. Then he said to Pat, "You come on up here and sit a spell. I wanna hear what you got to tell us about the conversation that led to both of these men ending up dead."

Pat hurried to get sworn in and sat down. He looked like he'd just been itching to tell his side of the story. Never knew what nationality Pat was, but he started right in with his backward English to tell what he had seen and heard.

He said, "Just like Miss Belle said it. Wild Jack had been saying all the day, 'he had shut her up, and she would no more nag him'. Then in come the Marshal, Marshal Bob not the new one. He asked Jack, 'How did you shut her up, Jack?'. Jack would not tell. Marshal told him, 'Hand over your knife and pistol, then you and me will take a ride up to your place and see'. I tell you, wrong thing for the Marshal to be saying.

"Jack said, 'No, I'll show you how I shut her up'. Jabbed him with the knife that rotten man did, right into his guts. Two times he stuck the Marshal."

Pat paused to catch his breath and then continued saying, "Club him down I was, but to my head he put that big pistol. In came the Deputy. Shot him down, Jack did. Walked over, was going to shoot the young Deputy in the head, he was. In come the big fellow. Called him a jackass, he did. To get his attention away from the young man on the floor, I am pretty sure.

"Raised up his pistol to shoot the big fellow

over there, Jack did," Pat nodded and pointed to Emmett. "His pistol he pulled out first, and shot him. That is what did happen and Wild Jack was no more." Pat got up and started over to sit back down with the crowd.

Judge Bryant stopped him by saying, "Just hold on a minute there Pat. Ain't nobody dismissed you yet."

"All I had to, I have said. I will be going to sit down here now," said Pat.

That is sure enough what Pat did, sat down where he was before and folded his arms in front of himself.

I guess Judge Bryant saw no purpose in pursuing the issue, so he said, "Thanks Pat, we do appreciate your eyewitness testimony." Pat nodded just once.

Judge Bryant addressed me now and said, "Deputy McCord, I think it's about time we heard you. Come on up and get yourself sworn in."

After I took the oath and sat down, Judge Bryant said, "Just tell us in your own words what happened that afternoon and what you saw, Deputy."

I started out by telling about Jim Hawkins coming into the Marshal's Office and how he was concerned with what Wild Jack Pike had been saying most of the day about his wife. I told how Marshal Coleman went to investigate leaving me to watch the prisoners at the jail. I told how I got to be at the Silver Stallion Saloon after Sally Belle had come crying into the office. I mentioned my error in judgment, not dealing with Wild Jack right off and how if it hadn't been for Emmett Cross, I wouldn't be alive to tell the story.

"That's about the end of it Judge," I said, "Except for you and Ben ridin' up to Jack's place and findin' his wife stabbed to death."

"Thank you Deputy McCord. That's all we'll be needing from you for now." The Judge dismissed me and I went over and stood by Emmett at the door.

Judge Bryant said, "For all of you who haven't already heard, Ben and I rode up to Jack's place which ain't no cabin, more like a lean-to. Anyway we found his woman run clean through. She was such a little thing, it wasn't a pretty sight.

"Emmett," the Judge said, "I reckon we'd better hear your side of this thing, so we can put it to rest once and for all. Come up and get sworn in."

Emmett sat down in the witness chair after being sworn in. Judge Bryant said, "All right Emmett, tell everybody here just how you got involved in this fracas."

I could tell Emmett didn't care a bit for the whole business of this inquiry, but he realized it was necessary because of the accusations made by Clarence Pike.

Emmett scooted around in the seat like it had splinters in it, but he just couldn't find how to get comfortable in the witness chair. After a few adjustments in the chair, he started telling how he came to be there when all of this took place.

"Well, back when this happened I was scouting for the Army, out of Fort Bowie. I'd decided it was time to move on to something else, maybe settle somewhere for a spell. I was tired of driftin' and working for the Army. Before I packed up to leave Fort Bowie, Lieutenant Carlson asked me if I'd ride over here to Cold Creek and pick up a couple deserters and bring them back before I parted. I agreed to do it only because the Lieutenant and me had become kind of close after fighting our way out of a couple of tough scraps with the Apache. Early the next morning I got some provisions and two extra mounts for the prisoners and headed over this way.

"I rode pretty hard, cause I wanted to get back so I could pack up and leave. Sure never expected to end up being Marshal here though," Emmett said.

"I got in town in the late afternoon. As I rode in from the south, I saw the Deputy headin' up the street with a shotgun. He seemed to be in an all-fired hurry about something. I rode up the street a bit, stopped, and tied off the horses.

"The Deputy went in the saloon and a few seconds later I heard a shot that sounded like it came from a large caliber pistol. I stepped up to the door and looked in. That's when I first laid eyes on that Wild Jack Pike fella. He didn't notice me standing behind the doors as he walked over to the Deputy who was sprawled on the floor. He said something threatening as he pointed his .44 at the Deputy's head. I figured I had better say something to try and stop him from pulling the trigger, so I yelled to him he should end it, but he wasn't for it. I thought if I called him some kind of a name, he'd get riled and turn his attention toward me instead of the Deputy. When he raised that .44 at me, I didn't have no other choice but to put him down. Not much more to tell, except I think this is a nice town, and I will tell you this, I don't intend to let people like that Pike fella ruin it. I wanna thank you folks too, for accepting me as your Marshal."

"One more thing," Emmett said, "There certainly was not any kind of a conspiracy on this deal. I never laid eyes on Jack Pike, Sally Belle, or anybody else in that saloon before the day all of this took place, and that's a fact."

"All right Emmett, that ought to bring this matter to a finish once and for all. I see no reason to carry it any further. The way I see it, Jack Pike killed his wife and Marshal Coleman in cold blood. The Marshal and the Deputy were only doin' their sworn duty as peace officers that day.

"Jack Pike killed Marshal Coleman and then tried to do the same to the deputy, and would have, were it not for Emmett Cross. He's our appointed Marshal now. Mayor Pots and I appointed him mostly because he's a man of reputation and a person who wouldn't stand by and watch another man murdered," Judge Bryant said to the crowd.

"Now about this so-called conspiracy and the matter of a claim and gold. I see no evidence at all except a claim that's been expired for way over a year. So, the way I see it, the only conspiracy here is in the minds and imagination of Clarence Pike and lawyer Thomas Boone."

Judge Bryant now addressed lawyer Boone saying, "You listen to me, young lawyer. If you intend to continue to practice law in this town, don't you ever come in my Court again with such trumped-up charges, or I'll see what I can do to have you barred from practicing law anymore, anywhere. Let me assure you, I carry enough weight in this territory to get the job done too."

Judge Bryant then said to Clarence Pike, "And, if I were you Mr. Pike, I'd hitch up those mules of yours and first thing come mornin', I be heading back toward Tombstone or where ever you crawled out from. You're not a popular fella around here you know. Marshal Bob Coleman was well liked around here and some of our good citizens might just decide to form a lynchin' party."

Pike looked around the room sheepishly.

"Now," Judge Bryant said, "I close this inquiry once and for all by declaring drinks all around. Lawyer Boone's a buyin' as a fine for contempt of court. Ain't that right, Boone?"

"I don't like it Judge, but if you say to," Boone said reluctantly.

Judge Bryant chuckled and said, "I say so, lawyer Boone, I say so."

Most everybody got a drink and left figuring that was the end of it. Boone didn't drink, but he did settle up with Pat afterward, and then he left. Emmett had a whiskey and I had a beer. Everyone else had whiskey too, since it was free. Me, I never touched the hard stuff, a beer or two was my usual. I like to keep my head clear.

Emmett and I made a check around town after having the drink. Then we headed down to the office for some coffee.

Clarence Pike left right after the close of the inquiry, I was kind of surprised that he didn't get his free drink before he left the saloon. I just figured he was going to hitch up his mules and leave like Judge Bryant had suggested. I didn't think we would see him around Cold Creek again.

CHAPTER FOUR
CONFRONTATION IN THE STREET

There were two other saloons in town besides the Silver Stallion. The Kings Palace Saloon, which sat on the west side of Main street, just a couple of buildings down from the center of town where my mother's boarding house was. It was a fancy place with all the trimmings. They had spared no expense when it was built, that's for sure. The bar even had brass trimmed rails and brass beer spigots. There was a stage where show girls danced three times a week, and it even had a crystal chandelier right in the middle of the place. Emmett and I didn't go there much, except on official business. Didn't much care for the atmosphere, a little too fancy for our blood, though most of the clientele was cowboys and gamblers.

The other place, a Cantina was owned and run by Manuel Gonzales, his wife and two daughters. Never had much trouble from the Cantina to speak of. It was mostly a place to get a five-cent beer and a fair price on a meal.

The Cantina was on the east side of Main street, across from the Marshal's Office, which was next to the livery stables, the last building in town.

It seemed like The Kings Palace Saloon was a place where trouble was always brewing, though the owner had intended it to be a respectable place of entertainment. The chandelier had to be sent to San Francisco for repairs twice in the last five years after some drunken cowboys used it for target practice. There were two Faro tables, a roulette wheel, a pool table in the back room, and always a couple tables of poker. Sometimes the poker games would last for days, and you would often find Casey March sitting in on one.

The Kings Palace was owned by Charles W. King, a well-to-do English gentleman from Chicago. He had been around town almost since its founding. It's a wonder they didn't call the town Kingstown instead of Cold Creek. It was actually named for the little river east of town that ran down from the mountains. The water was always ice cold.

King also owned fifty percent interest in the Silver Stallion Saloon. Pat and Sally Belle shared the other fifty percent.

Besides the two saloons he also owned the Cold Creek Hotel, which was west of the McCord Boarding House and across Tillman street, with a Chinese laundry in between them.

Cowboys from the Rocking 'W' ranch liked to spend a lot of time and money at The Kings Palace Saloon. One who especially liked to frequent the place was Terrance Wonderland, the younger of the two brothers who owned the ranch.

Terrance had been just a kid, about a year older than I was at the time, when his mother died of complications after giving birth to what would have been his sister, if the baby had lived. Old man Wonderland died about a year later. He was heading home from town drunk one night, passed out and fell off his horse, broke his neck. Jesse, the older brother found him the next morning after his horse wandered home without him. After his father's death, Jesse took over the running of the ranch and fixed the place up from the deteriorating state it was in.

Not long after Jesse started running the place there came to be questions as to where some of their stock was coming from. Nobody could prove anything of course, but there were many who were suspicious about how they managed to always have a good sized herd on the range.

Now, Emmett and I hadn't given much thought to where Clarence Pike might have run off to after the inquiry, but maybe we should have.

We both had a late supper at the boarding house. Mayor Potts and Judge Bryant were there too and we all had a few laughs about the way the inquiry had gone. After supper Emmett and I headed down to the Marshal's Office where we played a half-dozen games of checkers. Emmett won most of the time, as he usually did.

We started the evening rounds about 9:30. It seemed to be a pretty quiet night, not even a disturbance at The Kings Palace. We got back to the office a little before 10:30, and Emmett started getting ready to go to his room at the boarding house. I was to stay at the jail, and rest on the cot for the night.

Due to the fact that the saloons stayed open so late, sometimes all night, Emmitt felt it was a good idea for someone to stay in the office at night. I agreed and we planned to take turns staying at the office. It was my night.

Emmett had just finished cleaning his Colt Peacemaker and hadn't put it back together when we heard somebody shouting outside. We listened, and sure enough it was Clarence Pike. Emmett went right out the door and I followed close behind. The only weapon we had between us outside was the .45 caliber Colt Dragoon Conversion I carried on my hip. It had belonged to my father when he was alive and I had changed it to a cartridge outfit a couple years back .

Pike stood in the street so drunk he could hardly stand up. He called to Emmett, "Cum'on ou sheer, yuh jella belly law dog, and get shur come up'ens."

Pike had a 12 gauge shotgun, sawed off short at both ends, and was trying to sight it on Emmett. He just wobbled it back and forth, being as drunk as he was. "Cum'on, yuh murdered ma bruder, and alm a gonna shoot ja down, jess like yuh did him. Cum'on," Pike challenged.

"I'm not armed Pike. I think you had better go sleep it off before I have to deal harsh with you."

"Naw, I ain't goin' nowheres till I gets this here settled. Now cum'on yuh yeller dog, go get healed and let's have it out, ri'now."

Emmett walked right up to Pike eyeball to eyeball. "Look here you drunken fool. I don't need to be healed, you ain't got no guts. You ain't man enough to pull that trigger. You're just like your brother. If you can't bushwhack a man, you got no spine. So go ahead, pull that trigger.... See, no guts at all."

Emmett was standing toe to toe with Pike when I called, "Emmett, what are you doin'? That darn fool's gonna shoot you."

"Stay out of it Deputy," Emmett said without breaking eye contact with Pike. "This is between me and this drunken fool here. Ain't that right Pike?"

"Yeah... Yeah, shore it ess," said Pike.

At that Emmett slapped Pike across the mouth hard, and said, "Well then, go ahead Pike, if you got the nerve."

Emmett slapped him again, just like before. I couldn't believe it. Pike just stood there and took it. "Shoot fool... no guts." Emmett plucked the 12 gauge right out of Pike's hand. Pike glared at him, froze, not making a move.

Emmett then poked Pike in the belly with the little shotgun. "Now let me tell you Pike, I want you out of town by morning. And, if I ever see your face in this town again, I'll shoot you down in the street like a mad dog. Do you understand what I'm a tellin' you?" Emmett poked him again, "Well, do you?"

"Yeah Marshal, I understand, sheer I do," Pike hung his head looking down at the ground as he answered.

"Well then go find some hole to sleep that drunk off and get out of my sight, right now," said Emmett.

Pike turned and slowly staggered toward the livery stables with his head still down. As he walked away he mumbled, "Yes'r Marshal, alma goin'."

Emmett shook his head as he removed the shell out of the shotgun. As he walked back to the office he smiled and said, "Doggone close that time, huh Deputy?"

"Sure was Emmett. I was afraid you were gonna get gut shot for sure. How'd you know Pike wasn't gonna use that shotgun?"

"Sorry I talked harsh with you Deputy, but I had to keep my attention on that darn fool Pike."

"No problem Emmett, I understand that."

"It's like this Deputy. You just got to know how a man like that thinks. I knew when he didn't have the gun cocked and didn't use that shotgun right off, he didn't have the guts to go ahead if I stood up to him. I had to keep right on him, so he wouldn't have time to think about it. That's why I told you to stay out of it."

"I get you Emmett, but don't think I'd have tried it. Shucks, he'd a shot me."

"Well, no matter Deputy. I don't think Pike will be showin' his face around here for a long while anyway."

We went back inside and Emmett finished putting his Colt back together, then headed for the boarding house.

I slept uneasy that night. I kind of expected Pike to show up again, but he didn't. I looked around every dark corner when I made my rounds at two in the morning. I didn't see hide nor hair of him anywhere.

About daybreak, as the sun was just peaking the mountains, I heard the crack of a whip and, a "Hee-Yah" as Pike's team of mules and wagon rumbled out of town. I thought, 'Good riddance, if I never see that no-account again, it'll be too soon'.

I couldn't get back to sleep after that, so, in the little potbelly stove I started a small fire, just big enough to heat up some coffee as it gets warm pretty early that time of year. Emmett would want a cup when he came in and I needed it to keep my eyes open the rest of the day, because I sure didn't get much rest that night.

I was out back of the jail washing up at the pump when Emmett came in. He stuck his head out the back door and said, "Mornin' Deputy. How you doin' this fine day?"

I could hardly believe this was the same man who the night before backed down Clarence Pike while he had a sawed-off shotgun pointed at his guts, but it was. Emmett was a light-hearted soul most of the time, but he had no trouble at all getting really serious and being tough when it came time. He was a man who meant what he said when he spoke. I have little doubt that he meant every word of what he told Clarence Pike the night before.

Over the next few months, Emmett got to know the townsfolk pretty well and they got to know him and most everybody seemed to like him. Myself, I liked and respected Emmett a lot, he treated me as an equal, though I was young and made mistakes. Emmett was my friend, he was like a big brother to me.

Emmett and Ben Decker had struck up a friendship too. Ben wasn't the easiest person in the world to get along with, but he took to Emmett with no problem. You just had to know Ben to get along with him. Emmett had a way of reading people and he saw through Ben's outer crust. They had done some horse trading and I don't know what happened exactly, but Ben was always jokingly accusing Emmett of being a horse thief. Emmett traded in his Army mount and gear on a big two year old Paint gelding and a good riding saddle. Whenever Ben would tease him, Emmett would just chuckle and say, "I ain't no thief, just a good horse trader, that's all."

Ben would come back with, "Yeah well, I'm gonna see the Judge about getting' yuh hung just the same." Then they would both laugh.

Ben had watched what happened that night with Clarence Pike from the barn at the stables. It seems Pike had been drinking in the stables, getting his nerve up by talking to his mules and downing cheap rot gut whiskey. Ben hadn't realized what Pike was fixing to do or else he would have warned us.

The next day Ben spread through the whole town how the new Marshal had run Pike out of town, him not even being armed, while Pike had a shotgun.

CHAPTER FIVE
ROBERT BENJAMIN DILL

Things were quiet around town for quite a spell after that, except for one incident when Casey March, the town's resident gambler had to draw down on a half drunk cowboy one night at The Kings Palace Saloon. Seems this cowboy had lost a month's pay to Casey playing stud poker. There were plenty of witnesses to say the cowboy wouldn't give it up, even after Casey offered to give him back most of his money.

Stubbornly the cowboy made the mistake of drawing on Casey, leaving him no other way out but to live up to his reputation of being a fast gun. The cowboy died the next day from a wound in his abdomen.

Emmett took Casey down to the Marshal's Office for questioning. Casey went along peaceably with no argument. After questioning the witnesses, Emmett spoke with Judge Bryant. The Judge agreed Casey drew in self-defense. There hadn't been much else he could have done to keep from getting gunned down.

Judge Bryant told Emmett to let Casey go, unless he had reason to hold him. Emmett gave Casey back his gun and told him to, "Continue an honest game and we'll have no problem."

Casey said, "Sir, I wouldn't have it any other way." Then he left for the poker tables.

One morning in late summer, the steam engine pulled up to take on water and two men stepped down off the train. Seldom did anyone get off in Cold Creek. One man was dressed in an eastern pin-striped suit and bowler hat. The other man was in buffalo skins. They certainly were an unlikely looking pair.

The train stopped on the west side of town and the two men walked east on Center Street to the Cold Creek Hotel and checked in. After securing a room, they inquired as to where the Marshal's Office was.

A half hour later they walked into the office. It being a Saturday, Emmett and I had been lazing around playing checkers and making the rounds through town every three or four hours. The fellow in the suit walked right up to the desk where Emmett was sitting and threw down a wanted poster that had a hand-drawn picture of what looked like a teenage kid.

"My name is Jason Taylor. I have reason to believe this man lives here in town. He is wanted for…"

Emmett leaned forward in his chair and cut the man short. "Pinkerton, ain't you? Let me tell you something mister, I don't like the way you guys operate. And besides that, you got no authority around here. You see, me and this Deputy are the law here."

"That's right Marshal, I am a Pinkerton man, and as I was saying, I have a wanted poster here with a picture of Robert Benjamin Dill. He has a $500 bounty on his head. He is wanted for his part in a train robbery and murder of a Deputy State Marshal six years ago in Missouri. If he is here in this town, Mr. Jordon here," he gestured at the man in buffalo skins, "and myself are going to bring him to justice."

Emmett picked up the wanted poster and studied it, I did the same over his shoulder. Didn't look like anybody I had seen before.

"Nope," Emmett said, "No one around here looks like that, you can take my word for it. Besides, that was a long time ago. So I guess you fellas will be leavin' right away."

"No Marshal, I'm afraid it will not be that easy. As you can tell, that picture is at least six years old. So, we will be looking around town till we find this man, or at least find out where he went," the Pinkerton arrogantly told Emmett.

Emmett stood up from his seat behind the desk, and as he did, he kicked the chair back against the wall. At the same time he had drawn his Peacemaker, and stuck the barrel right to the Pinkerton's nose. Straight out Emmett told him, "Look here Jason Taylor, if you start roustin' the good citizens of this town, I'll be forced to deal real harsh with you. Like I told you, you got no authority around here. That Missouri wanted poster don't mean squat here. Now you and that smelly buffalo hunter can leave this office. Right Now."

When Emmett stood up, Jordon had made a move for a .44 Colt he had stuck in his belt. I put my hand to my .45. "I wouldn't," I warned. Jordon just nodded and put his hand back down to his side.

"Marshal, you have the upper hand for now, so we are leaving your office. But, be assured, if Robert Benjamin Dill is in this town, I will find him and bring him to justice, one way or another. Lets go Buff."

"Right, Cap'n," said Jordan and both men backed out the door.

Buff Jordon? I had heard that name before, but just couldn't remember where or when.

I had never seen Emmett so riled. I wasn't sure why he got so upset. Maybe he knew who this Dill fellow was. One thing for sure, he didn't like Pinkerton's. I had heard of them, but Taylor was the first one I had ever seen.

Emmett picked up the wanted poster from the desk and studied it.

"Emmett, what's goin' on here. You know somethin' about this Dill fella?" I said.

"Maybe Deputy, just maybe I do."

Emmett went over to the stove and took a piece of charred wood out and brought it over to the desk. With his pocket knife, he scraped some black onto the wanted poster. Then I began to see it too. Emmett had scraped the black so it fell around both jaw and chin of the figure on the poster. It was a pretty close likeness to Ben Decker, the town blacksmith who always wore a full beard. I don't know why I hadn't noticed it myself.

"Emmett that's the spittin' image of Ben Decker. What are we gonna do? You want me to go warn him about the Pinkerton?" I asked.

"No, not now Deputy. You really think it could be Ben do you? How long has he lived here in town?" Emmett asked as he picked up the poster and blew the black char off.

"Well, it sure looks enough like him to be his twin if it ain't him," I said. "Let's see…It seems Ben's lived here about.., oh say, four, four and half years." I thought for a moment, "That sure makes the timin' about right, don't it?"

"Tell you what we'll do here Deputy. We'll wait till after dark and you slip over to the livery without bein' seen, while I make the rounds. You have Ben come over to the office so I can talk to him about this and see what he's got to say. Listen, don't let on what I want, okay?"

"Sure Emmett, I'll do that. What about that Buff Jordon fella, you ever heard tell of him before? I know that name, sounds mighty familiar to me."

"Yeah, I heard of him alright. He's the scout that a few years back led an Army troop into an Indian village. They massacred the whole village, every soul, mostly women and children. I never cottoned to that kind of thing. That's one reason I left the Army," Emmett said.

"I knew I'd heard that name before. Sure had an uneasy feelin' when he was here, if you know what I mean?"

"Sure do Deputy. That other fella, that Pinkerton, prob'ly ain't much count neither. I've seen how some of them operate. They don't much care who gets hurt as long as they get their man. Back in Texas, a couple of Pinkertons killed a man's wife and son while tryin' to smoke him out. The law back there let them get away with it because they claimed, 'they were hiding a known criminal and fugitive'. So don't be surprised at what they might come up with in dealing with this.

Though that Missouri wanted poster doesn't carry much weight in Arizona Territory, that Pinkerton still gets paid just the same to get whoever he's after," Emmett explained.

At 9:30 that night Emmett went out to check around town, and I went out the back of the jail and over to the livery stables. I tried to keep out of sight as I came up to the door of the room in back of the barn were Ben slept.

I knocked. There wasn't any light coming from the room, so maybe he wasn't there. I knocked one more time and heard a voice from inside, "Yeah, who's there, I'm in bed, what d'yuh want?"

"Hey Ben, it's me Deputy McCord. Can I come in? I need to talk to you."

Ben answered, "Yeah Deputy, hang on a dang gone minute. Let me get my pants on."

The door opened and Ben was still trying to get his pants buttoned. "Here let me light the lamp," he said, fumbling with a match. "What's up Deputy, need me to watch a prisoner? Sorry, but I've been shoein' horses all day long and was pretty sound when yuh knocked. Anyway what can I do for yuh this time of night?" Ben rubbed his eyes and yawned.

"Well Ben, Marshal Cross has got somethin' he'd like to talk to you about over at the office."

"Tonight? Now?" he asked scratching himself with a curious look on his face. "What could be so all fired important that that old horse thief would wanna talk about tonight anyway?"

"I'm not at liberty to say right now, Ben. Emmett will explain the whole thing when we get to the office," I said.

Ben agreed to go along as he started searching for his boots under the bed, "Well, alright. I'll slip my boots on and be right with yuh." He grumbled as he was pulling his boots on, "Don't know what the heck anybody would wanna talk about in the middle of the night when a man's tryin' to get some rest anyway, darned old horse thief."

When Ben was ready, we walked the back way to the jail. Once inside Ben started to show a little concerned, "What this about McCord? Where's Emmett anyway?"

"Emmett's out makin' rounds, he'll be back in a bit. You wanna cuppa coffee while we wait? Got a fresh pot here," I said as I grabbed the pot off the stove with my kerchief.

"No thanks, don't need no coffee, just wanna know what's goin' on around here, that's all," Ben scowled.

"I'm gonna have a cup, if you don't mind. Like I said, Emmett will be here shortly, he'll tell you what's goin' on when he gets here," I said trying to ease his concerned curiosity.

We sat and waited for quite a spell before Emmett made it back. Ben's anxiousness was about to get the better of him when Emmett finally walked in the door. He had two cowboys with him, one in each hand.

"Sorry it took so long fellas, but these two cow punchers were bound and determined to kill each other, so I brought 'em in to sleep it off. I'll lock these two up and be right with you. Come on you, get movin'. I'll separate you two for tonight, and you can settle this tomorrow when you ain't all liquored up. Then what ever it was you were fighting about won't seem that important," he told the cowboys as he herded them back to a cell.

When Emmett stepped back into the office after taking care of the cowboys, Ben stood up, "Alright Emmett, what's this all about anyways? Just what's so darned important that yuh had to keep me up half the night for it?"

"So you wanna know what's goin' on do you Ben?" Emmett asked as he poured a cup of coffee. "Well how about this." Emmett pulled the wanted poster out of his shirt pocket with his free hand, shook it open and handed it to Ben.

Ben stuttered as he answered, "Wha…What's this? I don't na... know who this is. What's this here poster got to do with me?"

Emmett looked Ben straight in the eyes and said sternly, "Look here Ben, you can lie all you want to other people, but we're your friends here, so don't you dare stand there and lie to me. It's your picture on this poster, ain't it- ain't it Ben?"

"Yeah, dam-it. Yes, it's me, but it was a long time ago and I was just a runny-nosed kid tryin' to impress my two older brothers. Hell, I knew I shouldn't have sent that telegram to my ma to let her know where I was," Ben said.

"Sit down and tell me about it Ben," Emmett said, "We'll try and figger out what we're gonna do about this here mess you're in."

"Shoot Emmett, it was more than six years ago back in Missoura. I was seventeen years old and my two brothers were always in trouble with the law. They'd rob some place and come back home and brag about how they'd gotten away with it.

Then we'd all live high on the hog for a while, they'd be a buyin' me and Ma nice stuff and then when the money would run out, off they'd go and pull another robbery somewheres.

"Most of the robberies they were pullin' were blamed on the James gang. So they really thought they were smart and getting' away with it.

"Ma never really said much of anything about what they were doin'. We were poor. My Pa had got shot for cheatin' at poker in a saloon fight and died when I was thirteen years old. I guess Ma liked all the things my brothers were buyin' for us.

"I got to thinkin' the only way to have anything was to do like my brothers were doin'." There was regret in Ben's voice. "So when my brothers come in one day and said they thought it was time I went along and done my part, I figgered they were prob'ly right."

Ben admitted, "It wasn't right, I know, bad judgment on my part. Anyways, me, my two brothers, and another fella rode out to rob this train my brothers figgered would be an easy take. The train was supposed to have a big military payroll shipment on it, with little security. It turned out to be a set-up. A box car loaded with armed men was waitin' to ambush us when we showed up.

"My older brother, Joe, and the other fella, Zak Cole, were both killed as we attempted to hold up the train when they opened fire on us. Tom got one of the guards before bein' shot in the leg as we rode off."

Ben paused for a minute. You could tell he was fighting back his emotions. Ben cleared his throat and started again.

"Tom and me rode hard and fast till we came to an old abandoned trapper's shack that had a stream runnin' behind it. After we watered them, I tied the horses to a tree behind the shack where they were out of sight. Tom had lost a lot of blood and was getting' pretty weak. Since it was getting' dark, we bedded down in the shack for the night.

"Next mornin' Tom couldn't get up, and he told me that there was $300 in the poke in his saddle bags, and that he wanted me to take his horse and head on out. 'Go west,' he said, 'and make somethin' of yourself besides a thief, cause it's a rotten life runnin' all the time'".

"I said that I wouldn't go nowhere without him. He said he was in no shape to go on, and that he didn't want me to be involved in his kind of life. He told me that he felt pretty bad that he and Joe had made me go along in the first place. He just kept insistin', and told me that if I got caught he'd never forgive himself. He said that if he could just rest up for a day or two, he'd be alright, then would head out and catch up with me."

Ben paused and asked, "Yuh sure you boys want to hear all this?"

Emmett answered, "Tell us the whole story, so we know what were dealin' with."

"Well, Tom finally convinced me to go, so I saddled up his horse. He wanted me to take his because it was pretty strong. Tom always had a fast horse. This one was a well-seasoned buckskin and could really cover some ground in short order. I went out, got him ready and went back inside to say good-bye to Tom. Unbeknownst to us a posse rode up and had stopped down the road just as I hugged Tom to say good-bye. Someone shouted that we should give up peaceably and no harm would come to us. If we didn't, they'd come in a shootin'. Tom told me that because we'd killed a guard there was no way they wouldn't shoot us down if we went outside. Tom insisted I go and he'd stall them till I was gone and then he'd give up and take his chances. I didn't wanna go, but he just kept on tellin' me how bad he'd feel if I was caught or killed. Finally I give in to his urgin' and reluctantly snuck out the back. I led the buckskin across the stream, and mounted up. I rode that horse into the ground for a day and a half, never lookin' back.

"I found out later that Tom did give up, but when he went to trial they sentenced him to hang for shootin' the guard. There was nothin' I could do about it. About a month after the train robbery, they hung him in Abilene.

"I was pretty messed up for a while, and I went to drinkin' heavy. I drank up half the money I had, then I come to realize that it wasn't doin' me no good at all grievin' that way. Besides, Tom wouldn't have liked the way I was actin'; he gave his life so I could get away. After that I signed on with a couple of trail herds and saved all the money

I made. Then I headed out here to Arizona Territory, Tombstone in particular, cause I'd heard that a man could open a business there and do pretty good. A couple of days after I got there, I seen on a post office bulletin board there in Tombstone that this fella had a livery stable for sale up here in Cold Creek. Well, I loved horses and I'd done my fair share of blacksmith work back home and I liked it. So I come on up here. When I got here, I put a good size down payment on the place, and here I am.

"So what now Emmett? What are yuh gonna do?" asked Ben.

I ain't sure right yet Ben. I'll have to think on this for a spell. I sure ain't turnin' you over to that Pinkerton that's lookin' for you."

"Where'd yuh get the poster anyways?" asked Ben.

"Some Pinkerton agent brought it in here and said he knew you was living here in town somewhere. Let me warn you, he's pretty determined to flush you out. He has Buff Jordon, a rogue Indian Scout, with him. They came in here and shoved that poster in my face and I ran them out of the office, mainly because I didn't much care two hoots in a holler for either one of 'em.

"If you're bein' straight with me Ben, and I have no reason to think you ain't, I think we ought to go talk to Judge Bryant and see what he says. I mean anythin' you did six years ago in Missouri ain't held against you here in Arizona. There ain't nobody from back there got jurisdiction here in Cold Creek, Arizona, that's for sure." Emmett explained.

"I don't know Emmett, maybe he'll turn me over to 'em," Ben said.

"Judge Bryant's your friend and you know it. He's also a fair man and wouldn't just turn you over to some Pinkerton and murderin' buffalo hunter unless you had done something wrong around here or you really were a killer," Emmett assured.

Ben thought for a minute, "Yeah Emmett, I suppose you're right. Maybe it would be a good idea for me to go and get some advice from the Judge. Him and me have always got along real good. We've done a lot of huntin' and fishin' together as a matter of fact."

"Good Ben, glad you see it that way. We're gonna get you out of this somehow, you just wait and see. The Judge will come up with something that works," Emmitt assured.

"Tell you what we'll do," Emmett started explaining, "You go on back to bed for tonight. Then early in the mornin' before anybody is out on the streets, me and the Deputy here will check and make sure that there's no one around to see you. We'll all go down to the boarding house and catch the Judge before breakfast."

"Okay Emmett, if you think that's the best way to do it, then that's what I'll do," Ben agreed as he headed for the back door. Then he stopped, turned to look at Emmett and me. "Sure am glad I've got good friends like you fellas. Thanks for believin' in me. I ain't no criminal, I just made some dumb choices when I was a kid and didn't know no better. I'll see you fellas in the mornin'."

Emmett and I both stayed at the Jail that night. I slept in the desk chair with my feet propped up, while Emmett bedded down on the cot in the office. I think I got the better deal, though.

CHAPTER SIX
THE JUDGE'S LAW

The sun had not quite peeked the mountains when Emmett hobbled barefoot out back of the jail to the outhouse. I got up and put coffee on. Emmett was pulling his boots on when Ben walked in from the back.

"Mornin' to you fellas," he said.

We said good morning, then Emmett said, "I'm gonna make the rounds and see who's on the street. You fellas be ready to go when I get back, okay?"

"Sure Emmett, we'll be ready. You sure you don't want me to go with you?" I asked.

"I think it'll look more like normal if there's only one of us on the street in the morning. Just stay here for now, and keep Ben company till I come back and get you."

Ben and I agreed to stay and wait.

"Ben," I said as Emmett walked out the door, "How about a cup'a coffee?"

"Sure John," Ben said. "I'll have a cup with yuh this mornin'. You know, I should apologize for bein' a hard nose last night. I had a rough day yesterday and didn't know what was goin' on. I hope you'll accept my apology."

"AW, don't worry about that. I'll get even with you soon enough," I said, and we both laughed.

Ben and I were on our second cup of coffee and playing checkers when Emmett came back.

"I think it will be safe if we go now, but let's take the alley and go in the back door of the boarding house," Emmett suggested.

61

The three of us went out the back door of the jail to the alley. The alley ran parallel to Tillman Street where the Hotel was. It went behind The Kings Palace Saloon and down past the back door of the boarding house.

We went in and passed through the kitchen, where my mother was cooking breakfast. Surprised to see us, she said, "John? Emmett? And good mornin' to you as well Ben. What are all you boys doin' comin' through the back door like that?" She smiled, "I hope it's to help me serve up the hungry bunch that's gonna be in here about a half hour from now. I bet it ain't, is it?"

"No Ma, that ain't the reason. Maybe next time though."

Pointing a spatula at us she said, "Well, I'll be sure and hold you all to that you know. What do you fellas need then?"

"We need to know if Judge Bryant has come down yet," I said.

"No, I don't believe he has, but he's due anytime now. If it were me," she warned, "I wouldn't talk to that old cuss before he's drank his usual pot of coffee first, though."

"Sorry Mrs. McCord, but this just won't wait. We'll have to take our chances. We need to see him now," Emmett cracked open the kitchen door and looked out into the dining room. "I'll go up and get him. You fellas wait here." Emmett pushed on through the door and headed for the stairs that led up to the rooms.

"John?" my mother questioned with uneasiness in her eyes.

62

"Not now Ma. I'll tell you sometime, but I just can't explain right now."

"All right son." Still worried, she busied herself with the cooking.

Emmett was gone for quite a spell and the smells in that kitchen were enough to drive a man insane. My mother was one good cook and she brought in almost as much money from the dining room as she did from the rented rooms at the boarding house. It was a lot of work for her, but she loved it. She usually handled the morning and day crowd by herself, but in the evening for the supper time crowd, she had hired the new school teacher, Loretta Packard, to help out.

Miss Packard was a very beautiful lady with long blond hair, sparkling blue eyes and a lovely little smile that could, no doubt, melt the coldest heart. Other than saying 'Howdy ma'am,' I had only talked to her once since she had come to town, but that was enough to make me weak in the knees and stumble over almost every word I spoke. I had talked to tough drunken cowboys who were ready to kill me with less trouble than I had carrying on a conversation with her.

Those heavenly smells were just too much when my mother pulled a fresh batch of biscuits out of the oven. She set them on the table and I reached for a couple. The spatula threatened and my mother said, "You stay out of these here biscuits young man. They're for payin' customers, you know." Of course she was only teasing me as she was quite fond of doing.

She pointed at the butter crock and said, "There's the butter, you and Ben help yourselves, but save a few for the customers. You know how you are when you get started in on my biscuits." I grabbed two of the biggest I could find, pulled them apart and slapped some butter on them. I devoured half of mine as I handed the other to Ben.

As I poked the last bite of biscuit in my mouth, Emmett came through the door with the Judge right behind him.

"I thought this is what this would be all about," said Judge Bryant when he saw Ben standing there.

"You know what we want to talk about Judge?" Emmett asked.

"I've known who Ben really was almost ever since he came here to Cold Creek," he said.

My mother grabbed a big pan of scrambled eggs and said, "Excuse me, but I got work to do. I can't stand around jawin' all day like some people." She squeezed by into the dining room. I knew that was my mother's way of minding her own business, and letting us know she didn't appreciate us getting in the way of her making a living.

I figured it would be a good idea to take it outside, so I said, "Let's grab a cup'a coffee and set out back here to talk about this, so's my ma can do her cookin' in peace."

They all agreed, although Judge Bryant seemed irritated. I am sure he would have rather been in the dining room having his morning coffee and breakfast whilst reading the morning paper. I poured a cup of coffee for all of us, and we stepped outside.

Emmett spoke up first. "So how did you know about Ben, Judge?"

"I get a copy of all wanted posters that come this way. I saw the one on Ben back about two or three years ago," he said.

"Well then, what are we gonna do about it Judge?" asked Emmett. "Do you know about the Pinkerton and Buff Jordon?"

"I know about everything that goes on in this town. Let me tell you," Judge Bryant plainly stated, "I feel that anybody involved in a robbery where a man is killed ought to be punished to the furthest extent of the law."

Emmett, Ben and I just stood there with our jaws hanging down. "I'll make it clear to you," Judge Bryant said. "I think if Robert Benjamin Dill were to go back to Missoura, they should hang'm for his part in that robbery."

"Judge, I thought you and Ben were friends," I said, stunned at what he had been saying.

"We are, good friends, but that don't change the fact that he was involved in a robbery where a man lost his life in the line of his duty as an officer of the law. However, that was Robert Benjamin Dill, back in Missoura. So far, Ben Decker has kept his nose clean around here. "Men, I assure you, if Ben Decker were ever to break the law in such a manner in my jurisdiction, he'd swing by his neck just like any other criminal that has come before me for such crimes. As far as the law in Cold Creek, Arizona Territory is concerned, Ben Decker is a good citizen of this town. Now, if he is apprehended by that Pinkerton and taken as his prisoner, there ain't nothing we can do about it as long as no law is broken in his doin' it. If Ben was to bring any harm to the Pinkerton man, he would have to answer to the law here for any wrong doin' or harm he brought to him."

"Let me see if I understand this right," said Emmett. "As long as Ben doesn't break the law around here, we don't need to get involved in this thing? If the Pinkerton and Buff Jordon grabs him up somewhere, as long as they don't break the law a doin' it, there's nothin' no one around here can do about it?"

Ben and I stood there trying to make some sense out of what Judge Bryant and Emmett had just said.

Judge Bryant said to Emmett, "That's about the size of it Emmett. Now, I'll leave you men to worry about this. I'm gonna eat my breakfast." With that he turned and went back inside.

I suppose we should have realized that Judge Bryant would feel that way about this situation. Law and order was a serious matter with him.

"Well Ben, the way I see it, you otta go hide out somewhere's till those two bounty hunters get tard of lookin' for you and ride out," I suggested.

"I hate to disagree Deputy," Emmett warned, "but those two know their man is here in town somewhere and they won't be leavin' till they got him hog-tied across a saddle, dead or alive."

"Then what should we do, Emmett?" I asked.

Before Emmett gave an answer, Ben said, "Look, I ain't gonna let this worry me no more. Y'all just do what yuh want. I'm just gonna go about my business the way I always do. And, if those two come fer me, I'll just have to deal with it then."

"I think that's about the best thing to do for now, Ben," agreed Emmett. "What I mean is, I don't think they know who you are right yet anyway."

Ben headed back to the livery stables. Emmett and I went back inside and had breakfast. It was the first time I could remember eating in the boarding house dining room while Judge Bryant was there and not talking to him. It wasn't that we were mad about what he had said, I just think everybody was a little lost as to what to do about the situation. Most everybody in town liked Ben Decker and he was a good citizen and one darn good blacksmith.

We ate our breakfast and Emmett said he would make the morning rounds while I took a couple of meals to the jail for the cowboys he had brought in the night before. I was to turn them loose after they had eaten, as long as they weren't still in a fighting mood.

CHAPTER SEVEN
SHOOTOUT AT THE KINGS PALACE SALOON

I gave the cowboys breakfast and they were real appreciative. They sure wasn't expecting a meal before being turned loose. They ate like a couple of hungry hound dogs and were about as noisy too. They left together as though nothing had ever happened, though the night before they had been ready to kill each other. That's one reason I never took a liking to hard liquor. I like to stay in control of my thinking. A couple of beers once in a while is plenty for me.

Emmett was right about Taylor the Pinkerton man and Buff Jordon. Those two were out every day showing that wanted poster around town, asking people if they recognized the hand drawn figure on the front. I'm not sure if it was that nobody really knew who it was on the poster, or that they were just protecting Ben, but no one spoke up. Still, I figured it would only be a matter of time before someone told them what they wanted to know. Then they would be coming down on Ben with a vengeance.

Emmett started taking a lot of his meals over at the Cantina about this time. Not that he had acquired a taste for Mexican food, but he had acquired a liking for Manuel Gonzales' oldest daughter, Rosa Maria. She had taken to Emmett pretty well too. They were seeing a lot of each other.

One evening I was making rounds while Emmett was over at the Cantina. I was about to finish up when I heard gun shots and the sound of breaking glass. I had just checked the doors at Faye's Dress Shop next door to the Kings Palace Saloon. The commotion was coming from there and I figure it was some cowboy using the chandelier for target practice again.

I hurried over to the Palace and cautiously opened one of the double French doors a crack. Just then another shot echoed and shattering glass from the chandelier tinkled like tiny bells as it sprayed the glass in the French doors. When the glass stopped falling, I opened the door just enough to see inside.

Terrance Wonderland and two other cowboys from the Rocking W Ranch were doing the shooting. I wasn't too concerned about Wonderland, but the other two could give me more action than I really cared to jump into.

One of them was Billy McQueen, who had been building a strong reputation as a gunman over the last few years, he was known to run with some of the notorious Tombstone cowboys.

The other man, the one who had taken the last shot, was the one that really had me wondering if I hadn't ought to go get Emmett before stepping into this. His name was Burch Wendell and it had been claimed he was as fast a gun as John Ringo. Wendell had out-gunned a number of well-known shootists in his career as a gunman.

Apparently, he had fired the last round into the chandelier, because as I looked in, he spun one of his .45 Colts in his hand with the skill of a circus performer, then slipped it firmly to rest in his right hand holster. Another matching Colt was on his left side. His gunbelt and holster outfit had enough silver on it to pay my wages for half a year.

The three of them were laughing and having a good time at Mr. King's expense, not to mention scaring the daylights out of everyone in the saloon. The saloon bouncer, a large gruff fellow Mr. King had recently employed, was lying face down on the floor in front of the cowboys. He looked all right, though there was glass all over him from the chandelier.

I had just worked up my nerve to do my sworn duty of keeping the peace and had started to take a step inside when I felt a firm hand on my shoulder. I turned to assure myself it was Emmett, though I knew that it was.

"What's goin' on here Deputy?" asked Emmett. I leaned to one side so he could see inside the saloon.

"I'm sure glad you're here Emmett. What're we gonna do?"

"Go ahead in and break it up Deputy. I'm right with you," Emmett assured.

I swallowed, checked my shotgun and cocked back both hammers as I took a deep breath and stepped through the scroll-painted glass French doors.

By this time, Terrance Wonderland had the bartender by the shirt collar and stretched across the bar. Terrance was trying to balance a double shot glass on the bartender's head as we entered the room. No doubt, Terrance was about to attempt to shoot the glass off the barkeep's head. I would say it probably was a good thing for the bartender we showed up when we did.

McQueen was leaning back in a chair with his feet propped on a table top, reloading his .45 when we walked in. He sat the chair down abruptly and stood up when he spotted us.

Wendell was still standing by a table where he had taken the last shot at the chandelier. Few people were left in the saloon and I didn't take much note of them because my attention was on those three rowdies.

In as commanding a voice as I could muster I said, "Okay fellas, party's over. You've done enough damage for one night."

Wonderland let go of the bartender and turned his attention toward me. "Butt out Deputy. I'll pay for any damages done. We're just havin' a little fun here, and it ain't none of the law's concern."

"It is the law's concern," I responded, "when you're shootin' up someone else's property. Besides that, some innocent bystanders gonna get hit by a stray bullet if the shootin' don't stop."

Emmett stepped up to Terrance from beside me. "Hand over that pistol son, before someone gets hurt."

"I ain't yer son, and I ain't handin' yuh nothin'," snapped Terrance with a wrinkled lip. "If anybody gets hurt around here, it just might be you." Terrance took a wide stance to ready himself. "Yuh want my gun," he challenged, "just try and take it."

No more had the words come out of Terrance's mouth when Emmett drew his Peacemaker and back-handed him with the butt of it on the side of the head. Emmett grabbed the pistol out of Terrance's holster as he dropped to the floor. Emmett slipped his .45 back in its place and turned the cylinder of Terrance's pistol so that the shells fell out to the floor, then he tossed the pistol on the bar. That's when Burch Wendell decided he would get into it.

"No need yuh buffaloin' the kid like that Cross. Yuh really think yer somethin' wackin' him like that don't yuh? Yuh know, I heard of you back in Texas; about how yuh backed down ol' Bill Kelley. I tell yuh Cross, yuh don't rattle me none."

Wendell's spurs jingled as he stepped to the side a couple of steps to line himself up with Emmett. "As a matter of fact, I know I can take yuh. That there badge you're wearin' don't make yuh bullet proof or stop yuh from dyin' yuh know. Let's do it, right here, right now," Wendell challenged as he slowly placed his thumb to the hammer of his right hand Colt. People in the saloon started moving out to the edges of the room to stay out of the way of the action they knew was shortly to come about.

Emmett and Wendell's narrowing eyes locked in cold seriousness. Emmett warned, "No need for this."

"Oh yeah there is, lawman," Wendell responded as he positioned himself for action. "Come on, don't back off on me now." A self-confident smirk filled Wendell's face. "Let's see what yuh got facin' a real man."

The next instant was a blur. In a fraction of a second Burch Wendell's right hand tightened and pulled the .45 Colt up to action. Emmett cleared leather at about the same flash of time and fanned off two shots. Three loud explosions almost simultaneously rattled the walls of the saloon as sparks, smoke and fire streaked out of both men's weapons.

Wendell was knocked back onto the table he was standing in front of. It collapsed and crashed to the floor and Burch Wendell lay motionless with two scarlet-colored, silver dollar-size holes in his chest. Emmett was spun to his left side by the impact of a .45 slug slamming into his left hip. He dropped down on his right knee and toppled to the floor.

At the same moment, Emmett and Burch Wendell went for their guns, Billy McQueen drew his six-gun to fire on Emmett. I had no other choice but to let loose with a double blast from the Greener 10 gauge, which almost cut McQueen in half. It was the first time I'd ever killed, or even shot, a man and I was literally sick over it.

As the acrid-smelling smoke cleared, I flopped down in a chair at a nearby table trying not to lose my stomach. In a brief moment a dozen questions raced through my brain. Did I really have to shoot? Did I really need to use both barrels? Couldn't I have just wounded him? If I hadn't acted, wouldn't Emmett have been killed?

I was in a cold sweat and white as a sheet, but I realized I had to pull myself together and see how bad Emmett was hurt. I saw him lying on the floor at the end of the bar. "Emmett?" I called across the room, "You hit bad?

"Someone go get the doctor. Can't you see he's hurt," I shouted. It looked to me that everyone was just standing around staring instead of trying to help Emmett.

I hadn't noticed till then that Taylor and Buff Jordon were in the Palace during all the commotion. The bartender stood up from behind the bar and said, "I'll get the doctor, I'll get him in a hurry. Don't you worry Deputy," and he ran out the door.

"Deputy? You all right?" Emmett asked as he tried to get up, but winced in the effort.

"I'm fine Emmett." I hurried over to see what kind of shape he was in.

"How bad is it, Emmett?" I bent down to take a look.

"Oh, I think I'll survive Deputy. Just kind'a numb right now. Here Deputy, give me a hand getting' up."

I helped Emmett up and over to a chair to sit down at a table. I could tell it was painful for him, but a man like Emmett had learned long ago to get up and go no matter what the pain or hardship.

Terrance started to come around and pushed himself up on one elbow. He moaned as he looked around the room and tried to focus on what had happened. He asked as he looked around in amazement, "What the.., What happened? Is Billy and Wendell both dead? Yuh kill'm both?"

"Better take care of your prisoner, Deputy. I'll be all right till Doc gets here. Take him on over to the lock-up," Emmett told me as he applied pressure to his wound with his bandana.

"Okay Emmett, if you're sure you'll be all right. I'll take him to the jail and come right back."

"Come on you, let's go." I pulled Terrance up from the floor by his shirt.

"Good work by you two peace officers," the Pinkerton said.

"From anybody else, I would consider that a compliment, but coming from you Taylor, it don't mean a spit in the wind," Emmett replied.

"Yeah, thanks for nothin'. You sure did your part in helping keep the peace around here," I said with a bit of sarcasm.

"Well Deputy, that's just not my job, now is it?" Taylor sneered back.

Jordon had to throw his wit in, "First time yuh ever killed anybody, ain't it kid?"

"What if it is? I still got the job done. If it takes killin' a man to keep the peace, then that's what I'll do."

"Good answer Deputy. Don't let those two bother you, just do your job and take care of Wonderland," said Emmett.

"Right Emmett, were goin'." I nudged Terrance toward the door with my shotgun.

As Terrance and I headed down the street toward the Marshal's Office he asked me, "That Marshal out-gun Burch Wendell?"

"Sure did," I said.

"What happened to Billy? He didn't get him too, did he?"

"No, I had to take Billy out. He was gonna shoot the Marshal. He didn't give me no choice."

"Billy McQueen was my friend. This wouldn't have happened if you and that marshal hadn't stuck your nose in it. My brother ain't gonna like this neither. We was just funnin', weren't really hurtin' nobody."

"Destroyin' people's property and scarin' them half to death is against the law, and it ain't gonna be tolerated in this town," I said.

"Just the same, my brother ain't gonna like it that yuh throwed me in jail."

"Well, I reckon you and him will just have to live with it till the Judge decides what he will do with you."

I secured Terrance in a cell and he kept carrying on the whole time about it being unfair he was arrested and that his brother would take care of this thing when he came to town.

I went to the livery stable and asked Ben to come over and keep an eye on Terrance, while I went back to see how Emmett was. He grumbled some, as always, but did it anyway. He didn't mean anything by it, it was just his way.

After I explained to Ben what had happened, he said, "Aw don't worry about that old horse thief, he's too ornery to die."

I hurried back to The Kings Palace to see about Emmett. Doc Baker had just finished examining him when I got there.

"Is he gonna be all right Doc?" I asked.

"He will probably be fine in a few weeks outside of being stiff. That is, if I can get that bullet out of his hip. Otherwise we run the risk of infection and gangrene setting in. I had Murphy (that was the barkeep Terrance was going to use for target practice) go and get a buckboard to haul the Marshal here down to my office."

When Murphy got back from the undertakers, where he had got the buckboard, we loaded Emmett in the back of it and took him to the doctor's office which was across Center Street from the Chinese laundry. Doc drove the buckboard and I rode in the back with Emmett.

"Are yuh hurtin' much Emmett?" I asked as we headed down Main Street.

"Only when I laugh," said Emmett. "So don't you be tellin' me no funny stories."

"No problem Emmett," I said. I thought about it for a moment and added, "Hell, I don't think I know none anyway."

Emmett knew I was worried about him and trying to be serious. That big dummy thought what I had just said was funny and started laughing. "Ha Ha Ha, Oh…that hurts. See, I told you not to make me laugh."

"I didn't say nothin' funny. You just got one strange sense of humor that's all." He laughed again.

When we got to the doctor's place, Emmett said, "Run down to the Stallion and get me a bottle of rye. I got a feelin' that this is gonna be a long night."

I hurried over to the Silver Stallion, which was about a block away, and got Emmett his bottle. When I got back to Doc Baker's office, Rosa and her father were there waiting in the doctor's outer office.

"Is Emmett going to be alright, senõr Deputy?" Rosa asked. You could see the genuine concern in her dark brown eyes; she beautiful lady.

"The doctor, he will not let us come in," her father added.

"I'm not sure yet," I said. The Doc says he's got to get the bullet out of his hip or there will be trouble with infection. You two wait out here and I'll go in and see what's going on. Don't worry too much, Emmett's pretty tough. It's not the first time he ever took a bullet and I'm sure he'll pull through just fine. Stay here and when I find out something, I'll come out and let you know." I was hoping to calm their fears, as well as my own.

I opened the door to the examination room and saw Emmett sprawled on the table with Murphy trying to hold down his shoulders. "He's not like you John, he won't pass out so I can dig around and get to that bullet," Doc Baker said frustrated as he wiped sweat from his brow with his forearm. "Maybe you better give him that bottle to help him calm down. He won't let me put him out and I am afraid this is going to take a while."

I took the bottle right over to Emmett, pulled the cork and handed it to him. He took the bottle, but before taking a big swig Emmett said, "Don't let Rosa in here now Deputy. She don't need to be worryin' over me."

"I know Emmett, I've got it all under control. You just try and lie still and let Doc get that bullet out of you."

"Right Dep...," Emmett winced as Doc Baker probed for the bullet. "Dam Doc, I hope you're enjoyin' yerself."

"Shut up and lay still will yuh!" said Doc.

Emmett had three quarters of the whiskey gone when Doc Baker finally pulled the bullet out twenty minutes later.

"Boy, that was about the toughest time I ever had removing a bullet. I sure am glad it's over with," said Doc Baker as he flopped down in a chair.

"You're glad," said Emmett in a weak slurred voice, "I thought I wuss gonna have to send the Deputy affer anosser bottle."

"Shut up Emmett. You give me that bottle and lay down there and rest while I bandage you up proper," said Doc Baker.

Doc Baker took the bottle from Emmett and took a big swig and said, "You get on out of here now and let this man rest. I'll have you take him over to the boarding house tomorrow."

"That mean he's gonna be alright Doc?" I asked.

"Probably so. If I can keep the infection down and he gets plenty of good food and rest. Oh, he'll limp around here for a while and maybe need a cane. But listen, for the next three or four days I want him to stay off his feet."

"No problem with the good food part, but who's gonna make that big hoss rest?" I asked.

"Somebody better," warned Doc Baker. "He's not out of the woods yet by no means. Let me tell you something, if that wound gets infected, he'll end up with gangrene and die, and that is putting it mildly. It's too high up to amputate, so we have to watch it close. I mean what I'm saying here. This could still turn out bad in the next couple of days if we don't take it serious."

"I understand Doc, and I'll do all I can to see to it that he gets all the rest he needs, even if I got to hog tie him. You hear that Emmett?" Emmett just moaned faintly and closed his eyes.

"Can I let Rosa and her father in to see him for just a few minutes now, Doc?"

"Two minutes and no more Deputy. He has got to get some rest," insisted Doc Baker.

"Right Doc, two minutes, I understand. I'll tell them."

Murphy left, and after I explained the situation to Rosa and her father they went in, agreeing to make their visit no longer than a couple of minutes.

I waited in the outer office until they came out. Rosa looked worried as she and her father stepped out of the examination room.

"I am really worried about Emmett, senõr Deputy," Rosa said. "Is the doctor sure he is going to be all right?"

"Don't you worry Rosa," I said trying to assure her. "The worst is over now that the doc got that bullet out of him. Emmett's a good healer and I'm sure he'll be up and around and back to his old self in no time at all. We just gotta let him rest up a bit first, then you'll see, everything will be just fine," I said trying to make sure I didn't let on that I was as concerned as she was.

CHAPTER EIGHT
JESSE WONDERLAND

Next morning we moved Emmett to his room at the boarding house. He was weak and groggy the first few days, but started improving fast after that.

Judge Bryant came down to the Marshal's Office with Jesse Wonderland, Terrance's older brother, the day after the shootout. "Bring Terrance Wonderland on out here Deputy," said Judge Bryant. "I want to get this over with before I take off to Tombstone for a few weeks."

Jesse didn't look none too happy. He was quiet with a scowl on his face when I brought his brother out. Terrance wasn't as feisty as he had been the night before when liquor had been doing his talking. When he saw his brother though, he perked right up. "They got me here for no reason Jesse," he said, "Me and the boys were just havin' a little fun that's all."

"Sure, that's why Burch and Billy are dead. Don't think dyin's that much fun little brother," Jesse said.

"Yeah well, that Marshal had no call stickin' his nose in it anyways. That stinkin' law dog cracked my skull with his pistol, just weren't no call for that," complained Terrace.

"How much do the damages come to Judge?" asked Jesse.

"Don't be payin' them nothin'. I ain't done nothin' wrong here Jesse," Terrance whined. He was having little success convincing his brother he wasn't in the wrong.

"Just shut your mouth. We don't need no trouble with the law. We got to get along with folks, we got a ranch to run," Jesse said.

I looked at Judge Bryant. I think we both figured what Jesse really meant was that he didn't want the law to be nosing around in their affairs out at the ranch.

Terrance calmed down after that and Jesse asked again, "What's it gonna cost to settle up?"

Judge Bryant imposed a twenty dollar fine for disturbing the peace, and the damages at The Kings Palace Saloon were four hundred dollars; mostly because of the imported chandelier.

"Four hundred... damn-it Terry," Jesse complained and he pulled out a poke full of fifty dollar gold pieces and paid the bill as he gave his brother a hard look of displeasure.

"Get back out to the ranch before I kick your ass. You cost us enough money for one Saturday night's hell-raisin', not to mention two good hands.

"See you Judge... Deputy," Jesse nodded as he headed toward the door.

Terrance was standing in the doorway and he looked back over his shoulder. "I'll see you and that Marshal again Deputy," said Terrance.

Jesse pushed him on out the door before he could say anything more, but Terrance still stood stubbornly outside the door. "GET, I told you." Jesse shoved him so hard this time that he nearly fell out into the street as he stumbled across the porch. Terrance didn't buck his brother anymore. Jesse had a reputation of being a real hard man. They mounted their horses and rode out of town.

"Leavin' for Tombstone you say?" I asked.

"Sally Belle and I are going down there to check on a small business investment I'm thinking about making," the Judge said. "I'm also going to buy Sally Belle a new dress from New York. You reckon you'll be able to handle things without me for a few weeks?"

"Without Emmett, it might be a little challenging. But, I don't think there's anything I can't handle if I just stick to what's been taught me. If I need any help, I'll call on Ben to give me a hand," I said.

"Maybe you better get Manuel Gonzales or Dan down at the Nugget if you need help Deputy. Better tell Ben to keep to himself for now. I think that Pinkerton's getting pretty close to finding out something, if you know what I mean," cautioned Judge Bryant.

"All right Judge," I agreed. "I see your point. I'll keep that in mind."

"Well then, take care Deputy. I got to get going if we're going to catch the noon stage. Sally Belle prob'ly ain't half packed yet, so I had better get her going. I'll send a wire in a week or so and let you know when I'll be heading back," he said as he left.

"I'll see you Judge. Have a good trip, you and Sally Belle."

Emmett seemed to heal pretty fast. He was sitting in the swing on the front porch of the boarding house that first week and you would often see Rosa sitting with him in the evening. The second week Emmett was getting around with a cane, he kept asking me if he looked like Bat Masterson. I told him Masterson didn't wear a buckskin jacket. He asked, "How do you know he don't? Besides if he doesn't, he ought to."

On Wednesday, a week after the Judge had left, we got a wire from him saying he would be back in a week and he would be bringing his new bride with him. Of course we knew who that was, though he didn't really say in the wire. Everybody figured Sally Belle and him would be tying the knot sooner or later.

He also mentioned that some friends he had in Tombstone said that Clarence Pike had been telling it around he was going to come back up to Cold Creek someday and seek revenge on the people who had been responsible for his brother's death. Judge Bryant warned us to keep an eye out for him.

Taylor and Jordon wouldn't give it up. They made a nuisance of themselves every day, asking around about the Dill fellow.

Judge Bryant and Sally Belle got back in town late the following Wednesday afternoon. After they got settled in at the boarding house, the judge came down to the Marshal's office.

Emmett, Ben and me were having coffee when Judge Bryant walked in. "That all you fellas ever do is sit around drinking coffee?"

"Well Judge, sometimes we play checkers, especially when it's as quiet as it has been lately. By the way, welcome back, and I guess congratulations are in order too," Emmett said.

All of us congratulated the Judge on getting married. He told us it was a spur of the moment thing, otherwise, we all would have been invited.

Then Judge Bryant pulled something out of his pocket that looked like a short fat flute of some sort. He said, "I want to show you boys this. It's hand-crafted, came all the way from Germany. Well... what do you think?" He paused to allow us to look at it. We were all befuddled as to what it was.

Ben finally asked, "Well, what the heck is it, Judge?"

Judge Bryant looked at us like we were all crazy and said, "It's an elk call. It's hand carved. It makes a sound like another elk and they come right up to you. Ain't you never seen one before?"

"No, can't say that I have," replied Ben.

I just looked at the thing, I still wasn't sure what it was for. Then Emmett spoke up and said, "I've seen Indians use something like that now that I think of it."

"You fellas don't get around much," said the Judge with a scowl. Then he change the subject, "So I take it you ain't seen nothing of ol' Clarence Pike then?"

"No, not a sign of'm. You don't really suppose he'll show up around here after Emmett booted him out of town the way he did, do you?" I asked.

"You just never know about a man like that, Deputy. I'll be watching my back that's for sure. And, I suggest you boys do the same," the Judge advised.

We all agree on that point.

"How you getting on Emmett?" asked the Judge.

"I'm healed up pretty good now. I'd throw away this cane but the deputy says it makes me look just like Bat Masterson."

"Aw heck Emmett, I never said no such thing. You just got it in your head that you're pretty, but I think Rosa's the only one who will agree with you on that point," I said.

"Yeah that's right Emmett. Besides, Masterson might carry a cane, but he doesn't wear a buckskin jacket," Judge Bryant said.

Emmett smiled, "Now where have I heard that before?" Emmett and I both laughed as Ben and the Judge looked at us curiously.

The Judge turned to Ben, "How about you and me go up to the mountains and hunt us an elk or two, Ben? I might even let you use my new elk call."

"Sure, I got nothin' pressin' over at the livery right now," replied Ben. "Business has been pretty slow lately and, I wouldn't mind havin' some elk meat to make up some jerky. But, what's your new bride gonna think about you takin' off like that though?

"I just spent two weeks with her. It's time to get away and enjoy some solitude for a while. Besides, I bought me a Remington Rifle while I was in Tombstone and I can't wait to try it out."

"Fine with me. You're the one who has to live with her. When you wanna leave, Judge?" asked Ben.

"How about we leave early Friday morning," the Judge said.

"Sounds good to me. See you back of the stables…'bout daylight Friday mornin'. I'll have everything ready to go," Ben told the Judge.

"Well fellas, I'd better get back to the boarding house and spend a little time with Sally Belle before I take off into the mountains. I'm sure you can hold things together here a bit longer without me, can't you?"

Emmett and I agreed it wouldn't be a problem, to go ahead and enjoy himself, so he said 'good evening' and left.

CHAPTER NINE
THE FIRE

It had been three days since the Judge and Ben had left for the mountains. Emmett and I had just finished making a check through town, it was a little after eleven in the evening. Things seemed pretty quiet as they usually were on a Monday night.

Emmett headed over to the Cantina for a while before turning in. I had a nature call, so I headed out back of the jail to the outhouse to take care of business.

I was pretty well settled in on the seat when I noticed light flickering through cracks in the siding of the little shanty. I leaned closer to a crack in the boards so I could see what the source of the light was. What I saw was Buff Jordon carrying a lit torch in one hand and a can of kerosene in the other. He laid the torch across the rain barrel up by the door and dowsed the door of Ben's living quarters with the kerosene.

That door at the back of the livery stable was the only way out of the bunk room where Ben slept and ate. Ben had built it on the back side of the livery when he first bought the place. It had one very small window next to the narrow door and it wasn't big enough for anyone to get through.

Right then, I was in kind of an awkward position to do anything. By the time I pulled myself together, Buff had set the place ablaze. There was a roaring fire around the door of Ben's bunk room.

As I burst out the door of the shanty, I yelled at Jordon, "What the hell yuh doin' there Jordon?"

That's when I heard someone screaming for help from inside the bunk room. I knew it couldn't be Ben, because he was with the Judge hunting up in the mountains.

I had left my pistol back in the office when I had come outside. Buff pulled his pistol and took a shot at me and I dove back behind the shanty.

As I looked around the corner of the shanty from my lying position, I saw through the flames someone trying to open the door of the bunk room. Jordon fired off two shots at whoever it was, and they ducked back inside.

I yelled, "Yer not gonna get away with this Jordon." He took another shot at me as he ran to a waiting horse tied to a corner post of the corral, jumped on, and rode off into the night.

I got up and ran over to the door to see if I could get inside, but the fire was raging way too hot even to get close to the door. I figured whoever it was inside was probably gone by now anyway.

My concern now was trying to save the few horses being boarded inside and getting the fire under control. Most of Ben's stock was in the corral, about eight horses, I figured they would be safe there.

I went to the stables, swung open the barn door and went inside. The fire was already roaring inside the stables and I could hear the horses screaming and kicking in panic. It had been a while since there had been any rain and things were pretty dry.

There were three horses in the stables, but I could only get to one of them to let it out. To my sorrow, the other two perished in the fire. One of them was Emmett's Paint, and the other was Mayor Potts' new buggy horse. The Mayor's buggy was in the barn and it was lost too.

Seeing that I could do nothing else there, I ran around to the front of the barn where there were a dozen or so townspeople passing buckets of water trying to get the fire under control. They weren't having much success. That old dried out barn wood went up pretty fast.

Emmett was taking the lead in passing the water. He told everybody to start soaking down the Marshal's Office because the stables were too far gone to save. If the Marshal's Office went, it could easily spread to the whole town. Though the office and jail were adobe brick, the wood in the roof or windows could start the place burning.

By this time, there must have been near fifty or sixty people passing buckets and throwing water on the fire. Most of the people were still in their night clothes.

I noticed Taylor, the Pinkerton, was helping pass buckets and that's when I said to Emmett, "It was Buff Jordon set this fire. I saw him do it. Emmett, something else, I don't know who, but somebody burned to death in Ben's bunk room."

"Yeah? Is that right, Deputy?" Emmett was short on breath from passing water buckets. "Well keep it quiet for now. We'll investigate this after we get this fire out," Emmett said as he handed me a heavy pail of water to toss on the Marshal's Office.

We fought the fire till about three o'clock in the morning. The Marshal's Office got a little blackened, but we got it under control before it got a good start. The livery stables however, had been completely destroyed. The only thing left standing was the corral.

Emmett found Taylor after the fire was out. "Look here Mr. Pinkerton man," he said straightforwardly, "I don't want you leavin' town. I'm gonna be conducting a murder investigation and I'm sure you're involved in it."

"Me? Involved in a murder? That's plain ridiculous," Taylor answer sharply. "Just who was murdered, and when?"

"I'm not sure who, but somebody died in this fire that your pal Buff Jordon set. I'm sure you're the one who put him up to it," said Emmett.

"No, you got it all wrong Marshal," defended Taylor. "Buff Jordon was acting on his own. If he set any fires, he probably wanted the reward money for himself. We just found out yesterday that your blacksmith was the man that I have been looking for, Robert Benjamin Dill. I was going to come to you about it in the morning as a matter of fact."

"Sure you were. I don't think I believe you. Just who told you Ben Decker was this Dill fella anyway?" asked Emmett.

"Oh, I cannot reveal my sources of information," said Taylor. "But, let me assure you Marshal, Ben Decker is, or should I say was, most definitely Robert Benjamin Dill."

"This ain't over by any means Taylor. You stick around town or I'll come and hunt you down," Emmett promised.

"Sure Marshal, I'll stay in town awhile. You know you haven't got a thing on me. You saw me sitting on the porch of the Cantina when all of this took place and you know I had nothing to do with setting any fires," Taylor said as he lit a long cigar and took a long draw from it. Then he turned and headed down the street.

"He's probably right. I got no way to prove he had anything to do with this. Unless, maybe, I find Jordon and make him talk," Emmett said. "Let's go get cleaned up out back Deputy."

We went out back of the jail and washed the sweat and soot off at the pump. I said, "You know Emmett, I've been a thinkin'. I don't know who that was who burned in the fire, but that Pinkerton fella thinks it was Ben."

"You're right Deputy. He did say something that would lead a fella to think that, didn't he? Let's get some rest tonight, and tomorrow we'll poke around in the ashes and see if we can't come up with something that will tell us who it was that died in the fire.

"By the way, what happened anyway?" Emmett asked. "How'd you know that Buff Jordon set the fire and that somebody burned to death?"

"I saw Jordon soak Ben's room with kerosene and set it afire while I was out in the shanty," I said and explained everything that I saw and what had happened.

Then I told Emmett, "After Jordon rode off, I ran to the barn to see what I could do. I'm sorry I have to tell you this Emmett, but yours and Mayor Potts' horses were left inside and I just couldn't get them out. I'm real sorry, I tried my best, it just went up so darn fast."

"I'm sure you did Deputy, and I appreciate it too. I'm gonna track Jordon down and make him pay for this. I won't let it rest until I do neither. That was one good horse. I sure hate losing him." There was no doubt that Emmett meant what he said about tracking Jordon down.

"I don't believe for a minute that Taylor didn't put him up to it," Emmett said. "But, without Jordon I don't see how I could ever prove it. I knew there was something suspicious about him setting on the porch at the Cantina when I went in over there."

Emmett and I both spent the night at the jail. We were up at daybreak and having coffee, then we went over to what used to be the livery stables. The only thing left standing was the corral out back, which had horses in it, including the one I had rescued the night before, a big well-bred buckskin Ben had recently bought. All of them were horses that Ben usually leased out. As we arrived at the scene of the fire I spotted a mule I hadn't noticed the night before in with the horses in the corral. I might have over looked it easy enough with the fire and all going on. I wondered though, where did it had come from. I thought maybe Ben had bought it and I hadn't heard about it yet. Maybe he bought it to lease to prospectors. Ben usually told Emmett and me about all his trading deals, that is unless he got skinned by some shrewd horse trader. I never thought much more of it right then.

As I looked around, I just shook my head in disbelief at the sight of something that was so familiar to me being no more than a pile of ashes.

That barn had been there ever since I could remember, even back when I was a school boy. I wanted to see Buff Jordon pay for this myself.

At the spot where Ben's room used to be, Emmett started poking around in the ashes with a piece of wood he had picked up. The ashes were still smoldering, and it was uncomfortably warm walking around in them due to the steam from all the water that had been thrown on the fire the night before. The smell of the wet burnt pine was overpowering.

After about ten minutes, Emmett found what he was looking for and it was no pretty sight. It was the remains of the person I had seen through the fire in the doorway the night before. Who could it be? I wondered.

Emmett looked over the charred body. It looked as though the person had been wearing buckskin clothing. Emmett found some things in the jacket pocket that were not completely burned. They were papers of some sort in a leather folder, and Emmett held them up and said, "This is all I can find on the body. These papers were somewhat protected in the pocket of the buckskins in this wallet. I'm gonna take them over to the office and open them to see if they might confirm my suspicions of who this is."

"Why?" I asked, "Who do you think it is Emmett?"

"I'd just as soon not say until I know for sure. Tell you what I'd like for you to do. How about you go down and get the undertaker to take care of this body proper for burying. Be sure and tell him not to let out to nobody about what this body looks like. I don't want anyone to know that it ain't Ben. You tell him I said if anybody asks, it's Ben Decker as far as he knows. Then come on back down to the office and we'll see if I have any luck figuring out who this poor soul was."

I headed down Tillman Street to the undertakers. The undertaker agreed to Emmett's instructions as long as I guaranteed that the burial would be paid for.

When I got back to the Marshal's Office, Emmett was sitting at the desk with the papers from the body opened up and laid out on the desk in front of him. "It's just who I thought it was Deputy," he said after taking a big drink of coffee. "What he was doing in Ben's room last night I have no idea, but it's sure and the heck him all right."

"Okay Emmett, I give up, who is it anyway?"

"Look here Deputy," Emmett said as he pointed at the papers on the desk.

I walked around behind the desk where Emmett was sitting and took a look for myself. What I saw, still in good enough shape to make them out, was a receipt for the delivery of dynamite to some mine, and the expired claim papers that had belonged to Wild Jack Pike.

"You…You mean that was Clarence Pike that burned up in there last night?" I said. I could hardly believe my eyes.

"Well, these claim papers tell the whole story the way I see it," said Emmett.

"Yeah, I reckon they do Emmett, and that explains the mule in the corral too." I asked, "What are we gonna do now? Hey, do you suppose Pike was waitin' in the bunk room to ambush you Emmett?"

"I reckon that's a good possibility Deputy. I can't think of any other reason for him to be in there."

"And ol' Buff Jordon thought it was Ben that burned up in there, now didn't he?" I said.

"That's the way I got it figured," said Emmett.

Emmett started giving me instructions, "Here's what I think we'll do Deputy. You ride up to the cabin where the Judge and Ben stay when they're huntin'. Tell them what's happened here in town, and you tell Ben he's got to stay up there at the cabin until I send for him. Tell him there ain't nothin' he can do down here that will do any good. Let Ben know that I'll have Manuel Gonzales taking care of the stock he's got left, so they'll be in good hands for now. We'll help him figure out later what we can do about the loss of the livery stables.

"Listen Deputy," Emmett said insistently, "You got to see to it that Ben don't come back down here till I send for him. I see a possible way out of this for him, but he's got to trust me on this and be patient.

"You tell the Judge that as soon as he gets back to town I want him to swear out a warrant for Buff Jordon for settin' fire to the livery and murdering Clarence Pike.

"You should take some provisions with you when you go, so Ben can stay up there for a while. Don't let anybody know that you're takin' extra provisions with you. We don't want anyone to get suspicious. I'm gonna stay here and see if I can convince people that it was Ben that was killed in the fire."

I was about to walk out the door when Mayor Potts walked in the office. He was in quite a huff. "What the heck happened here last night anyway Emmett?" he demanded. "I understand that the whole damned town nearly burned down?"

Before Emmett could answer he brooded, "My horse and buggy burnt up in that fire last night, didn't they? I heard somebody died in the fire. Who was it? Do you know what started the fire?"

"Hold on there Mayor, take a breath. I can only answer one question at a time," said Emmett. "You know about the Pinkerton and the buffalo hunter Jordon that was with him, and that they were lookin' for some fella by the name of Dill?"

"Yeah, I know about all of that. Are they the ones set the fire? I knew you can't trust those hard-nosed Pinkerton's Why don't you get after them? That Pinkerton is over at the hotel. He's the one told me somebody died in the fire. I figured it to be Ben Decker, was it?"

"Now calm down Mayor, and listen to what I got to say before you go jumpin' to conclusions, okay?" said Emmett.

"All right, all right. I'm calmed down. Now tell me what's going on around here. I don't understand why somebody didn't wake me up last night and let me know that my horse and buggy was burning up. Do you have any idea what I paid for that outfit? Plenty, I can assure you, plenty. My wife wanted that outfit and now I'm going to have her crawlin' all over me about this. Explain it to me Emmett."

"Go ahead Deputy, take care of getting those provisions and stop back here when you get it done. I'll see if I can't explain the situation to the Mayor while you're gone," said Emmett.

I headed down to Cahill's General Store to get the supplies I needed to take up to the cabin. I had to buy a saddle from Cahill. Fortunately, he had one in stock. Usually, when I needed a horse, I'd just rent everything from Ben at the livery stables. I didn't have a horse of my own, didn't really need one too often. Now that everything in the livery had burned up I was hard-pressed for riding gear.

I thought about how upset Ben was going to be about losing everything in the fire. There was no doubt in my mind that he would want to get right back to Cold Creek. It wasn't going to be an easy chore for me to convince him to stay up there in the mountains. However, it would be the best way for him to leave that train robbery business behind. He would be able to go on with his life and not have to look over his shoulder every time a stranger came into town.

When I had everything together, I left it there at the general store while I headed back to the office in order to see Emmett before leaving. I figured I would pick a couple of horses out of the corral to carry the provisions up to the cabin. I thought, maybe I'll just use that mule to pack everything on. It was for sure Clarence Pike wouldn't be needing it anymore.

When I got back to the Office, Emmett was the only one there and I asked, "Well how'd it go with the Mayor?"

Emmett told me about his conversation with the Mayor. "He's a little calmer now that I explained the situation to him, but he's still pretty fired up about losin' his horse and buggy. He knew about Ben all along, just like the judge did. He said he realized that Ben was a decent man and that he didn't see any reason to turn him over to the likes of the Pinkerton and Buff Jordon. Ben had not broken any laws in Arizona Territory, he knew of, so he didn't say anything about knowing that Ben really was the man they had been looking for."

"I'm glad he sees it that way. Maybe Ben's gonna get clear of this business after all," I said.

"Maybe so," Emmett said hopefully. "The mayor doesn't want anybody to know he knew anything about it, because of his political position. I explained to him about Jordon being the one who set the fire and Clarence Pike being burned to death. I also told him about sending you after the Judge and having Ben stay up at the cabin for now. He agreed that was probably a good idea; at least until we see what the outcome of this thing is gonna be. He wants Buff Jordon brought in for setting fire to the livery and burning a man to death, even if it was Clarence Pike.

"I hate to give Jordon a three-day or better head start, but I want you along with me when I go after him. I think it's best for the Judge to be in town since both of us will be gone."

"I'll get goin' then, so's I can get back here as soon as possible."

"Good idea. I'm gonna look up that Pinkerton,

and see if I can't get him to admit to being involved in the fire. Or, at least I'll try and convince him Dill was the one who died in the fire. Then maybe he'll give it up. You be careful Deputy and get back here as quick as you can."

CHAPTER TEN
UP AT THE CABIN

After I had packed the provisions on the mule and a bay horse I had picked out from the corral, I headed north out of town toward the foothills. It must have been around eleven o'clock when I reached the edge of town, and I had a six-hour ride ahead of me. I was glad it was the cooler part of the year.

I would ride past where Wild Jack's place had been on my way up to the cabin. The cabin was an old abandoned prospector's shack that the judge and Ben had fixed up to stay in when they went hunting. There was a small mountain lake up there that was pretty good fishing. I never did much hunting myself, but I did try to make it up there once or twice a year to fish and enjoy the scenery.

I took my time and enjoyed the ride because I knew I would be staying the night anyway. I got to the cabin just as Ben and Judge Bryant were coming up the hill from the lake. The Judge was carrying seven or eight nice size trout on a stringer. As I dismounted and tied off the horse and mule, Ben and the judge were both full of questions about what I was doing up at the cabin.

"Hold on a minute," I told them. "I'll explain everything as soon as you help me get these animals unpacked."

"That Pinkerton is up to something I'll be bettin', ain't he Deputy?" said Judge Bryant. "I knew that man wouldn't give it up until he caused trouble in Cold Creek."

"Come on judge," said Ben, "let's get the deputy unpacked first. I'm sure he'll tell us everything." Then before I had a chance to answer. "Hey Deputy, what've you got all these provisions for anyway? There's enough stuff here to last two or three months, maybe longer."

"Well Ben, you said yourself, no answers till we get everything unpacked and I got some of that trout under my belt," I said; my mouth watering at the prospect of enjoying some.

"Yeah, you're right Ben," the Judge said. "But he didn't say anything about our trout bein' in the deal."

"That's right John, you sure didn't," Ben said agreeing with the Judge.

"You fellas are so anxious to hear what's goin' on that I figured I had better up the stakes a bit, while I could," I replied as I pulled the saddle off the bay.

The sun was low in the sky over the mountains, with brilliant streaks of red, gold, blue and pink reflecting from long clouds, when we got everything unpacked and stowed away. Ben went out back of the cabin to clean the trout as I put the horse and mule on the string with Ben and Judge Bryant's horses. Judge Bryant was inside building a fire in the open hearth fireplace for cooking the trout and heating up some coffee.

They didn't ask any more questions about my being there until we had finished a tasty meal of trout and pan cornbread. We were drinking coffee and enjoying the warmth of the fireplace afterward as night air in the mountains that time of year got down to near freezing. "All right Deputy," Judge Bryant started, "I think it's about time you told us what you're doing coming up here and what all those provisions you brought are for. Don't get me wrong now, I don't mind your company. But, you ain't up here to hunt and fish, are you?"

"And what about that mule you brought? I know you're ridin' one of my horses from the livery, but where'd you get a nice pack mule like that anyway?" Ben wanted to know as he struck a match to light his pipe and sat down in the rocking chair next to a window.

"Well Ben," I said, "that mule used to belong to Clarence Pike. Now, I suppose maybe it belongs to you."

"You wanna explain that Deputy?" said the Judge.

"You see fellas," I began, "It happened like this here..." I explained the whole dreadful story of the fire, how Buff Jordon had started it, and how Clarence Pike perished.

After I had told them most of the details I turned to Ben and said, "I tried to get the horses out of the burnin' barn. The fire was blazin' so hot inside by then I could only get one of'm out, and that was because it was in the end stall by the barn door. It was that big buckskin you just bought. I'm mighty sorry I couldn't save the livery or those other animals, Ben. I really hate bein' the one tellin' you all this, but the whole place burned to the ground in short order. The fire darn near took the Marshal's Office with it, but Emmett had everyone soak it down. He was afraid if it caught fire it would spread to the whole town. The only thing left was the corral and nine horses, countin' the one I pulled out of the barn. Emmett's got Manuel Gonzales takin' care of them for now."

Ben and the Judge Bryant just sat there numb with their mouths open. Then after a moment Ben leaned forward in the rocker and said, "I can't believe my whole business is gone. I do thank you Deputy for your efforts of tryin' to save the place. I just don't know what to say." Ben stared out the window into the darkness with a hollow look on his face as he bit down on his pipe.

"So I take it Clarence Pike's the one burnt up in the fire?" asked Judge Bryant.

"Yes sir, without a doubt. Emmett went diggin' round next day and found some papers that identified Pike. That's where I figger the mule come from. It must've been what he rode into town on. We figger he was lyin' wait to ambush Emmett from Ben's room. Can't think of any other reason for him bein' there."

Ben interrupted, "I'll be leavin' in the mornin'. I'm goin' down and get even with that Jordon fella," he said, still staring out the window.

"Hold on now Ben, least till you hear what I got to say about this situation. This might just turn out for the better in the end," I told him.

Ben stood up and paced across the floor, struck a match on the log wall to relight his pipe and said as he puffed smoke, "Sure Deputy, a man loses everything he's worked hard for, and that's gonna turn out for the better somehow? Well, sorry Deputy, but I sure can't see how that's gonna be possible."

"I'm real sorry about you losin' everythin' Ben, but there ain't nothin' you can do that will make it come back. Emmett and me plan on trackin' Buff Jordon down. We ain't gonna let him get away with it. He still murdered a man that he thought was you, and he'll pay for it.

"When I left town it seemed like even the Pinkerton, Taylor, thought it was you that burned up in the fire. So he'll prob'ly be leavin' town pretty quick unless Emmett finds some way of connectin' him with Jordon settin' the fire. That's what Emmett was a doin' when I left. We haven't let anybody know that it was really Pike that died in the fire, so the townsfolk think it was you, Ben, who died in the fire."

"Jordon was workin' for that Pinkerton, so you know he put him up to it," Ben accused.

"Shore, we all believe that, but Taylor says Jordon was workin' on his own, to collect the reward money for himself. That Pinkerton was smart enough to be where he could be seen across the street at the Cantina when the fire started. Emmett even saw him, so there ain't no way to prove Taylor put Jordon up to it, unless we find Jordon and make him admit it."

Then I explained Emmett's plan to have Ben stay up there at the cabin until we could see what the outcome of this situation was going to be.

"No sir, I ain't stayin' up here. I ain't got nothin' left and I'm gonna make those two pay for what they did. Sure I made some mistakes when I was a kid, but that ain't no reason to burn a man out. They're gonna pay," Ben said, blazing with anger, as he tapped his pipe to clean the burnt tobacco out on the fire place mantle.

"Listen to reason here, Ben. You can't take the law into your own hands when there's lawmen to do it for you," the Judge said. "Remember we was talking just yesterday about the seven-year statute of limitation running out in less than two months. Then you'll be clear of this thing. You know, that's probably why Jordon and Taylor made such a desperate move as setting a fire."

"Look here Ben, I don't know what we'll do about the livery, but you got a few head of horses to work with and I'd be willing to make you a loan to help you get back on your feet."

"That would be great Judge," I said. "And I'm sure there would be a number of townsfolk who would be willin' to help build a new barn and stables."

"You suppose they would?" Ben asked, trying not to show his excitement at the thought of having a new barn and stables.

"Sure Ben, you got lots of friends back in town. Why do you think it took Taylor so long to find out who you was?" I said, and the Judge agreed with me.

"I reckon maybe you might be right Deputy, but I don't want no hand-outs; It would just be a loan, right Judge."

"Right Ben, you pay me back as you can," replied Judge Bryant.

"But what about Jordon and that Pinkerton fella? They hadn't ought'a get away with what they did," said Ben

"I don't know for sure what, if anythin', can be done about Taylor," I said. "I mean, so far there's no proof he was involved. You and I know Emmett won't rest till he's got Buff Jordon behind bars."

"There ain't no way he'll get away with arson and murder as long as I can do something about it," Judge Bryant added.

With a bit more coaxing, Ben finally agreed that he would stay at the cabin until he heard from us or for at least six weeks. That was the time needed for the seven year statute of limitations to run out. Before turning in for the night, the Judge and I made plans for heading back to town the next morning.

Early next morning I woke up to the smell of coffee and deer steaks grilling. The steaks came from a buck that the Judge had shot a day before I got there. Judge Bryant was the one doing the cooking, as he seemed to enjoy it. Ben was just waking up at about the same time I was.

After a good solid breakfast of deer steak and beans, the Judge and I said our goodbyes to Ben. We reminded him of the importance of him staying put there at the cabin for a while. Ben said for us not to worry, he'd stay. Right before we rode off he said, "Tell Emmett to get that lousy no good murderin' Jordon for me." I yelled back, as we dropped out of sight over a hill, that I would be sure and give him the message.

It had been a long, hot, dusty ride. It was a pretty warm day for that time of year. Judge Bryant and I took our horses down to the corral, stripped the saddles and gear off of them, and stowed it in a empty jail cell. I was washing the road dust off at the pump in back of the jail when Emmett came out to greet us.

"Well, I don't see Ben," Emmett said, "so I reckon you convinced him to stay up at the cabin."

"It took some doin'. Finally we convinced him to go along with the plan, especially after the Judge mentioned the statue of regulations for seven years, or what was that you called it Judge?"

"You mean the statute of limitation, don't you Deputy?" Emmett chuckled.

"Well, I don't know what you call it. I just know in about six weeks from now, Ben will be clear of this trouble and they won't be able to hold it agin him no more."

"All right Deputy, I didn't mean to laugh at you. I hadn't even thought about there bein' a statute of limitation on this deal," Emmett said.

"I didn't take offense, Emmett. I'm just tired from the ride. It's a hot one out there today. I'm just glad there is such a thing as that, whatever you call it," I said.

Judge Bryant chided, "You fellas can try and figure out what the statute of limitation is all the rest of the day if you want to. But, I got a new bride a waiting on me and I know she'll be a lot more entertaining than you two scratching your heads and wondering over points of the law you don't seem to know nothing about. See you later." Judge Bryant turned and headed for the boarding house to be with

Sally Belle. Me and Emmett went in the back door of the jail.

"You rest up some Deputy," Emmett told me, "I'll take care of things for the rest of the day around here. I'd like to take out after Jordon in the mornin'."

"I'll be ready," I said. I stowed away the Greener shotgun I always carried and started for the front door, then Jason Taylor came to mind and I asked Emmett, "What's become of Taylor the Pinkerton man?"

"Sorry to say," Emmitt started explaining, "I haven't been able to find any solid evidence linking Taylor to the fire. I'm sure he put Buff Jordon up to setting the fire to at least to flush Ben out. I had a conversation with him yesterday and I told him I knew he had something to do with it, and as soon as I could prove it I would bring charges. Then I told him, if he was smart he'd get out of Cold Creek, and as far away as he could. I also let him know that Ben Decker, or whatever he wanted to call him, had been a good friend of mine and was well liked around town. Townsfolk around here didn't take kindly to losin' their blacksmith or the only livery in town.

"Taylor said with the man he was after dyin' in such a unfortunate manner, he didn't have any reason to stay around town any longer. Then he said he'd prob'ly be leavin' on tomorrow's noon stage. Then he gave me that story again about him not havin' anything to do with Buff Jordon settin' the fire and that Jordon was just tryin' to collect the reward money for himself. So, I reckon he'll be gone tomorrow. Least he'd better be, or I'll have the judge put so much heat on him he'll surely wished he had."

"Well, it'll be for the better if he's gone, that's for sure. I'm going down and get me somethin' to eat at the boardin' house and rest up a bit. I'll see you later on," I said as I left.

CHAPTER ELEVEN
OUT AFTER JORDON

The sun was just peaking the mountains as Emmett and I started following a trail that led from the corral at about the place where Buff Jordon had mounted up and rode off the night he set the fire. Emmett had found it after I had left town for the cabin to get the Judge. He had followed the trail southwest out of town that evening. When he had gone about two miles, it got too dark to see, so he had to head back to town.

As we started off Emmett pointed out, that it was an easy trail to follow. The horse Jordon was riding must have had a new shoe put on recently, because the track was clearly distinguishable. A trail could last for weeks out here as long as there wasn't a high wind or a heavy rain to wash it away.

After about three miles, it became obvious that the trail was going to lead us right to the Rocking "W" Ranch. I sure wasn't comfortable with the prospect of facing Jordon with that small army of cowboys that hung out with the Wonderland boys at the ranch.

We lost the trail when it went up to the main road about a quarter of a mile from the Rocking "W". Emmett and I rode down to the front gate. There a man we didn't recognize with a rifle asked, "What yer business here?".

"I'm Emmett A. Cross, Marshal in Cold Creek," Emmett said to the fellow. "This here is my Deputy, John McCord. We followed a trail left by Buff Jordon and it led us right here. He's wanted for burnin' down the livery stables and killin' a man back in town. I don't suppose you've seen him?"

"I don't answer questions, I just ask'm," the man said.

Emmett leaned forward in the stirrups and put his hand to his Colt. "You listen real close here mister. I followed a trail that led us right here to this gate. And, unless you want me to deal with you for obstructin' justice, I'd suggest you step aside and let us through. And, I'm tellin' you not to think on it too awful long, cause I ain't a patient man."

In an easier tone the man answered, "Well, seein' how yer the Marshal and all, I reckon I should let ya come on through." The man started pushing open the gate.

As we passed through the gate, Emmett said to the cowhand, "Glad you decided to see it my way. Much obliged."

We rode up toward the main house. There was a bunkhouse about thirty yards across from the main house and a couple of cowhands came out of it as we stopped our horses in front of the porch which ran the whole front of the house. Then another hand stepped out of the barn. I recognized him, it was Jake, the ranch foreman. The barn was at the end of the lot between where the house and bunkhouse were.

There we were setting on our horses facing the front door of the house with our backs to those two cowhands at the bunkhouse. Jake over at the barn was to Emmett's left and I couldn't see him from where I sat at Emmett's right.

I felt mighty uncomfortable about the odds and the position we were in so, I eased the Greener shotgun out of its boot on the front left side of my saddle. The Greener had become my close companion after being shot by Wild Jack Pike. I wasn't real handy with a six-gun, and the shotgun gave me the edge I needed to equal things out in this kind of situation.

As I rested the sawed-off shotgun across my lap behind the saddle horn, the door to the house opened and Terrance Wonderland stepped out. As he spoke he took a wide stance on the porch and slipped his thumbs in his gun belt. "What do ya think you're doin' out here lawman? You're not welcome here. I suggest ya ride on out the same way ya came in."

"We're not here for a social visit. We're on official business, Wonderland. We tracked Buff Jordon out here. Do you know where we can find him or where he's gone?" questioned Emmett.

"If'n I did, I sure wouldn't be tellin' you nothin' about it. Now I warn ya lawman, get off my land before I..."

Before Terrance got his threat out his brother Jesse came out of the house and interrupted, "Hold on Terry. We want to cooperate with the law. These fellas are just doin' their job. Ain't that right Marshal?"

"That's right. We didn't come out here for a fight. But, we aim to catch Buff Jordon and anyone who gets in the way will face the consequences and that's a fact," Emmett informed them.

117

"That sounds like a threat to me, and like I told ya before, I ain't scared of ya just because of that badge," Terrance spouted.

Jesse grabbed Terrance by the arm and lifted him up on one side. Jesse was tall and slim, but he was a strong man. He told Terrance, "Shut it up Terry. Go find somethin' to do. I'll handle this. Go on now, I ain't gonna tell you again."

As Terrance walked away, he gave Emmett and me a hard look. I knew that someday it was going to come down to a fight between him and us.

"The kid's a hot-head, he ain't quite growed up yet."

Emmett warned, "That's not healthy when you're wearin' a six-gun you know. Well, we didn't come out here to cause a rift between you and your brother."

"Yeah well, that's my problem to deal with. What's this about Buff Jordon? What's he done that you come out here lookin' for him?"

"He set fire to the livery stables back in town and a man died in the fire," Emmett explained.

"Is that right? Well he was here, spent a night anyways. It was a couple of days ago, but him and that half-breed they call Turquois left the next mornin' after Turquois collected his pay. Jake, my foreman," Jesse gestured toward the man over at the barn, "told me they mentioned somethin' about headin' down to Tombstone. I can't really say where they went for sure. If you wanna ask around, you can, but most of the boys are out on the range."

"No that won't be necessary, if you're sure he's gone now. Besides, I don't think we'd get much cooperation from your hands anyway," said Emmett.

Jesse bristled at Emmett's statement and he barked back, "Sure I'm sure. I got no reason to lie to you. I don't want no trouble with the law, but I don't take kindly to havin' my word questioned."

"Didn't mean any offense. Just don't wanna go chasin' my tail, if you know what I mean?"

"Well, that's all I can tell ya. I got work to do," said Jesse as he stepped off the porch and met his foreman coming from the barn. As we were turning our horses to leave we heard him say to Jake, "You take your tail on out to the gate and tell Baldwin to come up and collect his pay. He's through."

"But Jesse...," the foreman started trying to talk him out of firing the man at the gate. Jesse wouldn't give.

"I said, he's through," ordered Jesse. "Tell him to collect what he's got comin' and get to ridin'."

"Okay Jesse, you're the boss," Jake the foreman said. Reluctantly he started out toward the gate.

Emmett told Jesse, "I didn't give that fella at the gate any choice but to let us in."

"If you don't have any other business out here, I'd appreciate it if you'd ride on out," Jesse said bluntly. "I run my ranch."

"Your ranch, and it's your right to ask us to leave. Unless you're breakin' the law and hidin' something, that is. So we're goin, for now anyway. Thanks for your help."

119

"I ain't doin' nothin' wrong," Jesse snapped. "You can just keep clear of here from now on, unless you want trouble."

Emmett didn't answer, we just rode out as Jake was explaining to the Baldwin fellow that he didn't have a job anymore.

After we were down the road a piece, Emmett asked, "Pretty touchy wasn't he?"

"I ain't sure Emmett. I guess he did seem a little uneasy about us bein' there. You reckon he's hidin' somethin'?"

"Maybe not right now, but he didn't like the law comin' to his door, though he tried to put on otherwise. He might not have any rustled beef around right now, or he's changed brands so they can't be detected. I'd be willing to take bets that the herd he's got on the range ain't as clean as Jesse would like people to believe. I'd say you'd be able to find more than one set of running ir'ns around that ranch. Havin' all those gunslingin' cowboys from all over, comin' in and out is pretty suspicious in my book. Smells a lot like a rustlin' operation to me, if you know what I mean? Well, no matter for now. We got other business to tend to, right Deputy?"

"Right Emmett. Do you reckon we can pick up that trail again or do you think Jordon's still on the ranch somewheres?" I asked.

"Naw, I think Jesse was straight with us about that. Did you notice though, he didn't bother to ask who got killed in the fire? That's how I knew he was uncomfortable with us bein' there. Most people would've wondered who had died. Maybe when we get back we'll do some investigatin', but we don't have time now. Let's head down the road and see if we can pick up Jordon's trail again," Emmett said as we picked up the pace.

We hadn't rode far when Emmett spotted a track left by the new shoe on Jordon's horse. The trail lead us south along the San Pedro River toward a town called Benson that had recently sprang up since the Southern Pacific Railroad had come through that way. Before the railroad, there was only a depot for the Butterfield Stage Line.

It was cooling off pretty fast and night was coming on when we decided to make camp for the night. We would wait and make Benson sometime the next morning.

Emmett took care of the horses and I gathered up some loose mesquite branches laying around to start a fire. After I got the fire going I mixed cornmeal, lard, and water for corn dodgers to have with the beans.

"I've never been this far from Cold Creek before, outside of goin' up to the lake to fish. I'd be lyin' if I said I wasn't somewhat excited about goin' to Tombstone," I told Emmett as we sat by the fire drinking coffee.

"I ain't never been in the town myself, though I've scouted some in the mountains around there," Emmett said as he poked burning embers with a stick and then tossed it into the fire. He leaned back against his saddle and continued, "I don't imagine it's much different from any other boom town, wild and full of hard cases. A place like that is usually just waitin' for the right man to come and bring a little law and order to it."

"I hear that Wyatt Earp, from Dodge City, is down there now. He's got a reputation as a pretty tough lawman. You suppose he'll be the one?"

"I've heard tell of him. He just might be the one to do the job, but I don't know. That's a pretty wild bunch of cowboys and gunslingers they got around Tombstone. It ain't no small job that's for sure.

"You know the Judge likes spendin' time there, so it must have its finer points. Myself, I prefer Cold Creek, a small town where you know most everybody. That's why I decided to take on the job as Marshal there. I had all I wanted of wild towns and rowdy cowboys when I left Fort Worth, Texas. Although I must say, I never got shot while I was there," Emmett said with a chuckle. "You know Deputy, there's a possibility the trail might not lead us to Tombstone and we won't get to see it after all. Or maybe we'll catch up with Jordon before we get there."

Disappointed at the thought of not getting to see Tombstone, I said, "I never thought of that.., sure had my sights set on seein' it though. Well, if it ain't to be, it ain't to be."

"Let's get some sleep Deputy, and fret about that when the time comes. Maybe we can close the gap between Jordon and us tomorrow."

"Alright Emmett, good night. I'll see you in the mornin'." I mumbled as I grabbed my blanket, "Sure had a hankerin' to see Tombstone though."

Coyotes yelped in the distance as I lay down, wrapped myself in my Indian blanket and tried to find a comfortable place for my head on my saddle. It didn't take long for me to drop off to sleep and I remember dreaming about Emmett and me bein' lawmen in Tombstone that night.

I woke up chilled to the bone just as it was starting to get daylight. The fire was stone cold and there was a thin layer of frost on most everything, including our blankets. I couldn't even tell for sure which way Emmett was lying. He had his blanket pulled up over his head and it was covered with frost, top to bottom. First frost I had seen that year and it was a hard one.

I kept myself covered as best I could with my blanket as I sat up and searched around my saddle for my boots. I was shivering so hard that I wasn't thinking clear enough to check my boots before pulling them on. I got the first one on with no trouble. But, when I had my foot almost at the bottom of the second one, a sharp burning pain ran up my foot from my big toe. I howled like a calf being branded.

Emmett jumped to readiness with his six-gun in hand. He looked around searching for the cause of my trouble. He looked quite surprised that no one was there torturing me.

Sleepy eyed he questioned, "What's up Deputy? You all right? You ain't snake bit are you?"

"Sorry Emmett." I was hurting but I had to laugh because of the way Emmett had reacted. "I think I got something in my boot that bit me. I reckon I was more surprised than in pain, but it does hurt a bit."

I turned my boot upside down and shook it, and sure enough a two inch brown and yellow centipede came wiggling out and hit the ground. He must have taken refuge from the cold in my boot. He started crawling away with his tail in the air like he was proud of making a grown man yelp like a pup. I wanted revenge for the pain and embarrassment. It was MY boot he was occupying after all, so I crushed the ornery creature out of existence with the one boot I did have on. It really didn't give me much relief or satisfaction and it certainly didn't stop the pain in my foot.

"Dog gone Deputy, I thought Jordon and a half dozen more like him had rode right down on us. You should let a fella wake up a little before you let out a beller like that, you know?"

"Sorry Emmett, but I was so cold I didn't think to check my boots before puttin'em on. I bet you from now on, I won't forget."

We broke camp and rode the five miles or so on into Benson. The morning sun was warming things up as we approached the town. We came into town and stopped at a little inn with a restaurant at the edge of town, hoping to get some coffee and a home-cooked meal. We also figured to ask around about Jordon and the fellow called Turquois with him, because there had been a few tracks on the road that led us to believe they had come into town.

As we dismounted and looked down the main street, we didn't see any movement. We kind of felt the town should be a little livelier than it seemed to be, but then we figured it was still morning and nobody was up and around yet. Maybe it was just a sleepy little town. We tied off our horses at the hitching post and went inside the inn.

Inside was a small dining room. There were six tables with chairs and checkered table cloths. There didn't seem to be anyone around, so Emmett gave a little holler, "Anybody about, you got some hungry customers here."

A second or two later a young girl about twelve or thirteen stepped through a curtain in a doorway from a room in the back. She had long black hair down her back, and was wearing a plain blue floor-length washed-out cotton dress. She had a white apron tied in front.

"If you're here for the hangin'," she said as she walked through the doorway, "it's at the other end of town at the lumber yard. I'd reckon you'd be too late to see'm do it now though, but they might still be hangin' up there if you wanna go and look see."

"Is your town marshal there?" Emmett asked.

"I reckon he is. He's the one carryin' out the hangin'," was the reply. "Don't think folks ought to take delight in someone's punishment like that. That's why I don't care to be there with my pa."

"Well, we didn't come for that purpose. But, I would like to speak to the Marshal. We'll go down and see if we can speak with him. When we get back, you suppose we could get somethin' for breakfast?" Emmett asked.

"Sure mister, ham and eggs suit ya?"

Emmett and I both agreed that ham and eggs would be just fine with us, and we left the restaurant and started walking toward the other end of town.

Almost at the end of town, we came to the lumber yard. There was a crowd gathered and they were all staring at a man swinging from the rafters of the lumber yard's storage barn.

The man was hanging at the end of a heavy hemp rope wrapped several times to form a bulky knot at the end. It looked as though he had been standing on an empty nail keg, and someone had kicked it out from under him. He was hanging limp and his head was cocked to the side in an unnatural manner.

This was the third time I had seen a hanging. The first time was when I was about six years old. A man had killed another fellow in a fight over a saloon girl, and a group of vigilantes had dragged him out to the edge of town and hung him from a lone oak tree that used to stand there by the livery stables. It was when Cold Creek was still mostly a prospecting town and didn't have any appointed law officials yet. I saw the man hanging there the next morning after they had lynched him. It was an awful sight. They hadn't tied a proper knot and the man had strangled to death and his face was all contorted. He hung there all day long until evening when somebody finally cut him down and carried him off to be buried.

The second was a horse thief and cattle rustler that Judge Bryant had sentenced to hang. That had happened a couple of years before I became a Deputy. The oak tree had died and long since been cut down by then, so a carpenter was contracted to build a small gallows to carry out the execution. Although it was more proper than the first hanging I saw, it still wasn't a thing I wanted to remember.

The crowd started breaking up and some people were walking away shaking their heads and talking in low tones to each other.

I said to Emmett, "I think I kind'a agree with the little girl back at the restaurant about hangins."

"Yeah, I reckon she did have a point sayin' what she did about folks getting' pleasure out of someone dyin' for their wrongs. But, you know Deputy, if a man's gonna break the law, he's gonna have to suffer the consequences when he gets caught."

"I know that, and I agree. I just don't think it ought to be entertainment for folks," I replied.

"No argument there, Deputy."

About that time, Emmett spotted a man wearing a badge and said, "There's the Marshal, let's go over and talk with him." We walked over to a short, well-worn man who was wearing the Marshal's badge.

"Mornin' Marshal. I'd like to have conversation with you," Emmett said to him.

The Marshal answered, "Got plenty time now that that loathsome job's over with. How about we have coffee together down the street at the restaurant? I haven't had mine yet."

Emmett introduced us, "I'm Emmett A. Cross, Marshal up in Cold Creek, and this here is my Deputy, John McCord."

"Well now, pleased to make you fellas acquaintance. What brings you down this way?" the Marshal asked.

"We're on the trail of a fella named Buff Jordon. We wanted to ask you if you've seen or heard of him," asked Emmett.

"Well, don't know, name sounds familiar, but what's he look like?"

"He's about the size of my Deputy here, only more hefty and dressed in buffalo skins. He's ridin' with a half-breed Indian they call Turquois. The trail we've been followin' led us right in to town," Emmett explained.

"Sure did see them, they left town, though," the Marshal told us. "I believe they must have left early yesterday morning. There were three of them, though. There was a big fella with them, bigger than you, wider in the shoulders, well over six foot I'd say. I mean this fella was a bull. I noticed the big fella was carrying a 'Henry' rifle. I figure you should know that, because if they lay in ambush against you fellas, that would surely give them the advantage of range. That is, if that big fella knows anything about using it. I never laid eyes on any of them before they rode into town a couple of days ago. Didn't know they were running from the law or I would have detained them."

"That's okay Marshal, the only one I'm after at this time is Buff Jordon. He's the one wearin' the buffalo skins. He's wanted for settin' a fire and burnin' a man to death. Thanks for warnin' us about the fella with the 'Henry' rifle though."

When we got back to the inn and went in to have something to eat the girl had everything ready. It was a big breakfast of ham, eggs and homemade biscuits; reminded me of my mother's cooking. We talked with the Marshal, just small talk about our past and experiences. He explained that the trees in the area were short and flexible, that was why the hanging took place at the lumber yard. He wasn't able to tell us anything more about Jordon and the men that were with him.

We ate hardy because we weren't sure when our next good meal would come. Then we said our goodbyes to a new-found friend and headed south out of town along the San Pedro River. We followed the trail south past a Mormon settlement and on toward Tombstone.

With three horses, the trail was even easier to read for Emmett. Myself, outside of the tracks the new shoe on Jordon's mount made, I had a hard time seeing what Emmett would try to show me. I could see it took years of experience to be a good tracker and even to this day I can't hold a candle to Emmett's skills.

CHAPTER TWELVE
ON THE ROAD TO TOMBSTONE

We stopped under a grove of trees to get out of the sun and let the horses rest for a while. Not that it was too warm, it really was quite pleasant that day, as a lot of days are that time of year in the desert southwest. Nothing like the northern country and the mountains where they get all the snow. It's rare to have any snow; but if we do, it gone by mid-day. Night can be a different story though; it can drop well below freezing in the winter months and chill you right down to the bone.

I chewed on some jerky as we let the horses drink water poured from canteens out of our cupped hands. Then we heard what sounded like a woman screaming hysterically off in the distance. The sounds were coming from the other side of a ridge, not far from where we were.

"You hear that Emmett?"

"Sure do, sounds like a woman in trouble. Could be Indians. We'd better go check on it Deputy."

We secured our canteens and mounted our horses to ride over and investigate. We topped the ridge in just seconds, and could see down into a little valley where the main road ran. There was a freight wagon setting off to the side of the road a piece. As we rode closer, we could see that the rear wheel was off the other side of the wagon. A woman dressed in a canvass skirt and a burlap shirt ran around the back of the wagon. A burly, unshaven man was chasing after her with a thick leather strap in his hand. He beat the woman with the strap as she begged him to stop while trying unsuccessfully to crawl under the wagon to get away from him. The man strapped her again and again with no mercy, cursing her and saying something about her not being able to lift the wagon wheel.

"Ya dumb wench," he shouted, "come out from under there. I ain't through with ya yet. Yer as useless as they come. I get that wheel back on an' I'm gonna leave ya out here as buzzard bait."

Emmett kicked the big buckskin he was riding into a dead run toward the wagon. The man didn't notice Emmett coming, being more involved with trying to get the woman to come out from under the wagon.

Emmett hardly slowed down as he dove from his horse and grabbed the man in a flying bear hug. The man and Emmett went rolling and tumbling across the ground. As Emmett stood up, he dragged the man to his feet, only to knock him back to the ground again with a hard right cross to the jaw. Then Emmett picked up the thick leather strap and commenced to strap the man down to the ground. The man tried to protect himself by curling up in a ball with his arms covering his head, but had little success with Emmett whaling him the way he was. Emmett would have beat the man into unconsciousness if the woman and I hadn't stopped him by yelling at the top of our lungs for him to stop before he killed the fellow.

"Get up, you mess of dog puke. Any man that beats a woman ain't no man, he's a yella stinkin' coward. You hear me? I said, you're dog puke and a coward," Emmett shouted in the man's face.

The fellow didn't answer Emmett. I'm sure he was afraid to. I hadn't seen Emmett so upset since the day the Pinkerton and Jordon had walked into the Marshal's Office. The man was wise not to say anything back to Emmett, for it was plain to see that Emmett held him in no accord and would have probably killed him without a second thought.

"What's your name dog puke?" Emmett demanded.

"Conley, sir.., Jonas Conley," the man answered while still on his knees with his head down so as not to make eye contact with Emmett.

"Well, Jonas Conley. What's yer story here? What makes you think this women needs to be beat like that?"

"I was sleepin' in back of the wagon, sir. She lost control of the team comin' down that hill over yonder," Conley explained, his eyes still to the ground as he pointed. "Then the wheel come off and the wagon darn near flipped over before it come to rest where ya see it.

After I unloaded the wagon an' was under it liftin' with all my guts, I told her to slip the wheel back on the axle, but she couldn't lift it enough to get it on."

"So you think that's a reason to beat her? She yer wife or what?," questioned Emmett.

"Na, I wouldn't marry that wench," Conley started to look up, but decided against it. He continued, "I won her in a poker game back at the 'Rock Pot' minin' camp, up in Colorada. She weren't nothin' but an ol' ho' round there, nothin' ta bother yerself over mister."

"She's a woman no matter what her background is," said Emmett as he shoved Conley over backward with his foot.

"Ain't no man gonna beat a woman as long as I'm in ear shot least ways. Now if you want help with that wheel, me and Deputy McCord will help you out. Then we can all be on our way. And if the woman..," Emmett looked over at the woman standing by the wagon. "What's your name, Miss?"

"Phoebe Ann Dunn, from Saint Louis," the young woman shyly replied.

"And if Miss Phoebe Ann Dunn from Saint Louis wants to go with you, she can; and if she don't, you'll cut one of those team horses out and let her have it. Then she can go with us. That'll be up to her to decide," Emmett told Conley.

Conley objected as he stumbled to his feet with some new-found courage. "That ain't right mister. She's my property. I won her fair an' square."

"Nobody should own another human bein'. We fought a war over that issue. So forget it. She makes up her own mind where she wants to go."

Conley was burning about the possibility of losing possession of the woman, not to mention one of his horses. He just didn't have the nerve to challenge Emmett over the issue any longer though.

I tended to Phoebe's wounds. She wasn't hurt too bad, but did have some terrible looking welts on her arms and legs. There was one welt on her face that had broken the skin, so I dug some salve out of my saddle bags. After wetting my bandana from my canteen I wiped the wound clean and then gently dabbed some of the salve on it.

When Emmett saw the wound, I thought he was going to start in on Conley again; but he didn't. He only repeated, 'Nobody was gonna beat a woman as long as he was around to stop it.'

Phoebe wasn't what you'd call a beauty. She was dirty from road dust and dressed poorly; still a cute kind of prettiness shined through, especially when she smiled, which wasn't too often. I could understand why she wouldn't smile much, having to be in company with a man like Conley. She had brown hair cut pretty short for a woman and when she put on an old straw hat she had, she looked more like a young man than a woman.

Emmett and Conley lifted the back of the wagon while Phoebe and I put the wheel back on the axle. It wasn't too big of a chore with all four of us working together.

When we got done helping load most of the stuff back on the wagon, Emmett said to Phoebe who was sitting up on the wagon seat, "Well Phoebe from Saint Louie, what's it gonna be? You wanna go with this here woman-beater, or do you wanna ride with us to Tombstone, where we'll settle you in some place?"

She looked at Conley as she contemplated her answer. I could see she was real uncomfortable about making a decision with Jonas glaring at her.

Emmett said to her, "Now Phoebe, don't you worry none about ol' Jonas there. He's gonna abide by your decision, I'll see to that. Ain't that right Jonas?"

Jonas wrinkle his bristly face and growled, "I don't reckon I got no say so in the matter."

"That's right Jonas, you got nothin' to say about it. It's your decision to make Miss Phoebe. Don't be scared, just tell us what's your choice, either way."

"I...I think I had better go with Jonas. He did take me out of that god-awful mining camp, and he's going to take me to see my sister in Tombstone," she answered sheepishly.

It looked to me that Phoebe made her decision because she was still afraid of Conley. Emmett must have felt the same way because he said to her, "You realize Phoebe, that when me and Deputy McCord ride away, there ain't gonna be nothin' stoppin' this no-count from beatin' you again?"

Phoebe thought hard as she looked at Conley and then at Emmett. Then she looked at me, sighed, and looked back at Emmett and said, "I will stay with Jonas. I do thank you both for helping get the wheel back on and all though."

"Sure thing Phoebe from Saint Louie," said Emmett. "It's your decision, hope it works out for you."

Conley was putting a few things laying around on the ground back in the wagon. Emmett looked at him over the wagon and warned, "Let me tell you mister, folks don't take much to a man beatin' a defenseless woman around these parts. So if I were you, I'd think on it real hard before I'd do it again. And if I were to get wind of you beatin' Miss Phoebe here again, I'd come and shoot you on the spot. You think you understand that Jonas?"

Conley had just leaned a 'Sharps' Carbine rifle in the seat next to Phoebe, and hadn't taken his hand off it yet. He hesitated before answering, his hand still on the carbine. He couldn't have spoken the words out loud and said what he was thinking on any plainer.

Emmett just stared eye to eye with Conley from the other side of the wagon. Finally after a long silence, Conley took his hand away from the rifle and answered, "Yeah sure, I hear what you're a sayin'."

Conley went back to picking things up and putting them in the wagon. My horse was tied to a mesquite bush, and I went over to get it. Emmett's buckskin was tied to the back of the wagon and he was tightening his cinch strap and had his back to Conley. With my hand on the saddle horn and my foot in the stirrup, I was about to swing up on my horse, when Phoebe yelled, "NO". As I turned to see what was going on, I heard a blast from the carbine.

Phoebe was standing up in the wagon with the carbine raised in Emmett's direction, a stream of white smoke slowly pouring upward from the barrel. Conley was standing behind Emmett with a broad ax in his hands raised over his head. Turning slowly as he lowered the ax, he had a look of disbelief on his face. He didn't get turned all the way around to face Phoebe before he crumpled to the ground.

Emmett had turned quickly, his Peacemaker drawn, but there was no need for it. Phoebe had saved him from getting his head split open by shooting Conley in the back. Phoebe dropped the rifle as she plopped down in the seat and broke into tears.

Emmett walked back to comfort Phoebe and I retied my horse and walked to the wagon.

Phoebe explained through her tears, "I saw Jonas pick up the ax. I knew by the way he looked, he was going to do something awful. I learned to shoot a rifle when I used to go hunting with my father. I didn't think, I just picked it up. I tried to warn you.., but, I had to shoot or it was going to be too late...it happened so fast.

"Is Jonas dead?" Phoebe sobbed.

"Yes ma'am he is. Died quick. Didn't suffer none at all I'd say," I told her, hoping she would think he died without any pain and wouldn't feel quite so bad about it.

"Miss Phoebe," Emmett said, "I want to thank you for saving my life. Jonas there would've done me in for sure if you hadn't used that carbine. I know it wasn't easy for you, but you got to understand. You just did what was goin' to be done sooner or later anyway. A man like Jonas just keeps pushin' it, till somebody takes a stand and does what you did. He ain't worth you frettin' over. Believe me, I've seen plenty of his kind come and go the same way."

"Well I suppose that might be so, but I don't know what I'm going to do. Where am I going to go now that Jonas isn't around anymore."

"Don't you worry about that, Phoebe from Saint Louie," Emmett said as he lifted her chin up with his forefinger. "Me and Deputy McCord, here, will see to it you get to Tombstone to see your sister and then get settled in some place.

"I thank you for your kindness, but I don't have anything, not even any money. I don't want to impose on you or my sister. I'm not sure if she is even still in Tombstone."

Emmett let her chin go, took both her hands and held them, he looked her in the eyes and said, "Well you ain't imposin' on John and me. You just save my life. I owe you. Besides, we were headed for Tombstone anyway. Let's just get on down there and see what happens. If we can't find anyone that knows anything about Jonas in Tombstone, this here outfit, wagon and all, will be yours the way I see it. If you don't want to keep it, I'm sure it will fetch a fair price, and that will give you a stake to do something with."

"I am pretty sure Jonas doesn't have any family. He told me he was an orphan, and that he had run away from the orphanage when he was fifteen. He said he hunted buffalo for a while and then took up mining and prospecting.

"Do you really think, after me being the one that shot him, I would still be able to keep his wagon and belongings?"

"That's the way I see it if he hasn't got any next-of-kin. I'll fight with anyone who says different," Emmett told her.

We took a shovel and a pick from the wagon and dug a shallow grave a few yards from the road, put Conley in it, and covered it over with rocks. When we were done, Emmett pulled off his hat and stood there for a minute in silence. I followed suit respectfully.

Then Emmett slapped the dust out of his hat on his leg and said to me, "If you don't mind Deputy, why don't you tie your horse to the wagon and drive it on in to Tombstone? I'm goin' back to where we left Jordon's trail and see if it's gonna lead there. If it doesn't, I'll meet up with you in Tombstone just the same. We'll decide what to do from there when we meet up."

"Sure thing Emmett. I'll see you there then."

I tied my horse to the wagon as Emmett rode on ahead. I checked the rigging on the horses and wagon, climbed up into the seat beside Phoebe, and reined the horses onto the road. The wagon moved down the road at a steady pace. It was a well matched team.

"Any idea how Conley come up with such a good freight outfit as this?" I asked Phoebe.

"He won more than me in that poker game. He took the money he won and invested it in this wagon and the horses. He told me we were going to Tombstone and start a freight business. We needed to leave "Rock Pot" in a hurry because McMasters, the man he had won me and the money from, was trying to have him killed. He said he would put me to work as soon as we could find a decent place, and that he would split what I earned with me."

"Yeah, well, what was he gonna have you do?"

With a smile and a raised eyebrow she asked, "You're not serious with that question are you?"

"Well sure..," then my ignorance hit me between the eyes as I realized what she was talking about. I felt myself turn red with embarrassment. "Oh, you mean.., That ain't right for him to use you like that."

"Well that's just the way things were back in "Rock Pot"," Phoebe Ann told me.

"How in world did you ever end up in a place like that anyways?" I asked.

"Back in Saint Louis two years ago, I was a dancer on a riverboat. It paid good and the only thing I had to do to earn a living was dance and kiss a few fellas for good luck once in a while. Us girls were not expected to do anything more than that. I didn't realize what a really good thing I had going.

"Captain Stanley," she smiled as she thought of him, "was a very sweet man. He tried to warn us girls about being propositioned into going out West by some smooth talker. I was eighteen and all grown up, or so I thought, and besides, my sister had gone out west, so why shouldn't I? So then Lester McMasters came along promising a good job and gold, with lots of opportunities to own part of the action, maybe even find a young prospector who had struck it rich to marry. My friend..." she hesitated to hold back her emotions before she went on. "My friend Betsy and I jumped at the chance and signed a contract to work in a mining camp in Colorado."

"I reckon it wasn't what you had bargained for, was it?" I asked.

"No sir, certainly not at all what we had bargained for. When we got to "Rock Pot" after that awful trip across country, there was no dance halls like we had been told and everyone lived in tents. It was muddy and filthy with foul waste and muck running through the center of a tent city. Most of the men that worked there weren't any cleaner either."

"Sounds like a pretty nasty place for a young lady. Didn't you gals confront this Lester character about it?"

"Sure we did, but he just shoved our contracts in our faces and told us that we had agreed to work for him until we paid him back for transportation cost and expenses for our keep. He let us know in no uncertain terms that up there in camp a signed contract was law and there was no way we could get out of paying him. So we might as well face the fact he owned us until we paid up, in full. The charge for bringing us from Saint Louis, was a thousand dollars apiece and fifteen hundred if we wanted to go back. We were charged for everything, food and clothes, which there was none for women. We were even charged for clean drinking water. Betsy and I served food and drinks in McMaster's big tent, but what he gave us barely paid for our food. There was just no way to get free."

"Somebody ought to string a fella like that up, right in the middle of that camp," I said angrily.

"I would sure pay to see that, if I had money that is. Anyway, McMasters kept telling us the only way that we would ever get the money to pay him back and get away from there was to lay with the miners. He would supply us a tent of our own, for a price that is, and would give us twenty-five per cent of what we made. We told him that was unfair, but he said that was just too bad, that was the deal and sooner or later we would have to take it. At first Betsy and I would have no part in it."

"I can't hardly believe what I'm a hearin'. I'll tell you what, if I ever cross paths with this McMaster fella, I'll shoot him down. A man that would do such a thing to two young ladies doesn't deserve to live, the way I see it."

"Calm down now Deputy. He's a long way from here and he will probably never come down this way. Besides, he has two big men as bodyguards who are always somewhere close to take care of anyone that would try to cause him harm."

"Just the same, for his sake, he'd better never show up around here. Well, I guess you finally had to take him up on it?"

"I'm sorry to say, yes, we did finally give in. My friend Betsy got so depressed after a while that she cut her wrist with a razor one night while taking a hot bath. It was the next morning before anybody found her. Sh..She had bled to death," Phoebe Ann sobbed. "Poor Betsy, I miss her so."

She continued, "That left me as the youngest woman in "Rock Pot". The other three women were much older and one was very big, so I was the miner's first choice most of the time. Depression set in on me, it got so I didn't care anymore and the thought of suicide was on my mind. I felt it was a hopeless situation, that I was never going to escape it.

"I finally pulled myself together though. I decided to stop laying with the miners. That made Lester really mad, and he was going to beat me one

143

night, but a lot of the miners liked me, and they wouldn't let him touch me. The next night, Lester got to drinking pretty heavy while playing poker. That's when Jonas won me. Lester grabbed me and said he would use me to cover a big bet he had made.

"I don't know why I told you that whole story. I guess you're just easy to talk to," Phoebe Ann said.

"Don't worry Phoebe, I won't tell anybody what you've told me. Sometimes people just have to get things off their minds so's they can go on from there."

"Yes, you're right about that, Deputy. That's exactly how I feel. By the way, am I supposed to call you Deputy all the time, or do you have a name?"

"You can call me what you want, but my name is John McCord."

"I like the name John," Phoebe smiled. "It's a strong name with meaning, I feel. You are a pretty understanding fellow John. Thanks for letting me talk."

"Well thank you ma'am, it's nice of you to say so."

"Look John, quit calling me ma'am. You can call me Ann, that's what most of my friends call me."

"Sure thing... Ann."

Along the road to Tombstone we passed a stagecoach, two freight wagons, and a lone rider. We gave a friendly wave as each went by. It was a lot busier road than back home. I was a little worried that we might run into some highwaymen along the way. I kept hoping Emmett would show up some place soon.

Night was coming on and it was getting hard to see very far up the road. Tombstone couldn't be too much farther I thought. Then on a hill down the road I spotted a shadow. I could see the silhouette of a rider among the first stars in the evening sky. I slowed the horses and got ready to stop. I wanted time to ready myself if there was trouble. I slipped the Greener shotgun from between the seat and laid it across my lap and started to tighten up on the reins. Then I recognized the shadowy outline. It was EMMETT.

When we were close enough I said, "Emmett, good to see you. You had me wonderin' there for a minute. I thought maybe you was a highwayman."

"No, I'm not quite that hard up yet. It's too dark to follow the trail. I lost it awhile back. It looked like they were headed right into Tombstone, anyway," Emmett informed me.

As we cleared the hill, I saw a cluster of lights against the mountains about two miles off. I'd never seen so many lights at night before. It looked like someone had scattered a bunch of jewels across a piece of black felt. I was really anxious about getting there now. I couldn't wait to see the town. I just wanted to strap the horses and go; it was all I could do to keep myself under control.

CHAPTER THIRTEEN
TOMBSTONE

Finally, there we were at the city limits and starting down the main streets of Tombstone. I'm sure my eyes were as big as saucers as I filled them with every sight there was to see. Tombstone had sprung up in just a few short years, becoming a boom town due to the discovery of a rich deposit of silver.

We pulled up at a stables with the name "O.K. Corral". After getting everything checked in at the corral, Emmett told me he had found out that the town Marshal was named Earp and his office was down the street above a saloon called "The Crystal Palace".

We walked toward the center of town. I thought Cold Creek was a lively place at night, but there was absolutely no comparison. The street lights lit up everything almost like it was day time. There wasn't but two street lights in the whole town back home. As we walked along, it seemed like every other building was a saloon.

Then we came to the biggest, brightest, and the liveliest saloon in town. An outside stairway led to office rooms over the saloon. Emmett, Phoebe Ann and myself went up.

Once upstairs, we peeked through the window of the Cochise County Sheriff's Office, but there was no lights or anyone there. We stepped in at the Town Marshals Office where a blonde-haired man with a thick mustache sat behind a large wooden desk working on some papers.

Emmett spoke as the man stood up, "Are you Marshal Earp?"

"Yes, I'm town Marshal, Virgil Earp. How can I be of service to you?"

"Virgil? I thought Wyatt Earp was the Marshal here?"

"Wyatt's my brother. He's out of town on business. I don't know what to tell you as to his return. If your business is urgent, I'll do what I can to help till he gets back."

"No, if you're the town Marshal, you're the one I want to talk to. I do apologize for my ignorance sir," Emmett said.

"That's no problem. What's on your mind? Have a seat there and tell me how I can help." Earp extended a friendly hand and Emmett gave a firm hand shake as he introduced himself.

"I'm Emmett A. Cross, Arizona Territorial Marshal. I'm also Town Marshal of Cold Creek. This fella here is my Deputy, John McCord, and the young lady is Phoebe Ann Dunn, from Saint Louis." This was the first time I had heard that Emmett had a Territorial appointment. Apparently he hadn't wanted it to be common knowledge.

I shook hands with Earp and said that it was a pleasure meeting him. Phoebe Ann said hello shyly; Emmett pulled a chair over from the wall, and we all sat down.

Earp sat across the desk from Emmett; he relaxed in his chair and addressed Emmett, "Emmett Cross from Cold Creek? I've heard some about you. I know Judge Bryant from up that way. He speaks highly of you, and you too, Deputy

McCord. You know, the Judge spent some time here in town awhile back, got married here as a matter of fact. He sure is a pistol for sure."

Earp leaned forward in his chair. "Hey, seems I caught word here recent that you put Burch Wendell down. Wendell was a well-known gunman around here. While you're around town, I'd watch my back if I were you. Cowboys around here have a strange sense of vengeance sometimes. I wouldn't want you to get bushwhacked."

"Thanks for the warnin' Marshal," Emmett said, then explained the reason we were there. "I've tracked three fellas down this way. The man I'm after is Buff Jordon. He set a fire in Cold Creek that caused the death of a man and the town lost the only livery stable it had, nearly lost a lot more. Jordon's a heavy set fella, wears buffalo skins, just under six foot I'd say. He carries a .44 stuck in a sash around his belly. He's with two other fellas, but I don't have anything on them. One of them is half Indian, they call him Turquois. The other is a big man over six foot. Only thing I know about him is he wears a full beard and carries a "Henry" rifle."

After Emmett described the men, Earp said, "Those fellas were in town yesterday. I remember seeing them and would have took no note of them at all, except for the fact you're not the first person who has come in here asking me about that big fella carrying a "Henry" rifle."

"Somebody else is lookin' for them?" asked Emmett.

"No, not them, just the big man with the "Henry" rifle," said Marshal Earp. "Seems he stole it from a fella one night somewhere up around Benson. That fella came in here this morning and told me that he had offered the big fella the hospitality of his campfire and some grub. Next morning the big fella had disappeared with some cash and that "Henry" rifle. This fellow sure seemed mighty attached to that rifle I tell you."

"This man that lost the rifle, he still around?"

"Was a half hour ago when I finished my rounds."

"Are you takin' the matter up Marshal?" Emmett asked Earp.

"No it's not really a town matter. That fella did talk to Sheriff Behan about it. Behan put it to him rather bluntly that he had more urgent matters to tend to. So I would suppose he'll have to take care of it himself if he wants anything done. There's people around here that start getting upset when I take up things that aren't town matters. I haven't seen anything of the big fella, or the others since that one time I seen them yesterday. They didn't stay in town long. I would have liked to help the man out, but if they ain't in town any longer and they haven't committed violations against the law in town, there's not much I can do. Behan could've helped, but I guess he's got his own priorities.

"You won't have any trouble spotting this fella if you want to talk with him. He's a Buffalo Soldier, wearing a cavalry uniform. Got a Army jacket on that once sported Sargent stripes. He stands out pretty plain in a crowd around here. Let me tell you, he's not too friendly and he's pretty well fired up about losing that rifle. Seems to be a real tough nut."

Emmett asked, "You have any idea where I might find him now?"

"Was downstairs here at the Crystal Palace, before I came up a while ago. He just might still be there."

"Thank you Marshal. I'd like to impose on you a little further if you don't mind?"

"Depends on what you need Emmett. I'll do anything I can to help you here."

Emmett explained to Marshal Earp about the incident on the road with Conley and Phoebe Ann, emphasizing that Ann had acted in his defense when she shot Conley. I added what Phoebe had told me about Conley being an orphan. I didn't mention anything about Phoebe Ann's background. I kept my word about not telling anyone about her experiences back at the mining camp.

Emmett said, "I'd like to find a place for Miss Phoebe here to stay until she can find her sister and get on her feet. And the way I got it figured, unless Conley's got some relative here in Tombstone, the wagon and team outfit belongs to her."

"I have no problem with that, you handle it anyway you see fit Emmett. It's not a town matter and I don't know of any Conley's living around here. If you want, I can take her over to my place. My wife will get her some clothes and she can clean up if she wants. No offence intended ma'am," Earp said as he nodded to Phoebe Ann. With her hands in her lap she shook her head slightly with embarrassment while looking down at the floor.

151

"Tomorrow, we'll see what we can do about finding her sister," Earp suggested.

"One more thing," Emmett asked. "Can you recommend a place for me and my Deputy to stay for the night?"

"Tell you what Emmett, you go on down and see if you can find that Buffalo Soldier. I'll take care of Miss Dunn here, and make some arrangements for you and your Deputy while you're gone. When you get your business taken care of, come on back and see me. How's that sound?"

"That'll be fine. You've been a lotta help. I sure hate puttin' you to all that trouble, Marshal."

"No trouble at all Emmett, just courtesy to a fellow peace officer. I'm sure you'd do the same for me in your town. You go on, I'll take care of everything."

"Real nice man that Marshal Earp," I commented as Emmett and I walked down the stairs.

"He is Deputy. Been a lot of help to us. I just hope this Buffalo Soldier can do us some good too. I really got little hope of pickin' up the trail again after leavin' from here. The road's traveled so much that everything will be covered over."

As we entered the Crystal Palace Saloon, once again I was amazed by what I saw. I had never seen so much going on at one time in a saloon. It was just like "The Kings Palace" back in Cold Creek, only bigger with more people. There was every kind of gambling a fellow could think of. Men were dressed in suits like the kind Judge Bryant wore, although there were cowboys aplenty too. A thick layer of smoke hung just above everyone's head and the smell of liquor permeated the air. There was a pretty lady with a fancy laced dress, fashioned low across the bosom and high at the knee in front, for most every table. There was the sound of the piano playing and many people talking and laughing. All the noise blended into a low roar.

Once inside, Emmett hesitated as he looked around, taking in every person in the room.

There were two long beautifully polished mahogany bars, front and back, each lined with various types of patrons. One person I noticed right off was standing at the bar closest to the door. He had to be John Ringo. From the way I had heard him described to me many times by stories that circulated around Cold Creek, I knew it had to be him. He was a well-groomed, tall fellow; over six foot. What really gave him away was the two matching ivory-handled Colts hanging on his sides.

There was a man drinking with Ringo at the bar. He was much shorter than Ringo and had a patch over his right eye. I could tell he too, was a gunfighter, by the way he carried his .44 Colt backward in cross-draw fashion toward the front of his right hip, making him a left-hander.

Both men turned their backs to the bar and watched us intently as we walked in. It was obvious that the man with the patch was searching his memory as he watched Emmett.

After Emmett had observed the layout of the place, he brought his attention back to a table next to the wall. Though I'm sure he noticed the fellow

153

with the patch on his eye staring at us, he didn't act like he took much note of him.

A black man with a well-worn cavalry uniform sat alone with a whisky bottle in front of him and a double shot glass in his hand. This fellow was an older man and his uniform was somewhat frazzled. Still, he had a clean, neat, and orderly appearance, very military. He didn't take notice of Emmett and me as we walked toward him. I noticed that grin of Emmett's had come up on his face, but what he had on his mind, I had no idea.

The man looked up as we came up and stood at the table. At first he had a real bothered look on his face as if to say he wasn't to be disturbed. As he wrinkled his brow and studied Emmett's face, his expression started to change.

"Why.., I can't believe my eyes. I didn't think I'd ever run across you again," the man said.

"How are you Reese? It's been a long time ain't it?"

"It sure has, yes sir, it sure has. Sit, you and your friend. Let me buy you fellas a drink."

The fellow called Reese motioned to one of the saloon girls, and she promptly came over to the table.

"Get these fellas anything they want," Reese told the girl as Emmett and I pulled up some chairs borrowed from another table.

The dance hall girl was a mature gal with black hair pulled to one side in a long curl. She was very shapely; a good looking woman, and very lively. She gave us the prettiest smile, and asked cheerfully, "What'll it be boys? We got the best

154

whiskey in town. None more smooth tastin' or more guaranteed ta knock yer socks right off, that's fer sure."

"Just draw me a beer ma'am," I said.

"All I need is a glass. I'll help Reese here put this bottle to rest," Emmett told the saloon girl.

"Ma'am? Well, I'll tell you what cowboy," she said with both hands to her bosom, "You won my heart already. I'll get you those drinks and be back quicker than you can think of somethin' nicer to call me than ma'am." Then off she hurried to fill our order.

"Last I heard of you Emmett, you were still at Fort Bowie. So what brings you to Tombstone?" Reese asked.

"Well Reese, it's like this. I'm not at Fort Bowie any longer. Gave up chasin' Indian's. I left there awhile back to become the town Marshal up in Cold Creek. Matter a fact, this here fella's my Deputy, John McCord."

"Glad to know you son. You've teamed up with one heck of a man here. Saved my scalp more than once, I can tell you."

"Come on now Reese. Who saved who?"

"Well, I would say we were both lucky on more than one occasion," Reese admitted.

About that time the flashy black-haired beauty came back with the glass for Emmett and the beer for me. She sat on my lap as she put the shot glass and beer on the table. She turned and held my face in her hands. "Well now cowboy," she said, "Wait a minute, I don't wanna just keep callin' you cowboy, what's yer name?"

155

"John McCord, ma'am."

"Ma'am, I love him," she said as she looked at Emmett and Reese. Then she looked back at me, "Tell me Johnny, did you come up with anythin' else nice to call me while I was gone?"

I stuttered, "No m...ma'am, I'm sorry, I didn't." I could feel myself turning red with embarrassment.

"Well, that's okay honey, ma'am is about as special as a girl can get around here anyway. I told you I'd be back before you could think of anythin'. Tell you what though," she said; her steel grey eyes sparkling. "You just stay sweet honey, and if you do think of somethin' else, just give me a holler. My name's Lucy...Sweet Lucy is what they call me."

Lucy then planted a firm red kiss right on my mouth. I was thrilled and embarrassed at the same time. I wasn't sure how to react. I just knew everyone in the place had to be watching, but they weren't. She giggled, jumped up and was gone in the crowd before I was sure what had happened.

Emmett and Reese just laughed as I wiped bright red lip paint off my face with my sleeve and said, "That's some wild gal, I'll tell you."

Emmett gave a chuckle. Then he started talking serious to Reese. "I understand from talkin' with Marshal Earp, that you lost your 'Henry' rifle, is that right Reese?"

"LOST...Lost my ass end. It was stolen from me by some no-good, low-down, dirty four-flusher that ought to be hog tied and hung out to dry in the desert. Emmett, the law in this town ain't much

156

count for nothing. I wouldn't give a plug nickel for a dozen and a half of them."

"Hold on Reese, calm down now. You ain't gonna get nothin' accomplished if you get all riled up that way over it. Marshal Earp can't do nothin' about it, and it looks like the County Sheriff won't, so just maybe me and John can help you," Emmett explained to Reese.

"I don't think those fellas want to help, besides..." Reese stopped and thought for a second, "What's this now? Hey, you fellas didn't come all the way down here to help me find my 'Henry', that I know for sure. What's going on here, Emmett? What's your purpose here?"

"You're right Reese," Emmett said. "I ain't here just to help you. I'm trackin' a fella named Buff Jordon. Back in Benson, the big fella that stole your rifle joined up with him and a half-breed they call Turquois. Jordon set fire to the livery stable in Cold Creek. The livery burnt to the ground and a man burned to death inside. I aim to catch him and take him back. Trouble is, I lost their trail just outside of town and I don't know where they'll be headin' from here. When I asked the Marshal about them, he told me about a Buffalo Soldier havin' his rifle stole by the big fella up around Benson. I had no idea whatsoever the Buffalo Soldier he was referrin' to was gonna turn out to be you."

"Buff Jordon, ain't he the scout that led the massacre on that Indian village up north? The one where they killed all those women and children?" asked Reese.

"The very same one," Emmett answered.

157

"I never liked that kind of thing. It's one thing to hunt down a bunch of braves that have been on a killing spree, raiding ranches and the like. But, there ain't no call for killing defenseless women and children.

"I been asking around Emmett, and I found out that those fellas are heading down to Mexico, to team up with a bunch of rustlers that have been stealing Mexican cattle, then driving them up north to sell to the Army. Cost me a few dollars to get the information, but maybe it's gonna be worth it now that you're here."

"Wait Reese, who said you were goin' with us? I mean, this is a matter for the law and you'd better get back to Fort Huachuca, ought'n you?"

"The law you say. Well you better deputize me or something, because I intend to get my 'Henry' back, law or no law. My 'Henry' once belonged to Wild Bill Cody, and I ain't letting no thieving cowpuncher get away with coming right in my camp, eating my grub, and then stealing from me. Besides, I ain't in the Army no more. I'm retired. They kicked me out. Said, I couldn't see good enough anymore, but I can see good enough to take care of a man that steals from me."

"You mean Wild Bill Hickok," said Emmett.

"What?" questioned Reese.

"You mean your 'Henry' belonged to Wild Bill Hickok, not Cody."

"Oh…whatever. One of those Wild Bill's. Well, ya gonna deputize me or not?"

I suppose I could deputize you at that."

"Yeah, you could," Reese insisted with a wide smile.

"Havin' you along will make the odds even. You sure you can see good enough to do this? I'd hate to lose you," Emmett said.

"Since when has the Army ever known anything about a fella's health? I would have took off after them myself except for the fact Standing Eagle, and about twenty braves ran off from the reservation and joined up with Geronimo. That bunch of renegades have been running raids on isolated ranches and lone travelers between here and the border. I didn't think being out on the trail by myself would be too smart, especially since there are three of them fellas now. I was thinking about maybe hiring some derelict to go with me," Reese explained.

"You wouldn't be able to trust anybody like that Reese, and you know it," said Emmett.

"Yeah, I know. That's why I hadn't done it yet."

"Standing Eagle, you say? I hate to hear that, he's just signing his own death warrant runnin' off like that," remarked Emmett.

"Maybe he is, but can't say as I blame him for leaving the reservation. You know yourself Emmett, they've taken everything the Indians ever had away from them. A lot of the young ones, well, they're fed up with that kind of treatment. You know Standing Eagle don't you? In fact, didn't you save his mother from a beating by some trapper at the trading post back when you first come out here? Yeah, I remember, Standing Eagle was just a pup at the time and jumped on the trapper's back, got thrown to the ground and knocked out. That's when you stepped in. Darn near beat that trapper to death if I remember right."

"Yeah, I was kind'a hot headed when I was younger. I can't stand a man beatin' on a woman, any woman. A fella that does that, he ain't really a man, he's just a bully and a coward the way I see it."

I had heard that same thought earlier that day when Emmett had come to Phoebe Ann's rescue.

"Well, let's get started early in the mornin'. Those fellas got too much of a head start the way it is. You got some place you're stayin' Reese?" Emmett asked.

"I got a room for the night," Reese answered.

"What say we meet up at first light down the street at that O.K. Corral?" Emmett suggested as he pulled his watch out and checked the time. "That's where we got our horses boarded for the night."

Reese agreed and we finished our drinks. Then Emmett and I said 'so-long' to Reese and got up to leave.

CHAPTER FOURTEEN
FACE TO FACE

I hadn't given much more thought to Johnny Ringo and the fella with him until we started for the door on our way out. The man with the patch on his eye stepped in our path. Ringo stood back beside him.

"Ya know, a lot of fellas have poked fun at me since ya called me off that cowpuncher back in Fort Worth. Ya remember that don't ya?" the one-eyed man asked Emmett.

When he mentioned Fort Worth, the incident between Emmett and Bill Kelley came to my mind. This fella was Bill Kelley, a well-known gunman and a very dangerous man. The fact that the notorious Johnny Ringo was standing beside him made the situation even more deadly.

I was uneasy, to say the least, having to stand eye to eye with these two. Though concerned, I wasn't really what you would call afraid. I had learned from my experience as a Deputy Marshal that you just got to stand your ground in these kinds of situations.

Emmett answered, "I remember that I was tryin' to save you and that cowboy some grief, rather than have a killin' over nothin'. You were both drunk and I figured you'd forget it the next day anyhow. My intention wasn't to have folks poke fun at you, or him either, for that matter. I was just keepin' the peace by preventin' a killin', that's all."

I stood ready to pull my pistol and shoot at the first sign of any gun play. I figured no better than I was with a six gun, I would probably end up shot. At that moment I regretted that I had left the 'Greener' back at the corral with the wagon and gear.

Kelley kind of smiled and said, "Ah-h, don't need to concern yourself with it Cross. People don't bother me with their teasin'. I like to have a good reason before I kill a man, no harm done. Kind'a glad ya stopped me from killin' that cowboy. He wasn't much more'n a kid anyhow. I get touchy when I'm drunk. I just wanted ta see if ya remembered me. Maybe I can buy you fellas a drink?"

Before Emmett could answer, Ringo spoke up as he stepped forward, "Cross, from up in Cold Creek? Is that who you are?"

"That's me mister. Does that mean something to you?"

"You out-gunned Birch Wendell awhile back. Some say he was better with a gun than me. I don't share that feeling though. Tell me Cross, what's your opinion on that?"

"I don't have an opinion on it. Doesn't really matter to me. I do know that Wendell didn't give me no other choice but to put him down."

Ringo took a step back and readied himself, then said harshly, "It matters. It matters to me."

People started clearing out from behind Ringo and us. I thought, 'here we go, a show-down between us and two of the most infamous gunfighters there are'.

Just as Ringo was about to make his move, someone slipped between Emmett and me and said,

"Why, Johnny Ringo. I can't believe your lack of hospitality."

"Stay out of this Holliday. It ain't none of your concern," Ringo told him.

"It's Marshal Earp's concern," the man said coolly as he stepped toward Ringo. "He wouldn't take kindly to you picking a fight with his guest, now would he?"

This was no doubt the notorious Doc Holliday. He was dressed in a black suit with a long coat, the kind that a lot of gamblers wear. He had his hand under his coat to a nickel-plated, ivory handled Colt as he spoke.

"I don't care nothing about what the Earps think. What makes you think he's their guest anyway?" Ringo questioned.

Holliday coughed shallow a couple of times as he drew on a short cigarette, then answered, "Virgil just made arrangements over at the Grand Hotel for these gentlemen. I wouldn't be pushing this any further if I were you, Johnny."

Ringo and Holliday stood staring into each other's eyes. Holliday had half a smile on his face and a self-satisfied look in his eyes, like maybe, he was enjoying the confrontation. Ringo's expression was anger and once again he was about to make a move, only this time it would be directed toward Holliday.

Then Kelley interrupted the moment by saying, "Come on John, let's have a drink. We don't need no trouble with the Earp's, or the law right now."

With his concentration broken Ringo gave the situation a second thought, then said, "Yeah, okay. I never cared much for Wendell anyway. Maybe we'll take this up another time, when Holliday doesn't have his nose in it. What do you think Cross?"

"Not that it's what I want, but I do what I have to do. So ya might wanna think about it," Emmett warned.

"You're the one who better do the thinking. We'll just wait and see Cross. We'll just wait and see," Ringo said relaxing his tension. He and Kelly headed toward the bar.

"Don't pay Johnny no mind. He's just had a bad day," Holliday said with a smile and a bit of a chuckle.

"Doc Holliday is what they call me," Holliday said introducing himself. "Marshal Earp asked me to come and let you know that he had a room for you gentlemen across the street at the Grand. Just tell them over at the hotel that Virgil Earp, made arrangements for you. Everything has been taken care of. So whenever you want to check in, they are ready for you."

"Thank you Mr. Holliday. It sure is a pleasure to meet you," I said.

"My pleasure, sir. I would buy you gentlemen a drink, if you had a mind?"

"Thanks just the same Mr. Holliday, but me and John here have to be getting' some rest. Gonna be leavin' early in the morning."

"Then I think I'll indulge myself. Be seeing you boys," Holliday said as he nodded and headed for a lively looking poker table.

"I would like to have heard some of the stories he could tell," I said to Emmett as we stepped out the door.

"I don't know Deputy, a man like Holliday don't go around tellin' about everything he's done. Besides, I've heard stories about him that, I'd say, weren't what you would call honorable."

"Maybe so Emmett, but I sure am glad he came along when he did."

"Yeah, you're right there Deputy. Things were about to get real serious before Holliday distracted Ringo. I wasn't lookin' forward to a showdown with him, but like I told him, I would have done whatever necessary to deal with the situation."

"Emmett," I asked, "I got somethin' I'd like to do before turnin' in. Do you mind goin' on over and getting' us checked in and then I'll join you a little later on?"

"No Deputy, I don't mind. Go ahead, just keep an eye out for trouble. Don't forget we're leavin' around daybreak and we'll want to be rested up."

"Sure thing Emmett, I'll see you a little later."

I left Emmett, and headed back to the Crystal Palace to find Lucy. I had something I wanted to ask her.

Ringo and Kelley were coming out the door of the Crystal Palace as I stepped up on the wooden sidewalk. Ringo gave me a hard look, but didn't seem interested enough in me to start anything. That certainly was all right with me. I didn't have any desire to mix it up with the likes of him or Bill Kelley, for that matter.

When I was inside, I looked for the table where we had met up with Reese. He was just settling up his bar bill with Lucy and getting ready to leave as I approached.

"Hey, young fella, ain't you had enough excitement for one night?" Reese asked as I came over to the table. "You and Emmett sure know how to pick'm. Johnny Ringo, Bill Kelley and Doc Holliday. I don't know about you fellas. Thought I was gonna have to step in and give you a hand for a minute there."

"Wasn't our doin'. Ringo just wanted to pick a fight, and Emmett certainly wasn't gonna back down."

"Yeah, ol' Emmett is like that, ain't he? He'd take on a mess of wild cat's before he'd step aside. Well, I'm going to get some shut eye. Got a long day tomorrow you know. You'd better do the same, don't you think?"

"Yeah, I'll be comin' along as soon as I talk to Miss Lucy here. That is, if she's got a minute or two."

"Good night kid," Reese said as he left.

"Do you have a minute to talk to me, Miss Lucy?"

"Sure Johnny. I always got a minute for a well-mannered, good-lookin' young man like yourself. Sit down here and tell Lucy what's on your mind."

"Well Miss Lucy, I was a wonderin' if you knew of them needin' anymore girls right now? You know, to do what you do or somethin' around here?"

166

"Lucy's long hair was over her shoulder and she curled the end with her finger as she thought. "I don't know for sure, but I think they're always interested in someone with experience. I take it you got someone in mind?"

"Yeah, I do, and she's got experience as a dancer on a riverboat. Would that help?"

"A dancer, huh? I used to work on a riverboat myself. Well, there's always a job for a good dancer in this town. Why don't you bring this person around sometime tomorrow and I'll see what I can do to help?"

"Well ma'am, I won't be around tomorrow. I have to be leavin' town early in the mornin'. Maybe if I could send her to see you, would you still be willin' to help?"

"Sure thing Johnny, just send her over and tell her to ask for Lucy. Everybody knows me. I'll do my best to find somethin' for her," Lucy said with a smile.

"I sure appreciate it Miss Lucy," I told her. "You're one of the nicest ladies I've ever met."

"Nice of you to say that, and you're one of the nicest fellas I ever met. Listen now, you stay away from Johnny Ringo and that bunch of cowboys that hang around with him. They're nothin' but trouble."

"I intend to ma'am," I said. "I don't want any trouble with them fellas. Not that I'm afraid, but I ain't stupid either."

I said 'good-bye' to Lucy and left the saloon. When I was outside, I looked up to see if the light was on at Marshal Earp's office. It was, so I went up the stairs to ask where I could find Phoebe Ann, so I could talk to her.

Earp gave me directions to his house and told me he had found a buyer for the freight wagon if Phoebe decided to sell it. I thanked him for all he had done and for making room arrangements at the hotel for Emmett and me. When I offered to pay him for the rooms, he wouldn't hear of it. He just insisted we were his guests while we were in town.

I followed Earp's directions and found the house where he lived. I walked up on the porch, took my hat off and knocked at the door. When Mrs. Earp opened the door, she smiled, then politely asked who I was. I explained that I was one of the fellas that had brought Phoebe to town.

I asked to see Phoebe Ann, and Mrs. Earp went to get her after asking me to step in and sit down. I walked into the house, sat down on the couch, and started feeding the brim of my hat through my hands as I looked around the place.

The house was well cared for and decorated nicely. There was a dining room through double open doors and the kitchen was off the dining room. The kitchen was where Mrs. Earp had gone to get Phoebe Ann.

CHAPTER FIFTEEN
ANN

When Mrs. Earp returned, I thought for a moment there had been some kind of mistake. The woman who entered the room with Mrs. Earp was wearing a navy blue lace-trimmed dress with a bustle. She wore the slightest amount of face paint to accent her features.

I caught myself staring at this pretty young lady as I stood up. The young woman spoke, "Hello John. Is something wrong?"

"No.., No," I said, realizing that this really was Phoebe Ann standing before me. "It's just that you look so different."

She looked herself over and asked with a hint of concern, "Is there something wrong with the way I look?"

"Not at all Miss Phoebe. You look real nice. I mean, you really look great." And she did look good, although her short hair still gave her a bit of a boyish look. I wasn't used to seeing a woman with hair that short in those days. Still, Phoebe Ann looked better now that she was all cleaned up and dressed right. In fact, she was down-right pretty.

"Now John, I thought we made an agreement. You were going to call me Ann from now on."

"That's right, I forgot. I'll remember from now on though, Miss Ann."

She sat herself down lady-like at the other end of the couch. "You can forget the Miss part John. Ann will be fine. After all, we are friends."

169

I smiled and nodded in agreement. Then Mrs. Earp asked if I would like to have a piece of pie and some coffee. I hadn't had anything to eat, other than some jerky on the road, since morning breakfast in Benson. I sure did miss my ma's cooking, and home-made pie sounded great, so I accepted the offer.

Mrs. Earp went into the kitchen. Phoebe Ann ran her fingers through her hair, shook her head and said, "I sure will be glad when my hair grows out again. I had to cut it short back at 'Rock Pot' to keep the lice down. Before that my hair was down almost to my waist."

"That certainly was one terrible place for a lady to be," I said as I tried to imagine her with long hair. It was an impressive image in my mind. "That McMasters fella ought ta be shot. I mean, he's just a rotten son of a ...oh. I'm sorry, I ought not use such language in front a lady. What he did to you gals up there is just plain unforgivable."

"I'm sure I have heard a lot worse language than what you would use. That's over with now," Phoebe Ann said. "I just want to forget about that part of my life and start fresh from here."

"I think you will be able to do that here in Tombstone all right Miss Ann, ...I mean Ann. You know what? I talked to a saloon girl down at the Crystal Palace Saloon tonight, she said that there's always a job for a dancer in this town. And Marshal Earp mentioned that he had someone who was interested in buyin' the freight wagon and all. That is, if you want to sell it?"

I was nervous talking to this pretty young lady who I had found so easy to talk to on the way down here. I was feeding my hat through my fingers faster and faster and my conversation was trying to keep up. When I realized this I laid the hat on a nearby lamp table and tried to slow down my demeanor.

"I'll sell it, if it's still all right for me to do so. That way I won't have to look for work yet, at least not until I find my sister, Lucille Jeffers."

"I thought your last name was Dunn?"

"It is," answered Ann. "We are half-sisters. Lucille is a bit older than me. She was born to my mother's first marriage and her father died when she was young, then my mother married my father a few years later. Lucille worked on the riverboat before I did, and when some fella offered her a job out west, she jumped at the chance." With a tear in her eye she said, "I haven't seen her in over three years."

"Lucille?" I wondered out loud. "Why...that's kind of a coincidence. The lady I talked to at the Crystal Palace was named Lucy."

Ann perked up and wiped her tears with the corner of a handkerchief. "Really?" she said as her expression grew hopeful. "You don't suppose...no, it wouldn't be her. What do you think John, could it be her?"

"I don't know Ann, I reckon it's possible it could be her. She is supposed to be in Tombstone, right?"

"Yes. Lucille's got grey eyes and she always wears her long hair. There's a curl in the end. That's because she pulls her hair over her shoulder and curls the end of it with her finger all the time. She's always cheerful and has a smile for everyone."

"You know, I'd say that's more'n likely her," I interrupted. "Don't get your hopes up yet though." I looked into her hopeful dark brown eyes, "It's possible it ain't her too, you know? This gal had black hair and she sure was friendly and pleasant to talk to. She did have long hair with the curl in the end like what you're talkin' about."

Ann threw her arms around my neck and hugged me as she exclaimed, "John, it's got to be her. OH...You and Emmett have done so much for me. And now you've even found my sister. How am I ever going to thank you. I just know things are going to be better for me now."

I returned her embrace. The warmth and feel of her in my arms made me feel good, and the smell of the lilac perfume she was wearing had an intoxicating effect on me. If Mrs. Earp hadn't re-entered the room and told us to 'come on to the table', I really don't know what might have happened next. She smiled and lead me by the hand into the dining room.

I felt kind of guilty. 'What for?' I asked myself. I hadn't done anything. Was there something more to her embrace, or was I just taking advantage of an emotional moment? All I knew was, at the time, I certainly felt there was something more. I knew there was for me and I didn't know what to do about it.

Then something really strange happened. Loretta Packard, the new school teacher back home came to my mind. I remembered her sparkling blue eyes and her long golden hair. I mean, I had only talked to her that one time. I remembered how nervous I had been when I talked to her. My head was swimming in confusion. I tried to regain my thoughts as Ann and I walked to the table.

Mrs. Earp set the coffee and pie up in the dining room. She said, "It's ready, sit down and enjoy. There's cream for the pie if you care for it that way."

Phoebe Ann and I sat at the table in the dining room and I ate the pie and drank two cups of coffee as I explained to Ann about having to leave town early in the morning. I also cautioned her once more about getting her hopes up. There was a chance Lucy at the Crystal Palace might not be her sister. I didn't want her to set herself up for a big disappointment, though it did look pretty promising.

Ann insisted, "It just has to be my sister." She told me she would go the next day and see her at the first opportunity.

As I got up to leave, I thanked Mrs. Earp for her hospitality, especially for taking such good care of Ann.

Ann walked me to the door. "John," she said, then paused as she looked deep into my eyes. I felt somewhat uncomfortable with that, and it seemed to get terribly warm in there all of a sudden. My heart was jumping around in my chest, like I was scared or something. I wanted to look away, maybe even turn and run, but I knew it wouldn't be right. Besides I thought, what the heck was I afraid of anyway?

"You have to be careful, you and Emmett," Ann said as she put her hand on my arm. "And you will stop back here in Tombstone before you head back to Cold Creek, won't you please?"

"I can't say for sure whether or not Emmett will want to stop back by here or not. If we have a prisoner, he may want to get right back to Cold Creek. I'll talk with him and see what we can do. I ain't promisin' nothin', mind you, but I'll try my best." I felt so uncomfortable with her looking at me like that, all I wanted to do was leave.

"You tell Emmett I said he had better stop back here and say good-bye, or I'll be terribly disappointed."

"I'll tell him, but I still can't promise nothin'."

"I know John, do what you have to do. I'll just worry about you two until I hear something. So get word to me somehow, okay?"

"Sure, I think I can do that."

Ann lifted up on her tip-toes and kissed me on the cheek. "You better go get some rest," she told me. "I know you're tired and you'll have to get up early in the morning. Take care of yourself and be careful. And John, I really would like to see you again."

"Don't worry, we'll see each other again, one way or another." I thought, why did I say that as I headed back to the hotel.

It was cool outside, but I didn't mind. I needed to cool off anyway. Wasn't any stars out that night and you could barely make out the moon through heavy clouds. I felt moisture in the air, and I knew it would probably be raining before morning.

The Grand Hotel was sure a nice place and like every other place in town, there was still a lot going on for that time of night. Back in Cold Creek, about the only thing that would still be going that late would be The Kings Palace Saloon.

I got the room number from the desk clerk and found my room. Emmett was already in one of the beds, so I quietly slipped my clothes off and crawled in the other one. As I slid in between the blankets, Emmett's voice came through the darkness, "Bout time you showed up Deputy."

"Yeah Emmett, I'll tell you about it in the mornin'."

Emmett didn't say any more and that bed sure felt good. I fell asleep thinking about what had happened with Phoebe Ann and wondering if I wasn't having too strong of feelings for her. I fell asleep puzzling over what could have caused me to be so shook up.

Morning wasn't long in coming, and I woke up hungrier than a bear. I hadn't had a solid meal since the morning before in Benson. Wasn't much light outside, though I knew I had slept way longer than we had planned. I realized why it was so dim outside when I got up and splashed some water in my face from the wash basin. Looking out the window, I saw it was pouring down rain outside. I mean it was coming down in sheets.

Emmett wasn't in the room. I wondered where he had gone off to without me. I looked in the mirror and realized I was in bad need of a shave. About that time the door opened and Emmett came in, "Good you're up Deputy, thought you was gonna sleep all day."

"Sorry Emmett, I didn't mean to over-sleep like that. How's come you didn't get me up?"

"Well you was a sleepin' so pretty, I didn't want to wake you. Besides, with it rainin' the way it is, me and Reese figgered we would wait till it let up some before leavin'. That gave me a chance to send a telegraph message back home to the Judge. I let him know we were all right and should catch up with Jordon in the next few days.

"Tell you what, if you hurry up, I just might let you buy me breakfast at a little restaurant I found down the street." Emmett tossed me my saddle bags and I dug out my razor to shave and get cleaned up.

"By the way," Emmett said, "Phoebe Ann sold the freight outfit this mornin'. Got a pretty fair price too, thanks to the town marshal."

"I'm glad to hear that," I replied as I lathered up. "She sure can use the money."

Over breakfast I told Emmett about the night before and what had happened between me and Phoebe Ann. We talked about the finer points of love and courtship. Emmett told me a couple experiences of his own, and one thing he said that I tried to kept in mind was…"Take your time, don't rush into nothin' until you're sure that's what you want. You're young and you got plenty of time to make up your mind." Emmett also mentioned he hoped Lucy was Phoebe Ann's sister for her sake.

Emmett said there would be a good chance we would stop back in Tombstone on our way back, but a lot depended on what happened when we caught up with Buff Jordon.

After breakfast we stopped by the Telegraph office to see if Judge Bryant had returned a message, and he had.

The message read:

EMMITT:

'TAYLOR LEFT FOR MISSOURI ON THE STAGE SAME DAY YOU LEFT TOWN - BEN SHOWED UP THE NEXT DAY - COULD NOT STAND IT UP THERE ALONE - HE IS NOT GOOD AFTER SEEING THE LIVERY - FILL YOU IN WHEN YOU GET BACK - GOOD LUCK - BE CAREFUL'

JUDGE F.W. BRYANT

Emmett and I were both concerned with what Judge Bryant had said about Ben, but there was nothing we could do now.

The rain didn't let up until about two in the afternoon. We spent the day looking around town and buying odds and ends we needed to take along. I picked up a couple of boxes of shells for the Greener. Emmett and Reese bought some provisions for the trail. We loaded the stuff on the pack horse Reese had with him. We were well supplied when the rain finally did stop. We headed out of town, must have been around two-thirty in the afternoon.

I kept thinking maybe I would see Phoebe Ann during the day, but I didn't. We were always a block or so from the Crystal Palace, so maybe that was why I hadn't spotted her. I wondered if she had been to see Lucy yet and whether or not Lucy had turned out to be her sister.

Traveling was slow as we rode out of town. The rain had made the ground soft and slippery. Mud was up over the horses hooves. As we rode along, I just couldn't get Ann out of my mind.

We were heading south toward the Mexican border. Reese said we should try to catch up with Jordon and his bunch in a little hole in the wall place called Hades, just on this side of the border. He had found out they would be there for a few days waiting on the cowboys they planned to join up with.

CHAPTER SIXTEEN
REESE

Reese wasn't much on words, but he would answer when I asked him a question. I found out his full name was Washington Edward Reese, but everyone had always called him Reese. Originally he was from southern Tennessee, where his family had been slaves on a plantation. He said the plantation owner wasn't a bad sort, but freedom at any cost was much better than being another man's slave. So him, a friend, two older brothers and a younger sister ran off to the North shortly after the war broke out. He told me his parents wouldn't go because they were both too old. He had joined the Union Army, along with his brothers who were both later killed in battle.

After the war, there was no place for him to go. Both his parents had died so he decided to stay in the Army. He spent some time with his sister Thelma in Ohio before being transferred west to Fort Leavenworth, Kansas. There he was to join in the formation of the 10th Cavalry. Then he was transferred to Fort Bowie because of his excellent scouting abilities and that is where he and Emmett met. They scouted and fought together on a number of occasions, and a close friendship developed.

Being the only black soldier around, it wasn't easy for him to make friends. "Emmett never did seem to realize that there was any difference between the two of them," Reese told me.

Reese credited Emmett for saving his life and Emmett credited Reese, so I never really found out who did what. Neither man wanted to talk about their Indian fighting in detail. I figured it was because they both felt sympathetic toward the Indians, thinking they were getting a raw deal.

The Army needing good scouts to help track Geronimo and other renegades had transferred Reese to Fort Huachuca quite a while before Emmett had left.

We were never more than a mile or two from the San Pedro River as we traveled south. Reese told us Hades was on the edge of the river just a half miles or so from the border.

We rode steady all afternoon. The road had dried up about five miles out of Tombstone. It was obvious that Jordon and his outfit weren't trying to cover their trail. It didn't look like they were aware that anybody was trailing them. We pulled up to make camp on the back side of a ridge as night was falling. It was a beautiful evening, the sky was streaked with fire red and purple clouds as the sun slipped behind the mountains.

"You can look down on Hades with this field glass from the top of that ridge over there," Reese told Emmett as he pulled a collapsible spy glass from his gear and pointed it toward the ridge he was talking about.

"Good deal," said Emmett as he took the spy glass. Emmett kicked his horse to get a run at climbing the two-hundred foot or so to the top of the ridge.

Reese and I put up camp while Emmett took a look-see. Reese even had a tent big enough for two of us to sleep in. I stripped the horses and tied them off. Then I took water from the spare water skins from off Reese's pack horse and gave them some. Grass was pretty sparse, so after they drank a bit, I let them eat some oats and corn mix.

Emmett took a while up on the ridge. No doubt he was evaluating the situation down in Hades so there wouldn't be any surprises when we rode in. There was still a hint of daylight left and there was going to be a full moon that night, so he probably wasn't having any trouble seeing down into the town.

By the time Emmett came down from the ridge, Reese had a fire going and was fixing to cook up some salt pork and beans. "Coffee will be ready in just a bit," he told Emmett when he walked up to the camp fire. "I figure this far from Hades, and being this side of that ridge, no one would likely spot the smoke from the fire. I'll keep it burning so there won't be much smoke just the same," Reese explained.

"Ain't much of a town down there. Looks more like a way-station," Emmett said as he sat on his heels next to the fire. It was cooling off pretty fast now that the sun was down. "Only four buildings and what looks like a run-down blacksmith shop with a corral. I think they are there though, because one of the horses I saw in the corral looks like the one Jordon rides."

Reese pulled the salt pork pan from the fire as he started telling us what he knew about Hades. "Yeah, it ain't much of a place, just a hang-out for cattle rustlers and no-counts. There's a poor excuse for a Cantina at the south end of town. The building next to it is a boarding house, a couple of fallen flowers run it."

"Fallen flowers?" I questioned.

"Yeah, ladies of promiscuous and compromising principles. You know ladies of the evening."

"Oh, I get it... whores," I replied, once again embarrassed by my ignorance.

Reese gave me a bewildered look and continued. "Across the street from the Cantina is a mercantile. The building between it and the blacksmith shop is empty, least it was last time I was down this way chasing Apache. We stopped for water and to get a horse fixed that had thrown a shoe.

"The blacksmith is a unfriendly cuss. I don't see him sticking his nose into anything that ain't his business. The fella at the Cantina just might be a different story. I tend to think he might take up with the kind of hombres that hang around down there. The mercantile owner, he's an old fella. Him and his wife run the business and pretty well keep to themselves."

"It's good you can fill us in about the place like that Reese," said Emmett. "It will make it a lot easier to plan out how to handle this thing tomorrow. I'm sure nobody down there is expecting us, so it might be best to ride right in. Maybe one of us can stay behind cover somewhere in town, whilst the other two confront Jordon and his bunch."

Emmett took his bandanna from his neck and wrapped it over his hand, then grabbed the coffee pot from the fire. He poured some coffee in a cup he had brought with him when he came over to the camp fire. He reached over, filled Reese's and my cup too. "I'll sleep on it though," Emmett told us. "We'll anyway, let's see what mornin' brings. If either one of you fellas got an idea, let me know and we'll put our heads together and make a decision."

We ate supper and talked about our plans for the next day. We pretty well decided to do what Emmett had suggested. Reese would go into town a little before Emmett and me, leave his horse at the corral, and find a good spot for cover. Then he would stay there until we found out where Jordon and his bunch were.

We took turns keeping watch every two hours through the night. The watches kept the fire going while the other two slept in the tent.

When morning came, I was on watch sitting on a boulder wrapped in a blanket next to the fire. We had kept the coffee going all night and I had my hands wrapped around a cup to keep them warm. There was a thin layer of frost on everything that wasn't close to the fire. The sun was just getting warm enough to start melting some of the frost when Reese and Emmett started stirring.

"Coffee's hot fellas, and I'll have some bacon and pan bread fried up in just a few minutes," I told them.

"Good. I'm ready for that Deputy. I'll get up and saddle the horses," Emmett said.

"I'll give you a hand," Reese said, "Soon as I take care of some business over by that bush, that is."

We ate, not wasting any time and then packed up our camp. We went over the plan one more time. The plan was, Reese would ride in ahead of Emmett and me with the pack horse, leave it and his horse at the corral, then go around back of the empty building and come up between it and the mercantile building. He would stay out of sight and watch for anyone leaving, or until something happened where we needed his help.

Before we left the camp, Emmett told us to 'hold up'. He had Reese and I raise our right hands. Then he swore us in as Arizona Territorial Deputy Marshals. Now we were officially authorized to deal with Jordon and his bunch while they were in the territory.

We all checked the load and action of our weapons; Emmett his Colt Peacemaker, Reese a .45 caliber New Army revolver, and I checked my Greener and my father's Colt Dragoon.

"Let's be careful down there men," Emmett cautioned as we started off.

CHAPTER SEVENTEEN
DEATH IN HADES

We rode through a narrow pass at the end of the ridge that Emmett had climbed the evening before to look down on Hades. The opening dropped down about three hundred feet and leveled off right into the middle of town.

I saw Hades for the first time as we rode through the pass, and right off I understood what Emmett meant when he said it wasn't much of a town. It looked like, from where I sat anyway, the few buildings in the town were pretty run down. In fact, if I hadn't known better, I would have thought for sure it was a ghost town.

A dozen or so tumbleweeds lay scattered in the town's only wide dusty street. Every once in a while a breeze would kick up, and one or two of the tumbleweeds would roll down the street a few feet. It would hesitate like it was trying to get away from some invisible force holding it back as it struggled to press forward.

Without a word being said, Emmett and I slowed our horses and Reese kicked his into a canter to get ahead so he would be in position before we rode into town. The pack horse followed along like it knew what was going on. No doubt the animal was Army stock and was used to being called to action on short notice.

We rode slow to allow Reese time to get into position.

As Emmett and I entered the town we heard the ring of an anvil as the hammer stuck metal coming

185

from the blacksmith shop on the left side of the street. As we rode in front of the shop the Smith dowsed a glowing red-hot horseshoe in the water tank. It hissed loudly and a bellow of steam rolled up into the face of the burly Smithy. He gave us a hard look as we passed, then he went back to his business.

Emmett made a motion toward the Cantina and we rode to the end of the street where it was on the right. The Cantina stood directly across from the mercantile building.

An older, white-bearded man with a worn straw hat, sat on the porch leaned against the wall in a chair, next to the door of the mercantile building. He puffed whiffs of smoke from a long-barreled pipe and when I looked his way, he pulled it out of his teeth, smiled, and gave us a friendly gesture with it in his hand. I figured him for the owner of the mercantile. We gave the old gent a friendly nod as we passed. From what Reese had said about him and the looks of the old fella, I didn't feel he would give us any kind of trouble.

We pulled our horses up to the hitching post in front of the Cantina. Emmett hesitated before dismounting. Looking around cautiously, he took in the whole town, taking in all sides, especially behind us. Still, he never took his attention from the front of the Cantina. I tried to follow suit. I figured with both of us being observant, we were less likely to miss something.

Emmett looked over at me and gave a nod. We stepped off our horses, while keeping a keen eye out for trouble. Neither of us got in a hurry. Experience had taught us both that if we missed something or made an incautious move, it might be our last.

Emmett adjusted his gun belt, and I pulled the hammers back on the Greener shotgun. I held it tight against my right outer thigh, like it was part of my leg.

There wasn't much at all to the Cantina. The place was just a small run-down adobe building with a wide wooden door in front. An awning over the front of the building looked like the next stiff breeze that came along would take it off. A deep path was worn in the dirt from countless patrons coming and going through the doorway.

Emmett cautiously pushed open the door and stepped in. I walked almost beside him; the width of the door allowed us to enter together. The Cantina had a dirt floor and it was dark inside. It took a few moments for our eyes to adjust to the dim lit room. It was an uneasy feeling, not being able to see anything but shadowy outlines.

An unpleasant stench permeated the place, no doubt from years of cigar smoke, spilled liquor, and sick drunk cowboys. There would be no beer in a place like this, only hard rot-gut whisky, mescal and maybe tequila.

As my eyes grew accustomed to the lack of light the first thing that came into my view was the barkeep. He was standing behind a make shift-bar which wasn't anything more than two long wooden planks laid across three barrels, a barrel on each end and one in the middle. The barkeeper was a round-faced Mexican fella with about a week's worth of whiskers on his face. A black stub of a fat cigar was stuck in the side of his mouth. He gave Emmett and me an expressionless look, like it didn't matter to him whether we were there or not. Just the same, I felt it a good idea to keep an eye on him.

I looked over at Emmett. His attention was on two figures sitting near the end of the bar. They were sitting at a table in a corner of the narrow room. As I focused on the two figures, I recognized one of them as Buff Jordon. I didn't recognize the other man, but he was big even sitting down. He had a full beard, so I pretty well knew this would be the man that had stolen Reese's rifle.

Out of the corner of my left eye, I tried to keep the man behind the bar in sight as we approached the men at the table. He moved a step behind us as we walked the length of the bar.

Most of the light that came into the Cantina came through cracks in the door and from a small shuttered window behind the bar, and was to our side and behind us. By having the light to our backs and side, I don't think Jordon realized who we were until we stood across the table from him. The light situation gave us the advantage.

The 'Henry' rifle was leaning against the wall, next to the big fella. He gave us a mean look as we stood there. Jordon had a surprised looked on his face as he came to the thought of what we were there for.

"You're under arrest for arson and murder. Surrender your weapon right now Jordon," Emmett demanded.

As Jordon looked at Emmett, then over at the big fella, a sarcastic smile formed on his face. He got up slowly out of his chair and leaned on his knuckles across the tiny table, which put him almost nose to nose with Emmett.

Jordon set his jaw and spoke through clinched teeth, "I can't believe ya followed me all the way down here Cross. Ya must be loco to think I'm gonna let you and this wet-behind-the-ears Deputy of yours take me in. Besides, ya got no kind'a jurisdiction here. There ain't no law around here except what a man makes for himself. So, why don't you and this runny-nosed kid high-tail it back the way ya came before somebody ends up dead."

When Jordon got done saying his piece, he stood up straight, ready to make his move. The big fella remained sitting, but kept glancing beside him at the rifle leaning against the wall. I made eye contact with him. I could tell he was a cold man and I knew if Jordon made a move to fight he would too.

"You're wrong Jordon," said Emmett, "I got all the jurisdiction I need. As Territorial Marshal, I can arrest you anywhere in Arizona Territory. And, don't under estimate my young Deputy, him and his ten gauge can take care of business for sure. So, I'll tell you what you can do, either jerk that hog leg you got stuck in your sash and go to work or give it up and hand it over."

I readied my grip on the shotgun as Jordon gave brief thought to Emmett's challenge. He chose to go for the pistol, but he hesitated for a split second. More than likely, his hesitation was due to a fear of Emmett. After all, he did witness Emmett out-gunning Burch Wendell.

In an instant, Emmett had skinned his Peacemaker and backhanded the butt of it square to the temple of Jordon's head, much the same way he had done to Terrance Wonderland that night back in Cold Creek. As I knew he would, the big fella grabbed the rifle and brought it up to shoot, but Emmett followed through after striking Jordon across the head and put a shot point-blank into the big fella's chest, knocking him over backwards in the chair to the floor where he lay motionless.

I had raised the Greener to get off a shot at the big man, but movement, and the familiar sound of a pistol cocking, had caused me to take a half-step back and turn quickly to my left. I let go with a blast from both barrels of the shotgun. The blast knocked the barkeep hard against the wall and he jolted hard enough to squeeze off a round in the air, which ricocheted around the room a couple of times. The barkeep, with a numb look on his face, slid down the wall to the floor, dead.

This was the second time I had killed a man. I wasn't sick at my stomach this time, but I hoped that I would never feel comfortable with it. I didn't ever want to be that hard of a man. I know that most thought Emmett to be a hard man with no feelings, but he wasn't. He just did what needed to be done. He had deep feelings about people, he just didn't let it show too often.

"Where the...TURQUOIS? Where the hell is Turquois?" Emmett questioned.

"Outside somewhere? REESE," I replied.

Emmett reached down and grabbed Jordon's pistol and we both ran for the door.

When we got outside, once again our eyes had to strain to see and it took costly time to adjust to the brightness of the mid-morning sun.

What came into focus was a deadly disturbing scene. Reese was headed across the street toward us with his pistol drawn. He came from between the empty building and the mercantile. When he spotted us he slowed down his pace and seeing that Emmett and I were both alright, he smiled and waved at us with his pistol.

"REESE, behind you," Emmett and I both shouted at the same moment. We were trying to warn him of the impending threat. Right behind Reese, almost in his very footsteps, was Turquois brandishing a large Bowie knife. He was so close that Reese would be in the line of fire if one of us decided to take a shot. All we could do was watch.

Reese stopped with a puzzled look on his face. That's when he came to the deadly realization of what we were yelling about. Turquois buried the Bowie knife up to the hilt into Reese's back, just under his right arm. Reese jerked and yelled out in pain, firing his pistol into the ground. Turquois held him tight from behind, twisting the knife in place while it drained the life out of Reese. I actually think he enjoyed it. Reese dropped down on one knee, struggling. He pointed the .45 caliber Army revolver behind his back as far as he could and fired. It was Turquois' turn to scream in pain. A slug had struck him in the shin. He let go of Reese and tried to hobble away. Reese fell face down in the street.

191

I don't know why Turquois decided to go ahead and carry out his dastardly deed, but he did. He might have taken one of us out, but it cost him his life. When he was clear of Reese, Emmett from the hip, leveled the .44 he had taken from Jordon, and started fan-firing it at Turquois as he walked toward him.

Though Turquois hit the ground after about the third shot, Emmett went ahead and emptied the next three shots into him. He even tripped the hammer down twice more after the gun was empty. Emmett had a deadly aim and he had hit Turquois with every shot, though I'm sure he was dead after only the second or third.

We both ran over to Reese. Emmett got to him first. He bent down, rolled Reese over and lifted his head up, cradled in his arm. "Reese... hold on there old friend. We'll get you to a doctor."

"Come... Come on Emmett," Reese struggled to get his words out. "You know as well as I do, this is it. It's okay.., it's okay. I always knew it would be an Indian that would get me.

"Listen Emmett, I ain't got much time. Did you get my 'Henry'?"

"You damned bet ya we got it, Reese."

"It's worth some money. It belonged to Wild Bill Cody, ya know."

"I know Reese, you told us," replied Emmett.

"It's yours now Emmett, but listen..," Reese winced and coughed. He struggled to continue, "I got a money belt on me that's got twelve hundred dollars in it...please, Emmett...Emmett..., are you with me?"

"I'm right here Reese, I ain't goin' nowhere, I'm right here."

"Please see to it...that...the money gets to my sister Thelma, back in Ohio. Her address is in the money belt too, on...on some letters she's written to me."

"It'll get there Reese, don't you worry about that," Emmett assured.

Reese took a deep breath and looked at me, "Watch his back, Deputy."

I nodded and replied, "I will Reese."

Reese let out a last breath, closed his eyes and went limp in Emmett's arms. Emmett sat on the ground holding him and cursed under his breath as a tear rolled down his cheek.

The blacksmith and the mercantile owner showed up. They both agreed that it was an ugly way to die.

Emmett laid Reese down easy in the street after a few minutes. Going to the horses he jerked a set of shackles from out of our gear, went inside the Cantina and drug Jordon out and shackled him around one of the posts in the front of the Cantina. He made it clear to Jordon, if he even so much as thought about escaping, he was a dead man; and from the look on Jordon's face, I'm sure he knew Emmett meant what he said.

The fella from the mercantile told us the women at the boarding house also owned the Cantina. He informed us that the barkeep was their hired man and that he had drifted in about a year earlier. He also was sure to let us know that the ladies had a good relationship with the cowboy bunch that rode in and out of town from across the border, so he would appreciate it if we would leave as soon as possible. He didn't want any trouble with that bunch for fear they would burn down the town like they had threatened on one occasion.

Emmett, found two fifty-dollar gold pieces on the big fella. We figured it was part of the money he had taken, along with the rifle, from Reese. We only found two dollars on Jordon, and Turquois had about ten on him.

Emmett told the mercantile owner he would bury Reese himself, if he had a coffin; which he did have. Emmett arranged with him for the casket and he was to see to it that the others were buried for the price of one of the gold pieces.

Once again the man cautioned us about haste, since the cowboys were due to ride in at any time now. Emmett got indignant with the old fella and told him, if they did, they would just have to deal with him, because he was going to bury his friend and nobody was going to rush him.

There was a small spot with a broken down picket fence and a half-dozen or so grave markers in it behind the empty building, about fifty yards out. Emmett took a shovel and dug a hole by himself, he wouldn't let anyone help him, not even me. Emmett, the old man, the blacksmith and me carried the coffin with Reese in it out to the grave.

After we had lowered Reese into the hole, Emmett stood at the foot of it and took off his hat. He crumpled it in his fist as he stood there for a few minutes.

"I'm sorry, Reese," he said in a soft tone after a while. "Turquois just didn't come to my mind till it was too late." Then Emmett looked toward the sky, "Lord," he said, "I never was much on church goin' an' all. And, I don't know where my friend Reese is now, but he was a good man. Never did no harm to anybody that wasn't tryin' to do him harm first. He was a fair man too, he would do anythin' he could to help a fella in need. Saved my life a time or two, that's for sure. So, I hope you keep these things in mind. He was a good friend, and a straight-up kind'a fella. Well, don't know what else I can say, it's up to you now. Good-by Reese."

I said, "Amen", it just seemed appropriate. Emmett, straightened out his hat and started throwing dirt in the hole the with shovel. When the grave was filled Emmett forcefully planted the shovel on top of the grave. He then put Reese's hat on the handle and tied the chin strap to it. After that we headed back toward town.

We got a few supplies from the mercantile, and got ready to leave. We collected Jordon's gear; and outside of guns and ammunition from Turquois and the big man's things, we left the rest, including their horses. Jordon and his bunch hadn't been carrying much more than their weapons and water, and the horses weren't much more than ten-dollar horses anyway.

Emmett shackled Jordon's hands behind his back. He sure wasn't worried about his comfort. Jordon had started to complain, but one hard look from Emmett had shut him up. Jordon balanced himself by holding tight to the saddles cantle.

195

We rode back through the pass where we had come in earlier that day. We had Reese's saddle horse and his pack horse with us, so we moved at a slow pace. Emmett had put Reese's money belt on and put his own rifle on the pack horse, then he had slipped the "Henry" rifle in the scabbard on his horse.

CHAPTER EIGHTEEN
STANDING EAGLE

We were a few miles southwest of Bisbee, riding in a narrow stretch of flat land with rocky hills on each side. Just before it opened out into a valley filled with various desert plant life and cactus, I remember thinking that it would be a good place for an ambush and was glad we were about to get into some open country. No more had the thought left my mind, when the whoosh of an arrow cut through the air and struck with a dull thud into the breast of Jordon's horse. The horse reared and Jordon being unable to hang on rolled off backward. From out of the rocks appeared twelve to fifteen Apaches, yelping war cries as they rode hard toward us from both sides.

My horse spooked at the sudden excitement and took off at a dead run. Before I could get him under control, he tried to clear a dry wash and landed us in a large mesquite bush growing out of the edge on the other side. I heard his front leg snap as we landed in the tangle of limbs. The horse and I both fell back and tumbled into the middle of the wash. I was dazed from the fall and my horse was snorting and fighting furiously to stand up, but couldn't because his leg was broken.

I heard an Indian war cry, but couldn't tell from which direction it came. Before I could gain my senses someone jumped on my back pinning me to the ground. My head was yanked back hard by the hair. I saw a hunting knife flash in front of my face. Believe me, I shudder at the very thought of what

197

almost happened next. Thanks to Emmett I kept my hair that day. A shot was fired a split second before the blade made contact. The Apache that was about to remove my scalp moaned and fell off my back.

As I pushed myself up on my knees I saw Emmett standing down in the wash holding down his rearing horse by the reins with one hand and his pistol was in the other. He yelled, "STANDING EAGLE, STOP THIS. It's me Emmett Cross. STOP."

He was yelling at a stout Indian brave with stripes of bright colored war paint on his face, sitting on a pinto atop the edge of the eight-foot deep wash. The Indian turned, shouting something in Apache to the others and they stopped their charge.

The one Emmett had called Standing Eagle rode the top of the wash toward me and my panicking horse. The horse was still struggling furiously to get up. The Indian aimed his rifle and put the pitiful animal out of its misery.

Emmett said, "Stick with me here, Deputy."

"Like glue," I replied.

We climbed up out of the wash and reached the top as one of the Indians came riding up dragging Jordon by a rawhide lariat behind him on the ground. He wasn't taking any care as he dragged Jordon, screaming and cursing, through cactus and thorn bushes.

"Tell me, Emmett Cross, why should I stop? Is not this the way it is done? First white man kill Apache women and children. Then Apache kill white man. Then soldiers come and kill Apache.

We die with honor, as warriors avenging our dead families."

"Standing Eagle, you know it doesn't have to be done like that. I'm not out here for that purpose," Emmett answered.

"No, Apache could stay on reservation and starve in humiliation like dogs and turning the ground like old woman. Better to die in battle with honor. If it is not done like that Emmett Cross, then why are you and that killer of women and children out here? You are here to hunt down Apache. That is your job."

"Think about it Standing Eagle. Look, Jordon is in shackles, and there is only three of us. What chance would we have against you and your warriors? You know the Army always sends lots of soldiers to fight Apache."

"Why is killer of women and children in shackles?"

"I'm not a soldier any more. I'm a town Marshal and Jordon is my prisoner. He killed a white man and I'm takin' him back to be tried in white man's court of law, and then he'll hang if found guilty."

"He has slaughtered Apache women and children. White man has approved, so I will try him under Apache law," Standing Eagle said sternly.

"You don't wanna do that," Emmett argued.

About that time another brave rode up with Reese's pack and saddle horses. They had run off when I lost the reins in all of the commotion.

"I can do that Emmett Cross, and I will. As long as I have a breath, I will avenge my dead brothers. You give me your guns."

Emmett hesitated, "You can't win Standing Eagle, you know that."

Standing Eagle said something in Apache again. All the other braves snapped their weapons on us. We didn't have any choice but to comply. We would have most certainly died on the spot, had we tried to make a stand.

"You are right Emmett Cross, maybe I will not win. Then I will die in battle, with honor as a warrior, not like a whipped coward of a dog."

The Indians bound our hands with rawhide and led us on foot behind their horses. Jordon had a tough time of it. He wasn't in very good shape after being dragged the way he had been. Somehow though, he managed to keep up, stumbling along and almost falling several times. If he had fallen, the Indians wouldn't have stopped to let him get up; no doubt Jordon pretty well knew that so he struggled along. Though I certainly didn't care a bit for Jordon as a man, I had to admire his grit.

They led us through the rocks about two miles to a canyon where there was a camp. When we got there, they sat Emmett and me down against a large boulder out of the sun.

Two of the Indians took Jordon and after kicking and hitting him, they tied his hands to the shackles on his feet behind him. Then they pulled the bonds tight so that he was laying on his belly with his feet in the air behind him. Jordon kicked and cussed, even challenged them to let him loose so he could fight. That wasn't what the Indians had in mind for him, though. He kept trying to fight back as they tied him, but he only managed to wear himself out.

Then one of the Indians took a long piece of new rawhide strap and soaked it with water. When it was completely wet through and through about a half hour later, he tied it twice tightly around Jordon's neck and dragged him on his belly out in the sun and then left him.

At first, Jordon tried to talk, but he couldn't get anything understandable out of his mouth with his wind mostly cut off the way it was from the rawhide strap.

"Emmett," I said, "That's a hell of'a way to die. When that rawhide dries around his neck like that, he'll choke to death."

"Yeah Deputy, that's the idea."

"Well what are they gonna do, make us watch him choke to death and then do the same to us?" I asked, thinking what a hard way to die.

"I ain't sure. I don't think Standing Eagle has anything against me that he would torture me like that. If he's gonna kill me, I think he will do it in a more humane way, like walk up and shoot me, maybe even give me a runnin' chance. He prob'ly feels havin' my scalp would be a pretty good prize to show off his medicine to Geronimo. I don't suppose that really answers your question concernin' yerself though, does it?"

"Well, I was hopin' to die of old age, not out here in an Apache camp, with no hair."

While Emmett and I talked and Jordon slowly gagged and choked to death, the Indians were going through our gear, dividing things up. After they had everything divvied up, they sat around and talked while watching Jordon slowly choke. Once in a while one would go over and stick him with his knife a couple times, just enough to pierce the skin like you would test a piece of meat to see if it was done. They would all laugh as he jerked and kicked to get loose.

Standing Eagle didn't join in the fun. He sat cross legged on a large boulder on the side of a hill and watched while cutting off pieces of our jerky with his knife and chewing it. Every so often he would signal one of his three sentries stationed around on top of the hills to see if everything was all clear.

I had never seen a man in so much distress as Jordon was. His tongue was swelling, making it even more difficult to breath. His face was turned red. I was actually feeling sorry for him. It hadn't taken the afternoon sun long to start drying out the wet rawhide and for it to start shrinking ever tighter with each half-hour that slowly slipped by.

One time Emmett called to Standing Eagle, and offered five-hundred dollars, if he would let him go. Standing Eagle didn't even bother to answer. He just looked at us like we were crazy for even thinking he would consider it.

Jordon was quiet, conserving each breath of air he managed to gasp into his lungs. The Indians left him alone now. They just sat and watched while talking among themselves.

Finally Emmett had seen enough. He called, "HEY, Standing Eagle. You won't get away with this, the soldiers will come and hunt you down. They will hang you and your braves for murdering that man," Emmett pointed with his head toward Jordon.

Standing Eagle got up and walked over to us casually. "What am I going to do with you Emmett Cross," he said as he bent down and sat on his heels. Looking into Emmett's face he said, "You know, I have been sitting over there thinking about that very thing. As a boy, I remember you and the Buffalo Soldier, Reese? Yes, that is what he was called, Reese. The two of you were the only men among the Army scouts I can remember who treated me and my mother with any kind of respect. I have not forgotten the day you stood up for my mother when the trapper was beating her. I owe you Emmett Cross."

Standing Eagle pointed with his knife at Jordon as he stood up. "That killer of women and children there, I owe also. For my cousins and brothers I owe him. That was many moons ago and now I am paying him what I owe. And the cost is high Emmett Cross. So let the soldiers come, and let them kill me or even hang me. Still I have paid what I owe. You say, let him go for money. NO- money will not pay what he owes, not five-hundred, not even a thousand of your dollars would pay what he owes. Soon now, he will have paid what he owes. Now, how am I to pay you? I have not decided yet. I will only pay back one thing at a time, and the killer of women and children has not yet been paid in full, but soon I will owe him no more. Then...then I will consider how I am to pay you for my mother's life and your respect for us."

"Listen to reason Standing Eagle. You know this is only going to end with more blood spilled. You and your braves will just be run into the ground and killed. What honor is there in that?"

"Tell Three Feathers over there," Standing Eagle said as he pointed to one of the braves who had tied Jordon up. "You tell him to listen to reason. Tell him he is not to avenge his mother and father who were slaughtered because of that man. You tell him, he will not listen." At that, Standing Eagle went back to the rock on the side of the hill and sat once again.

The sun was setting and it began to cool off. Jordon had not moved or made a sound for quite some time and the Indian that Standing Eagle had pointed to got up and walked over to Jordon. He shoved on him with his foot, and Jordon didn't move. He shoved him once more and there still was no movement. The Indian pulled his knife and gave a war cry before cutting off Jordon's scalp.

So, that was that. No more Jordon, and we hadn't even asked him whether or not the Pinkerton had paid him to set the fire that night at Ben's place. Now with the Statute of Limitations about to run out for the train robbery that Ben had taken part in, I guess it didn't really matter anymore. I must admit Jordon had certainly paid the price for burning Clarence Pike to death in the livery that night, not to mention what the Indians had against him.

It got to be mighty uncomfortable sitting with our hands tied behind our backs by rawhide. No matter how hard we tried, we could not loosen the knots. So we sat and tried to make ourselves as comfortable as possible. Night set in and the temperature dropped and frost started to form.

I awoke chilled to the bone, shivering uncontrollably. I had slipped off to sleep, but the cold had awakened me. It was pitch dark now, not many stars out that night. The Indians had a fire going. Emmett and I barely felt any warmth from it though; we were too far away. Wrapped in blankets the Indians slept sitting up around the fire.

One time Emmett yelled at them and asked for some blankets, but they all ignored the request and went back to sleep. Emmett and I huddled together in an effort to keep warm. It helped some, but not all that much. It was a long night and though we did get some sleep; because of the cold we didn't really get any rest.

At the first hint of day-break, someone walking toward us brought Emmett and me around. It turned out to be Standing Eagle, who came over and once again bent down to talk.

"I will pay what I owe now, Emmett Cross. You gave my mother her life and I give you yours. I will cut you loose and give you your horse and pistol and you can go," Standing Eagle told Emmett.

"What about my Deputy here? He's not done anything to you or the Apache people."

"He can go with you. I have no reason to harm him."

"I want the 'Henry' rifle, Standing Eagle."

"No, your pistol is all I will let you take."

"That rifle belonged to the Buffalo Soldier, Reese. He was my friend. When he died he gave it to me, and I won't leave until I get it."

"My Pa's pistol," I interrupted, "I got to have it."

"And his pistol too, he's got to have it."

"You ask much Emmett Cross."

"Ain't your mother's life worth a couple of guns that don't belong to you anyway?"

"You push hard. Maybe I should scalp you and show your scalp to Geronimo. I will not this time.., I owe you no more, just like I owe killer of women and children no more. You do understand?"

"I understand. And you understand, I don't approve of the way you killed Jordon, even if he did deserve it."

"It does not matter to me that you do not approve. He had to pay for what he did, Apache way." Standing Eagle spoke Apache to one of his braves and he brought over Emmett's horse, the 'Henry' rifle, and our two pistols, as Standing Eagle cut us loose.

"Come on now Standing Eagle, where's the other horse for my Deputy here?" Emmett asked.

"He has no horse," Standing Eagle said sternly. "It had a broken leg and I shot it. You do remember?"

"I remember we had five horses all together, before you and your braves showed up and took them."

"You have what you are going to get. You have one canteen of water, your horse. You have your rifle and pistols. Now you go, or I will let my braves do what they want with you."

We had got all we were going to get from Standing Eagle and Emmett realized it. So Emmett stepped into the saddle and I climbed on behind him. Before we rode off, Standing Eagle said, "Next time we meet, I will owe you nothing. You will be just another white eye."

"Let's hope that next time doesn't come about, Standing Eagle." At that Emmett turned the big buckskin and we rode out of the camp.

We rode out of the canyon and when we were sure we were clear out of sight of the Indian camp, we stopped to evaluate our situation. First, we checked our guns. The rifle had five cartridges in it. Our pistols were empty, and when we checked the saddle bags they were empty too. The only ammunition we had was what was in our gun belts and the loads in the 'Henry' rifle. Fortunately, they hadn't taken our gun belts and we at least had that ammunition and Emmett still had Reese's money belt strapped around him under his shirt.

"I sure hate not havin' my shot gun," I told to Emmett.

"Didn't you have it on your horse?" he asked.

"Sure did, you don't suppose it's still there do you?"

"There's only one way to find out. I didn't notice any of them botherin' with your horse after Standing Eagle shot it. Let's mount up and go see."

We rode double the two miles back to the wash. Good thing we had the buckskin. He was a big horse and could handle carrying the both of us for a while.

Sure enough, when we got there, the dead horse was still lying in the wash. Coyotes were fighting with some buzzards over the carcass when we arrived. We shooed them off and I checked for the Greener. It was there. I also checked the saddle bags and found that nothing had been taken. There was about twenty rounds of .45 ammunition for my revolver, a box of shells for my shotgun, eight dried biscuits, a small skillet, a good-sized piece of fat back and some beans. So, at least we wouldn't starve for a while. Fortunately, I had a full canteen of water on my horse too.

"What about the saddle, Emmett? It's brand new. I just bought it at Cahill's General Store. It was the last one he had."

"Strip it off Deputy. We'll tuck it away some place and hope nobody finds it before we get back here to get it."

After we got everything together and hid the saddle in a thick growth of mesquite, Emmett suggested we head for Bisbee about eight miles away.

Going was slow. We took turns walking and riding so there wasn't too much strain on the horse.

CHAPTER NINETEEN
A MOMENT OF PASSION

We finally reached the outskirts of Bisbee. Most of the town was built on steep hillsides. It looked like most any fellow with a chaw in his jaw could sit on his front porch and spit down the chimney of his neighbor's house.

It was an interesting place, but we didn't stay any longer than it took to get a meal, rent a bath, and buy me a decent horse. We also bought enough supplies to get us back to Cold Creek including more ammunition.

I decided to buy the horse myself, I figured being Emmett's Deputy was going to require a horse a lot more often than it had working for Marshal Bob Coleman. Emmett made me a loan for the horse. I would pay him back when we got back to Cold Creek. I picked out a long-legged sorrel I thought would be a good ride for me. I rode bare-back on a horse blanket back to the wash. I hadn't rode that way since I was a kid. I was certainly glad when we got back to that wash and I found my saddle still there. The thought of riding bare-back any farther wasn't a pleasant one. I didn't waste any time getting it on my horse.

After we picked up the saddle and I had slipped it on the sorrel, we headed straight for Tombstone. Emmett wasn't going to concern himself with Standing Eagle anymore. There really wasn't much we could do about him and, 'It was a matter for the military,' Emmett had said. Although he didn't appreciate losing the pack horse and Reese's gear.

We knew Standing Eagle would be long gone from around that area by now anyway.

We made it about half way to Tombstone, before we made camp for the night. We ate, and were sitting by the fire drinking coffee when I decided to ask Emmett about the Territorial Marshal's appointment he had mentioned to Virgil Earp, back in Tombstone.

"Emmett, what's this deal about a Territorial appointment that you told Earp about?"

"Oh, yeah that," he said. "You remember that day we first met at your mother's boardin' house?"

"Sure, I remember that day. I asked you if you would take the Town Marshal's job. You said you didn't want to be a lawman again."

"That day, after I left the boardin' house, I ran into Judge Bryant and he invited me into the Silver Stallion Saloon. He bought me a drink and started tellin' me that he had been lookin' for a man like me to look into the going's on out at the Wonderland ranch. He said he 'was sure the Wonderland boys were involved in some kind of cattle rustlin' operation.' He told me there had been cattle stolen from ranches between Cold Creek and Tombstone for quite some time now. He strongly suspected that cowboys, after rustlin' a herd, would drive them up to the ranch where they would change the brands and keep the cattle out on the range until they could sell them off. He figured that was why there was always such an influx of cowboys in and out of there all the time.

"So the Judge told me," Emmett continued, "he had gotten government permission to appoint a

Special Territorial Marshal to look into and deal with the situation. He had it figured, if I would accept the town Marshal's job and keep the Territorial appointment quiet, no one would get too suspicious and I would be able to investigate the rustlin' operation without drawin' too much attention to myself. He also told me that soon the railroad was goin' to start stoppin' in Cold Creek to pick up cattle for shipment back east. With the railroad stoppin', it was urgent that any cattle rustlin' operations be brought under control so's the honest cattlemen could benefit by it."

"So that's when you decided to take the job?" I asked.

"Well, not exactly. I told the Judge I wasn't sure I wanted to be a lawman again, but I would give it some serious thought and get back with him in a few days to let him know for sure.

"I thought about it all the way back to Fort Bowie. I wanted to settle down and call someplace my home. I felt Cold Creek was a nice enough town, and I would have a job there with a respectable wage. I decided I really didn't have any reason not to take on the job. So here I sit."

"Well, I'm sure glad you made that decision," I told him.

"Outside of this deal here with Jordon and all, I am too Deputy. It just goes with the territory, I reckon. I sure hated losin' a friend like Reese though." Emmett paused for a second. I could see the pain in his expression. "He was a good friend for a lot of years.

211

"Let's get some sleep now Deputy. I'd like to make Tombstone early tomorrow and get our business taken care of there so we can head on back to Cold Creek. I want to see what's goin' on with Ben."

"Sure thing Emmett." I threw the rest of the coffee in my cup into the fire. It popped and hissed as I made myself comfortable in my blankets.

Next morning we hit the trail heading for Tombstone at first light. The wind was kicking up a ruckus that day which put quite a chill in the air. Herds of tumbleweeds of all shapes and sizes, scurried across our path from every which-a-way. There were a lot of clouds in the sky so that the sun had a hard time warming things up. It wasn't until we rode into Tombstone and got out of the wind that the day had any hint of warmth to it.

We decided to leave the horses at the same place we had the last time we were in town. As we rode down the street toward the O.K. Corral all my thoughts were on that night at Marshal Earp's house with Phoebe Ann. I remembered she had told me to call her Ann, and I liked that. Every time I thought of that woman I would start to get nervous, I couldn't understand that. It hadn't been that way on the ride down to Tombstone, when we had talked in the wagon. 'No', I thought, it was since I had seen her all polished up and in that blue lace-trimmed dress. She was a pretty woman and I really liked talking to her. Also, Ann's search for her sister came to mind. I wondered if Lucy, the saloon girl at the Crystal Palace, had turned out to be her sister.

We squared away our horses and gear, then found a room at a boarding house for the night. The place had a dining room restaurant similar to my mother's place back in Cold Creek.

Emmett and I had just sat down to a steak with all the trimmings when Marshal Earp came in. He spotted us and came over to the table. "I haven't had a good steak in a while. You mind if I join you?" asked Earp.

"Sure, have a seat Marshal," Emmett answered as I nodded agreeably.

"I reckon you didn't catch up with that bunch you were chasing," Earp said as he sat down.

"As a matter of fact we did," Emmett replied. "Lost a good man to that bunch of no-counts."

"You're talking about the Buffalo Soldier with the stolen rifle that was with you I take it?"

"Yeah," Emmett said as he over-exerted his effort at cutting his steak; no doubt reliving Reese's murder in his mind. "We used to scout together, he was a damned good friend, even saved my life a time or two. Wasn't able to return the favor this time though. The Indian they called Turquois caught him from behind and knifed him."

"Sorry to hear that about your friend, Emmett. He seemed like a decent sort. He sure was upset about that big fella stealing his rifle."

Emmett filled Marshal Earp in on what had happened in Hades and on the road with Standing Eagle and Jordon. Earp said he would send a wire to the Army to inform them about Standing Eagle being on the war path in the area.

I asked Earp about Phoebe Ann, and he told me she was staying in a rented house with her sister, Lucy. I asked, "That the same Lucy that works at the Crystal Palace?"

"The very same one," he told me.

I asked Earp for directions and he told me how to get there. "It's not far," he said, "just a few blocks away."

I quickly finished my meal, washed it down with a quick drink of cold coffee and excused myself to head over and see her.

"Don't be in such an all-fired hurry there Deputy. You're liable to end up getting' hitched up if you don't slow down a bit," Emmett teased.

"Married? Me married? I got no intentions on marryin' nobody. I just want to see if she's gettin' settled in okay," I answered defensively.

"Sure, sure Deputy. Wait.., What's that I hear, bells? Yeah, that's it, I hear weddin' bells. You hear the weddin' bells Virgil?"

"Maybe, I do hear something faintly," Earp said as he cocked his head as if to listen for something.

"Ah go on. You fellas are full of it," I said as I left the restaurant.

Once outside, I headed for the street Marshal Earp had given me directions to. In an effort to convince myself about my feelings, I thought, 'I don't REALLY have marriage on my mind, do I? No, I'm just concerned about how Ann is getting along, that's all. Besides there's a lot of women to consider before I ever think on getting' married. Why there's.., the new schoolmarm back in Cold

Creek.' Try as hard as I might, I couldn't think of her name. Every time I tried to picture her blond hair and blue eyes, I could only see Ann in that blue-laced dress, and remember how I felt when we embraced that night at the Earp's home. I tried to think of another eligible young lady, but no one came to mind.

When I got within a few houses of where Lucy and Ann lived, that nervous feeling started coming over me again and my stomach started fluttering. Why was I getting so darn nervous? She was just a friend I made on the trip down here, nothing more. Again, I was trying to convince myself I had nothing more on my mind than to see if she was settled in all right.

Now, there I was, standing in front of a white washed little cottage with a knee-high picket fence around the front. I was breathing heavy from walking at such a fast pace. My heart was pounding too, though I don't know whether it was from the brisk walk or from my nervousness. I had been in a hurry to get there, up until then, but now I just stood out front of the place for the longest time wondering what I was going to do this time when I saw Ann.

My thoughts came to a sudden end when the front door popped open. Ann burst out hurrying over to me as she wiped her hands on the front of the apron she was wearing. She called and motioned, "John, John. Don't just stand out there. This is the right place, come on in, come on in."

She met me half way up the path to the house and grabbed my arm. "I have been so worried about you," she said as she pushed up on her tip toes and kissed my cheek. Then she led me by the arm into the house. I hardly said a word. I wasn't sure what to say other than a greeting.

"Lucille," she called as she pulled me through the front door. "Look who's here. It's John. He made it back safe."

Ann stood beside me and still had a tight grip on my arm when Lucy appeared in the doorway of the kitchen. "Well, look here; if it ain't that handsome gentlemanly young fella I met at the Crystal Palace awhile back. How are you?" Lucy asked in that cheerful tone of hers.

"Me? I'm doin' just fine Miss Lucy." Then I asked, "So you did turn out to be Ann's sister after all?"

"Yes John. Isn't it wonderful," Ann said as she squeezed my arm. "And I got you to thank for finding her for me. Now come sit down and tell us about where you have been. And where is Emmett? He is all right, isn't he?," Ann asked as she pulled me over and sat me down with her on a comfortable green velvet settee.

"Emmett? Sure he's all right. We did have a tough time of it though," I said. Then I told them what had happened while we were on the road and down in Hades. I tried to leave out most of the gruesome details, though.

After I was through telling the story of what had happened on the trail, Lucy jumped up. "MY PIES. I hope they're not burnt." She rushed into the kitchen.

Ann said, "That's a terrible story, Emmett losing a friend like that. Those Indians, it's a wonder you weren't scalped.

"John, you have to go and get Emmett. You two will join us for supper," she insisted. "Lucille is making a roast and has baked some pies."

"Well Ann, I wouldn't want to impose on you ladies like that and I do appreciate your hospitality. Fact is, we just finished a big steak down at the boarding house. I mean, you gals weren't expectin' us or nothin'."

"That won't keep you men from having some fresh baked apple pie. You and Emmett are my friends, you could never impose on us. You both have done so much for me. The Earp's have too; but you were the ones that asked, and then seen to it I was taken care of. A good home-cooked meal or a piece of pie is the least I can do for you fellas."

"Well, I'm sure Emmett won't turn down a fresh homemade pie. I'll go and talk with him."

"Good," said Lucy who had returned from the kitchen. "I'll take the pies out to cool. Go get Emmett and come right back." Lucy went back to the kitchen.

Then Ann looked deep into my eyes like she had at the Earp's home that night. I started getting that nervous feeling in my stomach again. I stood up, and Ann stood up with me. Her brown eyes seemed to sparkle as I looked deep into them. We were close. Once again the smell of lilac perfume intoxicated me. I could feel her breath in time with mine. Without a thought of what I was doing, I slowly pulled her close and her soft warm lips met mine. As our lips pressed together, it was like she just melted in my arms.

'What am I doing?' I thought after the embrace had lasted for what seemed like a long while. I let go rather abruptly and said, "Well, I need to be leavin', to get Emmett." As I turned I said nervously, "I'll be back shortly,"

I just walked right out the door and was halfway down the street before my head cleared. I thought, 'Why did I walk out like that. It wasn't polite. I do like Ann, a lot. Maybe I'm even starting to love her.' I really wasn't sure yet. 'What was I going to do about it though? Does she feel as strong about it as I do?' I wondered. It sure seemed that she did.

CHAPTER TWENTY
STRONG FEELINGS

I caught Emmett up in the room resting on the bed and he was all for fresh apple pie and we got to the house in about twenty minutes. Lucy met us at the door. "Come on in fellas," she invited. "Annie's getting freshened up a bit and the coffee's about ready. You fellas can have a seat there in the dining room while I cut the pie and bring in the coffee."

Lucy brought a pot of coffee and some cups for us and went in the kitchen. A few moments later, Ann entered from what was more than likely the bedroom. Ann was wearing the blue lace dress I liked so well. Emmett and I both stood up, showing our manners, when she came in the room.

"Well Phoebe Ann Dunn from Saint Louie, look at you," Emmett complimented, "quite an improvement over the last time I saw you."

"You really look special in that blue dress Ann," I added.

"Do you really think so John?" questioned Ann shyly.

"Shore I do. I wouldn't say it if I really didn't think it."

Ann curtsied politely and thanked us for the compliments.

Then Lucy brought the pie and some cream and set it on the table.

Ann put some linens and forks on the table; I really enjoyed her fussing about. She started telling us about her and Lucille's plan to put their money together and start a hat shop in town. She told us

219

that they were both tired of the saloon life and that Tombstone could use a good ladies hat shop. Emmett and I agreed with her. We reckoned it sounded like a good idea for them to invest their money that way, though neither one of us knew a doggone thing about ladies hats.

After the pie; Emmett ate two wedges, Lucy poured more coffee and sat at the table and talked. Shortly Ann invited me into their small parlor where the settee was. Ann grasped my hand in both of hers and held it as we sat down. "John," she started, "I want to thank you once again for all you have done for me, especially for finding my sister. Really now, do you think Lucille and I are doing the wise thing putting our money together and investing in a business?"

"Sure, I think it's a great idea if you're plannin' on stayin' here in Tombstone."

Ann raised an eyebrow and looked into my eyes as she asked slowly, "Where else could I be John?"

"I… I didn't mean you should be some where's else," I said, having a hard time of it. "I just meant if you had no plans of movin' back to Saint Louie or somethin'."

"Oh. Well no, I have no plans of going back there." She smiled softly. "You just never know what might come up in a girl's life, though, do you John?"

'Just what did she mean by that?' I wondered. "I suppose not.., I reckon that's true. You never know what tomorrow will bring," I said trying to avoid her giving me any explanation on that subject.

"I'd say," I continued, "if you think you got a good deal goin', then go right ahead. Then, if you wanna change your mind later on, you can always sell out. I'm sure there's lots of folks that would just be achin' to buy a goin' business in Tombstone."

Ann gave a little sigh of disappointment, though I didn't understand why. "Well, I guess you're right John. I just didn't want to obligate myself to a business if there was a possibility that something more important in my life might come along. Once Lucille and I invest our money, we won't want to be changing our minds and moving off somewhere else."

She hesitated for a brief moment, "John, you will write to me? Won't you?"

"I… I never was much on words in a letter Miss Ann."

"Oh John," she scolded, "Quit trying to wiggle out of things all the time. I know you have feelings for me, some anyway. I am going to write you. And you don't even have to say much, just let me know that you have received my letters, that's all."

"Oh sure.., sure Miss Ann, I can do that all right. It'll be real nice to hear from you. I'm sorry, I didn't mean to offend you. I just don't write much since I've been away from school, you know, book learnin' an' all," I said trying to excuse myself, for I had obviously hurt her feelings. "I can let you know I got your letters. In fact it'll be great keepin' in touch with you.

"You know Ann," I looked into her eyes, those sparkling dark brown eyes of hers that always made me say things I wasn't sure I wanted to say. So what

221

I said next just came out without thought, "I like you a lot Ann. And I will sure look forward to those letters."

"Really John? I want you to know I like you a lot too, and I will write often. Please don't forget to write me in return."

"Don't worry. You'll hear from me, I promise."

Emmett and Lucy entered the parlor as Ann kissed me tenderly on the check.

"Hey there Deputy, don't mean to be interruptin', but we had better get. We need to be leavin' early in the mornin'."

I agreed as I stood up. We thanked Lucy and Ann for the pie and apologized for having to leave so soon. Emmett explained that we had urgent business back in Cold Creek. The ladies said they hated to see us go, but understood and walked us to the door. They both wished us a safe trip. Ann reminded me one more time about returning her letters, and once again I assured her I would. Then she squeezed my hand as she pushed up on her tip toes and kissed the corner of my mouth tenderly. Her eyes watered as she said, "Good-bye John. You two take good care of each other." Ann turned and hurried back through the door before she broke out in tears. I didn't know what to say or do.

"She'll be all right after you're gone," Lucy told us. "It's just that you fellas mean a lot to her and she hates to see you go. I mean, you two are all she's talked about since she found me at the Crystal Palace. Especially you John. She's got some strong feelings for you, and if you're gonna do anything about it, ya better get at it soon. Well, 'nough said for now. Don't like ta poke my nose in other people's affairs. You fellas take care."

We thanked Lucy again and left.

That kiss was still with me early the next morning when we rode out of Tombstone. Ann was right when she said I had feelings for her, and I was really confused about those feelings too. Especially after what Lucy had said at the door the night before. 'Just how strong were my feelings, marrying strong?' I asked myself. I just wasn't sure at that point. I figured I would talk with Emmett about it later as we headed for home.

Emmett said he 'wanted to ride hard and make Cold Creek before night fall. We had been gone long enough'.

We stopped just the other side of Benson, not far from where we had made camp on the way down. We watered the horses and let them rest awhile.

"Emmett," I asked, "Can I talk to you about somethin' that's been a botherin' me?"

"Sure Deputy, but if it's about what I think it is, I ain't gonna be much help on that subject."

The horses had their fill so we mounted up and talked as we rode along at a walk for a while.

"Well Emmett, it's like this. I just don't know what I should do about Ann. I know I got feelin's for her, an' she's sure enough got feelin's for me, but I'm not so sure about marryin' anybody. What do you think I should do? I don't want to hurt her, she's a sweet gal and I do care about her feelin's."

223

"I can tell you this for sure Deputy. A one-sided love ain't no good to anybody. People just end up gettin' hurt worse and bein' miserable. I think what you got to decide is whether or not you love her. If you do, then marry her and make yourself and her happy for the rest of your lives. If you don't, then leave her alone so's you both can go on and find someone you do love to make a life with."

"I follow you Emmett, and that makes sense, but just how do you know if you love someone or not?"

"That's somethin' you'll have to figger out for yerself. Ain't nobody can find the answer to that one but you."

"I reckon that's so, too. Ain't easy though."

"Love never is Deputy," Emmett kicked his horse into a canter as he repeated, "Love never is."

I thought about what Lucy had said and the conversation with Emmett. I thought about it real serious all the way back to Cold Creek. I came to realize that I did love Ann, that I wanted her to spend the rest of her life by my side. I had never felt that way about anyone before. It was something strange to me and I didn't know how to handle it. I suppose that's why I always got so nervous whenever things started to get a little serious.

How was I going to make a home for her though? A deputy salary wasn't that great and I was sure she would want a house and things. I would have to do some serious thinking on this. 'Talk to my ma,' I thought, 'that would be a good idea.'

Then I remembered what Lucy told me, that I had better do something soon.., 'or what' I wondered. Maybe there was someone else a calling on her. I couldn't stand the thought of losing her. I had to figure this thing out and I couldn't waste any time doing it.

CHAPTER TWENTY-ONE
BEN'S ARREST

There was only a trace of daylight left as Emmett and I rode into town. It was good to see home again, I had never been that far away from Cold Creek for that long before. It had been quite an adventure, with some unforgettable good experiences and some bad; the worst being the loss of Reese and of course for me, the best was meeting Ann and getting to know her.

I had seen Tombstone, Bisbee, and even met up with the likes of Virgil Earp, Doc Holliday and Bill Kelley. I certainly wouldn't soon forget John Ringo, though I didn't really care to run across Ringo's path ever again. I was almost been scalped, had been captured and let loose by the Apache, not many can say that. To end it; or should I say to begin, I had met Ann, fallen in love and I hadn't even realized it until that very day.

A close lasting friendship had been formed between Emmett and myself. Though only a few days had gone by I had grown and matured some from the experiences on the road.

We stripped our horses down and let them out into the corral behind what used to be Ben's livery stables and blacksmith shop. Someone, probably Gonzales, had built a small storage shed for hay, so I threw some in the corral for the horses. We stowed our riding gear in the back room of the jail and then washed off what road dust we could at the pump out back of the jail.

"Deputy, I'm goin' over to the Cantina," Emmett said. "I want to check with Gonzales and find out what's goin' on with Ben. Then we can head down to the boardin' house and get some supper, maybe even check in with Judge Bryant."

"Sounds good to me Emmett, I'll come along."

Things were pretty lively at the Cantina, with a full house of mostly Mexican cowboys. When Rosa saw Emmett she dropped what she was doing and shrieked, "EMM-E-TT...You are back." She ran and jumped into his outstretched arms. Emmett grabbed her up and swung her around a half-dozen times until he about fell over from dizziness.

Emmett sat her down and her expression turned serious. "What is it," he questioned, "what's wrong Rosa?"

"Oh, it is not good what has happened to your friend señor Ben."

"What has happened Rosa? What's wrong with Ben?"

"After everyone thought he had died in the fire and that man Taylor left town, Señor Ben came back, he was not dead. When he saw his business, he became very angry about it being burned down to the ground. He began drinking very much, every day. My father, the Judge and many others tried to talk with him, but he would not listen to anyone; he only would drink more and act very hateful.

"Yesterday morning that man Taylor, he came back into town with another man and arrested Señor Ben. They have him in chains at the Cold Creek Hotel."

"I've got to see about this." Emmett gave Rosa short kiss and said, "I'll be back later. Come on Deputy, let's find out what this is all about."

Emmett stormed out the door of the Cantina and took long strides down the street. I almost had to run to keep up with him. He mumbled something under his breath as we hurried along, "Somebody's gonna end up gettin' their head blown off over this deal."

We rounded the corner onto Center Street, and came up in front of my mother's boarding house. We hurried past and on down to the hotel. Emmett picked up the pace almost to a run; we got there in about half the time as normal.

Emmett burst through the double doors into the lobby of the hotel, marched right up to Dave Vail the desk clerk, and demanded, "What room is that stinkin' Pinkerton in?"

Dave shied back a few steps and said, "Room eleven.., BUT, Mr. King don't want no trouble in here Marshal."

"Then you all had better think twice before you let somebody keep one of my friends in shackles in this place," Emmett barked in his face.

Emmett forged up the stairs, taking them two at a time. He was at the top before I even got to the staircase. I caught up just as he busted into the room. I stepped in, Ben was sitting on the bed shackled to the iron bed post. A man that I figured to be a Texan, from the way he was dressed, sat in a chair beside the bed with a double barreled shotgun pointed at Emmett's belly.

"That's far enough mister. I don't know who you are or what your beef is; but if ya take another step, I'll open ya up."

Emmett stopped, even he wouldn't challenge a double load of buckshot at close range. I looked around the room over Emmett's shoulder. Taylor was sitting at a table, It looked like he had been writing a letter or something when Emmett had busted into the room. He was turned sideways in the chair, facing Emmett.

Emmett addressed Taylor, "Just what do you think yer doin' Taylor? You know you ain't got the authority to do this. You let Ben out of those irons right now or I'll have your hide nailed to the wall."

"I don't think so Marshal Cross," Taylor smirked calmly. "You see," he pointed with the quill pen he had been writing with, "That gentleman with the shotgun is Noah Whittaker, he is a United States Federal Marshal, and he served a Federal Warrant for Mr. Dill's arrest yesterday morning. I'm going to assist Mr. Whittaker in taking Dill back to Missouri to stand trial for his part in the attempted robbery of a government payroll. There's nothing you can do to stop it Marshal Cross, so I suggest you leave us alone in our duty to serve justice before you get in trouble with the United States Government yourself."

"Justice? Just what do you call justice, almost burnin' down the town and causin' a man's death? That's the kind of justice you deal in."

"I told you before, I had nothing to do with that fire. Jordon was acting on his own to collect the reward money. Don't you remember, I helped pass water buckets that night?"

"That don't mean squat Taylor. That was just a put-on. You put Jordon up to settin' that fire; and if I ever prove it, I'll track you down wherever you are.

"I want to see this so-called, Federal Warrant," Emmett demanded.

"You'll have to go see Judge Bryant," Taylor explained. "He's the one who has it right now."

"What's Judge Bryant doin' with it?"

"I'm not telling you anything more. If you want any more information, you'll need to talk to the Judge. You and your Deputy can take your leave now. I have got more important things to do than waste my time explaining everything to you."

Emmett looked over at Ben, "Are they treatin' you all right Ben?"

Ben kept his head down, not wanting to make eye contact with Emmett. "Yeah Emmett, I'm fine. Ya shouldn't bother yerself with me though, I ain't worth it. There ain't no chance of me getting out of this anyway. I reckon I'm getting what I deserve."

"Come on Ben, keep your chin up, friend. This ain't over with yet. I'll do somethin' to get you out of this.

"I'm leavin' Taylor. But, let me tell you, this better be on the level or I'm gonna come back here and shove O' Noah Whittaker's shotgun down your throat and pull both triggers. Let's go Deputy."

We turned and walked out as abruptly as we entered. Emmett was fuming as he headed straight for the boarding house to find Judge Bryant.

At the boarding house, we found Judge Bryant and Sally Belle in the dining room. They had just sat down to supper. Emmett and I quickly pulled up some chairs to sit with them.

Emmett leaned toward the Judge to talk, but was interrupted. "Where's you fellas' manners anyway?" Sally Belle wanted to know. "I mean, we ain't seen you boys in almost a week and you don't even so much as say hello."

Emmett and I both apologized to Sally Belle for forgetting our manners, and gave an appropriate greeting. She thanked us saying, "That is more like it, it's good to have you two home safe."

With that out of the way, Emmett leaned toward the Judge again. This time, before Emmett could say anything, the Judge interrupted him, "Good to see you two finally made it back safe," he said without looking up from the piece of meat he was cutting. "I know what you're all fired up about, so just calm down a minute and I'll explain what's goin' on. First you got to tell me what happened with Jordon, though."

"Sorry Judge, I got plenty of time to fill you in on that." Emmett's expression showed his patience with all the small talk was worn to the limits. He wanted answers about Ben's situation right then. "I want to know about this Federal Warrant that was served on Ben, and I want to know what we're doin' about it."

"Well, all right Emmett; but I'm telling you, I got it all under control," Judge Bryant assured him. The Judge began explaining the events of the previous day concerning Ben and the federal warrant, as he filled his mouth with bites of his supper. "It's like this... Taylor and that Federal Marshal showed up here at the boarding house and looked me up. They informed me that," the Judge paused briefly to swallow a mouthful, "they knew it wasn't the blacksmith, Ben Decker, that had died in the fire. They also let me know that they were aware of the fact that Ben Decker was Robert Benjamin Dill. That's when they shoved the federal warrant in my face. Wasn't anything I could do to stop them from arresting him.

"You know Deputy McCord," Judge Bryant said to me, "if Ben would have stayed up there at the cabin like we told him to, maybe this wouldn't have happened. Well, no matter, they arrested him and there ain't much we can do about it now."

Emmett's anger was stirred again. "Oh yeah there is. I can run those two out of town real quick. Who in the hell told Taylor that Ben wasn't the one that died in the fire anyhow?"

"You know better than that Emmett," the Judge pointed his fork at Emmett. "That's a U.S. Federal Marshal you're dealing with. You can't just go off half-cocked and do something you'll regret for a long while. Might even end up in Leavenworth yourself. You got to stay within the parameters of the law and you know that. Just stay sitting there for a minute, and I'll tell you what can be done here. Taylor didn't want to tell me where he got his information, but I kept insisting till he did."

"Well, who told him; and how do you know for sure that Whittaker fella's even a real U.S. Marshal? Just cause he's got a badge don't mean nothin'"

233

"Give me a little credit for knowing something will you Emmett? I wasn't born yesterday. I ain't been an Officer of the Court for fifteen years for nothing," snapped Judge Bryant. "I know Noah Whittaker, I know he's a U.S. Marshal. Has been for quite some time."

Seeing that the Judge was irritated, Emmett backed off a little. "Yeah, maybe you're right Judge, but I'm so dog-gone fed up with this deal. I mean, I don't want Ben to hang…and that Pinkerton has got me mad enough to kill'm."

"Okay Emmett, I understand all of that. Just let me talk for a minute, and maybe it won't seem as bad as you think it is."

"All right Judge, I'll listen," Emmett was desperate for a solution. "What have you got in mind? What can I do to help… and who the hell was it that told about Ben?"

"It was Terrance Wonderland," the Judge told us. "He had been in town the day Ben came back."

"I'll get even with him for that one of these days," Emmett promised.

"Just don't do it today, Emmett." Pointing with his fork again, Judge Bryant started to explain. "I know a few influential people back in Missouri; and if I go with Ben and act as his Attorney, I can pull a few strings. I think I can get him off with only a five-year sentence. You know, in view of his age an' all at the time of the robbery."

"FIVE years? That's a long haul Judge. A man can lose his identity in prison after five years," Emmett lamented.

"Well Emmett, I know five years is a long time, but it's a lot better than the gallows. Besides, he did commit the crime; and a man has got to pay for his wrongs sometime or another."

Reluctantly, Emmett agreed and shook his head, disgusted with the whole situation. He knew the Judge was right, though he hated admitting it. Going to prison for five years was better than being dead, but having a friend locked away in prison was still hard for us to swallow. We all knew five years penned up would be terribly hard on Ben. He loved to get out and go up in the mountains to hunt and fish at every opportunity.

Emmett and I ordered some supper. While we ate, we took the time to tell Judge Bryant about everything that had happened to us on the road and with Jordon. I filled the Judge in on the deal with Standing Eagle and the events in Tombstone. He didn't seem much impressed when I told him about meeting Doc Holliday and Johnny Ringo. He did perk up when I mentioned meeting a lady that I was pretty sure I was going to ask to marry me, though.

"That's real good, Johnny boy. It'll make you more respectable, LIKE ME." We all got a chuckle out of that, except Emmett; he wasn't in the mood for any kind of joking around.

Then the Judge frowned, "Hey, what's so dab-blame funny. I think I've settled down a lot since me and Sally Belle, been hitched." We did have to agree with that.

"Now, all we got to do is get ol' Emmett here to pop the question to that pretty little daughter of Gonzales'. Then we'll be all set. A town with all the officials respectable." Judge Bryant looked questioningly over at Emmett.

"What? Married? I don't need marriage to be respectable. The institution of marriage is fine; but right now, Rosa and me just enjoy one another's company. We've done no talkin' on that subject. We got us an understandin'."

"Maybe it's time you did some talking about it Emmett. Your Deputy, here finally came around."

Emmett was getting terribly upset with the subject, he had more serious matters to think about. "That's for you and the Deputy. I got no weddin' plans in my future right now. If you all will excuse me, I got a town to check on," Emmett said in a gruff tone as he got up to leave.

"I'll join you pretty soon Emmett. I wanna say hello to my ma first though."

"That'll be fine, take your time," Emmett said, heading for the door.

Emmett had eaten less than half of his supper when he got up to leave. He had only been picking at it anyway. He had a hard time dealing with the situation with Ben and was used to being in control; there didn't seem to be anything he could do.

I finished my meal; then got up and helped Miss Packard, my mother's supper-time helper, clear off a couple of tables of dishes. I carried the big tray of dishes back to the kitchen.

My mother sure was glad to see me back home safe. I didn't tell her too much about what had happened on the trip, because I knew it would just worry her the next time I had to go out and perform my duty as a Deputy Marshal. After a big hug, she kept busy washing dishes as I talked with her.

I told my mother about rescuing Phoebe Ann on the road. Then I said, "Ma, I'm in love with her. I wanna ask her to marry me."

"What's that? Did I hear you right son? You want to marry this girl you met on the road? Why John, you've only known her less than a week. Don't you think you're bein' a bit hasty? Besides, I thought maybe you and Miss Packard might..." She paused, stopped washing dishes, and looked me square in the eyes with a loving look that told me that her only concern was for my happiness.

"John," she asked, "do you really love this girl? I mean, really love her? You know, so that you wanna spend the rest of your life with her and never part until you die, take care of all her needs no matter what?"

"I do Ma, I really do. I'll admit, at first, I wasn't really sure; but now that I've had time to think about it seriously, I know she's exactly what I want. And, I will love her till I die."

My mother, dried her hands on her apron and came over and hugged me. She kissed me on the cheek and looked into my eyes with tears welling up about to fall and said, "Then you have my blessing son." She pushed back and held my shoulders in her hands. "I can't wait to meet her son," she said as she wiped her eyes with the shoulder of her dress. "When is she gonna be up here?"

"Well Ma, I ain't asked her yet. She might turn me down you know."

"How could any girl in her right mind turn down a handsome young fella like you?"

"Aw Ma, you're just sayin' that because I'm your son. I'll send a wire tomorrow and we'll see what happens."

CHAPTER TWENTY-TWO
CATTLE RUSTLER'S IN ELROY

The next morning, Judge Bryant, with Sally Belle on his arm, Taylor, and Ben, shackled to Noah Whittaker, all boarded the train as it stopped for water. Cut timber and supplies that had been shipped in were laid out along the tracks on the edge of town; however, construction on a railway station had not yet begun. The train left billows of black smoke and steam behind as it slowly chugged out of town right on schedule at nine o'clock. They were on their way east, to Missouri, where Ben's fate would be decided. I wondered if we would ever see him again.

Emmett wasn't much on conversation that day as we checked in around town. We wanted everyone to know we were back on the job. Folks were really glad to see us and most everybody asked about the situation with Ben. Emmett wouldn't say much on the subject, just mumble a bit. I would give as brief of an explanation as I could, and then we would go on about our business.

After the train pulled out that morning, I stopped in at the Telegraph Office and sent a wire to Tombstone. The message was to Ann asking 'If she would come up and meet my mother'. I also mentioned that I had something important I wanted to ask her, if she decided to make the trip. I was sure she would have a pretty good idea of what I wanted to ask her.

I told Emmett what I had in mind when I sent the telegram. I wanted his thoughts on the matter of marriage. He had made a lot of sense when we had talked on the road.

We talked and it seemed to get his mind off of Ben's plight, for the moment anyway. I knew it wasn't easy for Emmett to lose his friend Reese; then when we came home, to have another close friend going off to be hanged, or at a minimum get a long stretch in a federal prison.

"Well Deputy, it's your business what you do. You can make your own decisions and I reckon it's a good idea, if that's what you want." Emmett's advice was, "You should step right in there and get it done. I mean, Phoebe Ann's a nice enough gal and I'm sure she'll make you a good wife.

"Just don't start pushin' the subject of marriage off on me Deputy. Okay? I mean, Judge Bryant was startin' to get under my skin last night. I got a lot of things goin' on, bein' Marshal an' all. I don't need a wife sittin' home worrin' about me. And I sure don't like the thought of leavin' a widow behind for someone else to look after if something should happen to me. You do understand what I'm tryin' to say here, don't you?"

"Sure Emmett, I wouldn't think of pushin' you into nothin'. Like you told me, that's for every man to decide for himself. So, I apologize for my part in the funnin' last night. From now on I'll resect your feelings an' stay out of it."

"I thank you for that Deputy," said Emmett.

We ate an early lunch, or a late breakfast I should say, at the Cantina. We were having coffee after eating and Emmett said, "I slept lousy last night, had Ben an' all on my mind. Everything seems pretty quiet in town, so I believe I'll go on over to the jail and take me a nice long afternoon siesta. That is, if you don't mind lookin' after things for a while?"

"Go ahead Emmett," I agreed. "I can handle it okay. I'll wake you if anything comes up I need help on. Right now, I'm gonna get back down to the telegraph office and see if Ann has answered my message yet."

The telegraph office was the next building west of the Cold Creek Hotel, on Center Street across the corner from Doc Baker's Office. As I walked down Center Street toward the telegraph office, a young cowboy I didn't recognize and Terrance Wonderland came riding in. Terrance was slumped in the saddle and he looked pretty well worn. His left pant leg was covered with blood from just below the hip, and a blood-soaked bandanna was tied around his upper thigh.

The cowboy leading Terrance's horse stopped at the hitching post in front of Doc Baker's Office. I hurried across the street to help him take Terrance off his horse. "What happened?" I asked as we struggled to put Terrance on the ground.

"He's been shot in the leg," the cowboy told me. Of course, that was pretty obvious. He seemed to get rattled when he noticed my badge. "It was…was an accident.

"Yeah, what kind of accident? How'd this happen?"

"Well.., ah...," the cowboy groped for an explanation.

Terrance came to life and in a slurred, weak voice said, "He was cleanin' his gun and it went off. It was...an accident...he tol' ya.., an accident."

"That's right. I was cleanin' my pistol and it went off. I really feel bad about it," the cowboy said agreeing, obviously relieved to have a reasonable explanation.

"Not too smart, cleanin' a loaded pistol you know."

"Yeah, really dumb of me," said the cowboy.

There certainly was something questionable about that story. I couldn't picture anybody shooting someone while cleaning a pistol. Besides that, I'm no expert of course; but that wound looked more like something a rifle shot would make, not a pistol.

The cowboy and I helped Terrance up the steps into the Doctor's Office.

Noticing how stiff the pant leg was from dried blood, I asked, "When did you say this happened, how long ago?"

"What makes any difference," Terrance snapped. "Why all the damned questions anyhow? It was a stupid accident, that's all. We...we ain't broke no laws; so why don't ya just back off McCord, and go find someone else to hassle? Help me get in to the Doc's office Miller."

I opened the door and we all went inside. Doc Baker came in from the other room with one of the town's womenfolk; an older lady who was hard of hearing. He was almost shouting at her as he explained about some medication she was to take when he saw Terrance. "Take him on into the treatment room and put him on the table. I'll be right there," he ordered.

Miller and I helped Terrance into the room holding his arms and then we lifted him up on to the operating table.

"Thanks for your help McCord. We don't need ya anymore now," Terrance said insistently. "The Doc will take ca...care of things from here on," he grimaced. "You can juss go on... now, an' take care of yer own business." Terrance made a gesture with his hand for me to leave and fell backward. The young cowboy Miller, caught him before he hit the table and laid him down gently.

I figured I might as well go on about my business like Terrance suggested, for the moment anyway. I would check back with Doc Baker later on.

"Okay, I'll leave you alone. I still don't see how a man cleanin' a loaded pistol would end up shootin' someone with it though. Hey Miller, you sure you was cleanin' your pistol?"

A bewildered expression on his face, Miller said, "What?" he was lost for an explanation as he looked desperately to Terrance for an answer.

Terrance gathered enough strength to raise his head a couple of inches and say, "He made a damned mistake; it was a confusing situation; his rifle, he was cleanin' his rifle. Now, will you get on out of here McCord, before I shoot YOU."

"All right, I'm a leavin', for now anyways. Don't need to get yerself so worked up. I'm goin'."

I stopped at the door, "Miller, what kind of rifle ya got?"

"Huh?" responded Miller.

"DAMN McCord, a .44-40,"shouted Terrence with what little strength he had left.

I had Terrance shook, and that's just what I wanted to do. There was something going on that the law should know about, I was sure of it.

I opened the door and Doc Baker rushed in. I went on outside and as I passed Miller's horse I pulled the rifle from the scabbard; a .45-60 Winchester, fully loaded. 'Imagine that. Interesting, ain't it?', I said to myself. I slipped it back in place and went around to Terrance's horse and looked at his saddle rifle; a .44-40, I wasn't surprised.

'I'll leave it for now,' I thought, 'and just head on over to the telegraph office to see if there has been a return message from Ann.'

I walked in and the telegraph operator said, "Good, you're here Deputy. Now I won't have to leave the office to take the Marshal this telegram I just received from the County Sheriff down in Elroy." Elroy, was a small mining settlement about twenty-five miles south east of Cold Creek, across the San Pedro River. There was a fair-size cattle ranch, the 'Lazy J', in the area too. The 'Lazy J's' brand was a J leaning forward at a forty-five degree angle sitting on a bar.

I read the telegram; it told about a 'Lazy J' ranch hand who had died of gunshot wounds received the previous evening while trying to stop two rustlers from stealing around a hundred head of cattle from the ranch. Before the ranch hand died he told the County Sheriff he had hit one of the rustlers in the leg with a rifle shot. The rustlers had a head start and had fled into the mountains with the cattle. The Sheriff and a small posse had tracked them up this way, but had lost the trail in the mountains when night fell. There was a thousand places to hide in the canyons, washes, and valleys south of here, especially if you knew the country. At night it would be next to impossible to find somebody, even if they did have a hundred head of cattle to hide. That is, unless you ran into a band of Apache renegades.

Right off, I knew it had to be Terrance Wonderland and the cowboy with him. Better let Emmett in on this I thought; so I headed the back way over to Tillman Street, and down the alley toward the jail. I didn't want that cowboy spotting me and leaving town before Emmett and I could get back to Doc Baker's Office.

I threw open the back door to the jail, it banged the wall hard as I rushed in. I almost ran over Emmett as we met in the doorway between the office and the jail cells. I had rattled him awake when I came in. "What's all the noise about Deputy?" he asked all sleepy-eyed. "Why'd you come stormin' in the back door like that?"

I handed him the telegram from the County Sheriff; he looked it over. "What? You know something about this?"

"From what I just left back at Doc Baker's office, I'd say I sure enough do." Then I explained to Emmett about the cowboy, and about Terrance Wonderland coming in with a leg all shot up.

"They tried to feed me a made up story about an accident while cleanin' a pistol at first, which changed to a rifle and well.., it just don't hold water Emmett."

"You reckon they're still down there?"

"Prob'ly so. Ol' Terrance was hurtin' pretty bad when I last saw him."

"I'll pull my boots on and we'll go down and check this out. Sure looks like Wonderland and that cowboy are in this hip deep without any doubt. I knew sooner or later those Wonderland boys would slip up, and we'd have'm."

After Emmett got his boots on, he strapped on his gunbelt and checked the load and action of his .45. I grabbed the Greener shotgun out of the gun rack and loaded it. As we hurried down Main Street headed for Doc Baker's Office, I told Emmett about how I had checked out the rifle story and what I had found out.

The cowboy was getting ready to mount his horse when Emmett and I came up on him in front of the Doctor's office.

"Hold on there Miller," I said. "We need to ask you a few questions."

The young man turned around and backed up against his horse as he put his hand to his six-gun. Emmett's hand went instantly to his Colt, and he warned, "I don't think you wanna die today, sonny."

The young man's mouth tightened and his eyes narrowed. Realizing he was no match for a seasoned gunfighter like Emmett, and the shotgun I was carrying, he relaxed his hand down to his side.

"What kind of questions?" he asked. "I already told ya the shootin' was an accident."

"Well that story just don't wash. So, maybe you better tell it again to the Marshal, here," I said.

"How about you come on down to the Marshal's Office with us and give a little more detail on it," Emmett said.

"I hain't got no time for that. I gotta get back out to the ranch. Jesse will be a wonderin' where we are. I gotta let him know what's happened to his brother." Beads of sweat started forming on the young cowboy's face. He was getting mighty nervous.

"I'm tellin' ya," said Miller, "I hain't done nothin', and y'all hain't got no call a holdin' me up here. So, I'm gonna mount up and ride on out and get back to the ranch before I get fired."

"You'd just better hand over your six-shooter and we'll go on down to the Jail and have a little talk about this," Emmett directed.

"I tol' ya I was a leavin', unless you're arrestin' me or somethin'."

"I'm holdin' you on suspicion of murder and cattle rustlin'. Now, this is the last time I'm a tellin' you. Hand over that iron and come with us."

The cowboy eased his hand up to his pistol. "Slow and easy now," Emmett cautioned. "Now hand it over butt first."

Carefully, so not to be mistaken for gun play, the young man handed Emmett his six-gun, butt first like he was told.

Once again, he denied doing anything wrong, "I tell ya, I hain't done nothin'. I hain't murdered nobody or rustled no cows. I swear to ya, I hain't. The only thing I done wrong was shoot Terry, whilst cleanin' my rifle."

"Your rifle huh? You sure you don't mean your pistol?" I asked.

Emmett and I had the young man by the arms and were marching him down toward the jail.

"It was my rifle," he insisted, "That was just a slip of the tongue earlier."

"That the .44-40 in your saddle scabbard?" questioned Emmett.

".44-40? No, it's a Winchester .45-60," Miller insisted.

"You shore yer not just a bit confused about the story you're tellin'?" I asked.

"I'm just a little shaken over shootin' my friend Terry, that's all." Miller said. "Why? What are ya tryin' to get at?"

"Yeah.., how is good ol' Terry, anyway?" asked Emmett.

"The Doc gave him somethin' to make him sleep. The Doc said Terry had lost a lot of blood and needed to rest."

"That a fact. Well, we'll, just let him rest awhile and talk to you then. How's that sound? We'll drop in and see how he's getting' along a little later," said Emmett.

When we got into the Marshal's Office, Emmett said, "Throw this hombre in a cell Deputy." Emmett grabbed a pair of wrist shackles off the wall and told me, "I'm goin' back to Doc Baker's Office and make sure Terrance don't go nowhere when he wakes up."

"Doc Baker told me that the bullet went clean through Terrance's, upper thigh," Emmett explained when he returned. "He said, from his experience with gunshot wounds, he had strong doubts that the wound in Terrance's leg had been made by a pistol. His guess was a rifle shot at close range."

"That's pretty well the way I had it figgered myself," I said. "What did you do with those wrist shackles you took along a while ago?"

"I shackled Terrance to that big heavy operating table he's layin' on. I don't think he'll be up to draggin' that around when he wakes up. The Doc's gonna send word when he comes around. Don't expect to be hearin' from him before mornin' though.

"By the way, I noticed red mud caked on that cowboy's and Terrance's boots. Anywhere you know of they could've picked it up?" Emmett asked me.

"The only place I know of where there's red mud like that is down at a little stream in Miner's Gulch. It's about three miles east of the Rocking 'W' Ranch house."

"I think I'll take a ride out that way and see if I can find anything. They hid those cattle somewhere. You okay with keepin' an eye on things around town till I get back?"

"Sure Emmett, you know I will."

"Okay then, I'm gonna saddle up and take off out that way if you give me a little more detail on how to get there. I'll try to make it back before dark."

"You be dog-gone careful out there with no one to watch your back Emmett."

"Sure Deputy, thanks for the warnin'. I'm just goin' out to check around and see if I can find any evidence."

"Hey Emmett, I wanna check and see if Ann has answered my telegram yet. Maybe I could ask Gonzales to come over and watch the prisoner while I'm gone."

"I'll check with him and send him over, if he's available, before I leave town Deputy."

CHAPTER TWENTY-THREE
MARCUS' CONFESSION

DEPUTY JOHN MCCORD-

DEAR JOHN –
  I WOULD BE VERY PLEASED TO MEET YOUR MOTHER - LUCILLE WANTS TO COME ALONG WITH ME - I HOPE THAT IS ALRIGHT - WE WILL ARRIVE ON NEXT WEDNESDAY'S STAGE - LOOKING FORWARD TO SEEING YOU AND EMMITT AND FINDING OUT WHAT YOU WANT TO ASK ME-
                            LOVE - ANN

  The telegram from Ann had me so excited that I did a little jig right there in the telegraph office and I almost turned cartwheels as I hurried over to the boarding house.
  I wanted to stop by and tell my mother about the telegram. It was getting close to supper-time, so I thought I would get some supper to take back to the prisoner at the jail.
  My mother was excited about the prospect of meeting Ann when I told her she was coming up. We talked while she dished up two plates of some heavenly-smelling, fresh-made stew. There were dinner rolls too. It sure was nice being back home and enjoying my mother's cooking. I had two plates of stew and a half-dozen rolls to take down to the jail. My mother had put the two plates of stew in a basket covered with a checkered linen to keep them warm. She caution me, 'not to spill it' as I left; and

once again she said, 'she could hardly wait to meet Ann'.

I relieved Gonzales and thanked him for watching the prisoner while I was gone. After Gonzales left, I took the stew back to the young cowboy and pulled up a chair next to the cell he was in. I made sure not to sit where he could get a hold of me, had he a mind to.

"Here you go," I said as I shoved one plate of stew under the bars. "It's some really delicious stew my ma made. She's the best cook around these parts. And those dinner rolls will for shore just melt in your mouth." I sat down to eat my plateful while I talked with him.

"Thanks mister. I hain't had nothin' to eat all day. It sure looks good, and I hain't had no homemade rolls since I can't remember when."

"What's your name cowboy?"

"Marcus.., Marcus Johnston," he answered around a mouthful of stew.

"Mine's John McCord," I reached through the bars and shook his hand.

"You know, you don't seem like a bad sort of a fella Marcus. Why don't you come clean about this cattle rustlin' deal down in Elroy? Maybe if you cooperate with me and the Marshal, I can talk to the judge and he won't go so hard on you."

"I told ya before, I don't know nothin' about no rustlin', or nobody getting' shot; 'ceptin' for the accident with Terry, that is."

"Gonna stick to that lame story, huh? Well, I can't do nothin' for you if you ain't gonna tell me the truth, Marcus. I'll tell you this though, we pretty well got you and Terrance nailed down for this one. And since a man was killed, I know that you'll both hang for murder. Now on the other hand, if you was to help us get evidence on the whole rustlin' operation goin' on out there at the Wonderland Ranch, why, I just might be able to get the judge to let you off with a light sentence. I tell you, I'd think about that real serious if I was you. It sure would be a lot better'n swingin' at the end of a rope," I explained shaking my head in a pitiable gesture. Marcus remained silent, I figured that meant I was starting to get to him.

"You know Marcus, I saw a man hanged here recent. It sure ain't no pleasant way to die, 'specially if they don't tie the knot right. If it's tied right, it just snaps your neck and it's all over with. Boy, if it ain't tied right; well, man," I said shaking my head again. "You just gag and kick while you're swingin', till you just choke to death."

"Why don't ya just SHUT UP mister. I hain't kilt nobody, and there hain't no reason I should be hanged."

"Well, maybe not." I stood up, and as I turned to go back into the office, I said, "It sure don't look good for you Marcus, it sure don't. Like I said, hangin' is sure a tough way to die if they don't do it right." With that I closed the door between the office and the jail cells.

I figured I had given him plenty to think on for a while.

It had been dark for a half hour or so; and I was starting to get concerned about Emmett, when I heard him come in the back door of the jail and stow his gear. I went back to meet him.

"Hello Deputy. Everything quiet around here since I've been gone?"

"Pretty well. Terrance was still out last time I checked in at the Doc's office. Doc said he wouldn't come around enough to talk at least till mornin'."

"Good. I didn't want to mess with him tonight anyway."

Emmett walked over to the cell that Marcus was in and said, "Get your boots off and hand'em out here."

"What for? I don't wanna be without my boots. What's the deal with my boots anyways?" Marcus wanted to know.

"Hand me those boots or I'll come in that cell and take'm," threatened Emmett.

"Okay...okay," said Marcus, as he sat on the edge of his bunk to pull off his boots. "I don't see what's the big deal about my boots." He handed them to Emmett.

"Look here cowboy. I'll show you what the big deal is."

Emmett held Marcus' boots down to the floor beside his own.

"What? I don't see nothin' but two pair of boots, yours and mine." Marcus tried to look like he didn't understand what Emmett was trying to show him.

I saw what Emmett was getting at with the boots, and I think Marcus did too. He just didn't want to think that we had any evidence linking him and Terrance Wonderland to the murder down in Elroy.

"You do see the red mud on your boots?" Emmett asked. "And you do see that it's the same red mud that's on my boots, don't you youngster?"

Still acting dumb, Marcus answered, "Yeah, I see that both pair of boots got mud on them. So what?"

Talking to Marcus like he was a child that you had to explain every little detail to, Emmett said, "Look here now…red mud on your boots, and red mud on my boots, and there's also red mud on Wonderland's boots."

"So everybody's got red mud on their boots, that don't mean nothin'." Marcus' voice trembled as he spoke. He knew Emmett was getting at something that was going to be incriminating.

"Well, I'll show you what it means," Emmett said and stepped out the back door.

I heard iron clank together, and Emmett stepped back inside with three branding irons in his hand.

"You see, it's like this. The only place you can pick up red mud like that is up at Miners' Gulch. It just so happens that I found about a hundred head of cattle corralled up there with the Lazy 'J' brand on them. I also found these brandin' irons with the Rockin' 'W' brand on them. You notice, they're different sizes. That's so they can cover over other brands of different sizes." Emmett held one of the irons up. "You see, this one here fits right over the leanin'' J of the Lazy 'J' brand, just about perfect. I'd say these irons, along with the three runnin'

255

irons I left outside, and the red mud ought to just about be enough evidence for you and Terrance to hang."

"I didn't do no shootin'," exclaimed Marcus excitedly. "I didn't kill that ranch hand. Sure, I rustled some cattle; but I didn't kill nobody."

"Cattle rustlin' is still a hangin' offense around here cowboy," Emmett told him.

"I'll tell ya anythin' ya wanna know Marshal. Please, I don't wanna hang." Marcus was pretty shook, about to break down.

I'd say Marcus wasn't much older than eighteen or nineteen, and I felt kind of sorry for him. I really didn't like the thought of him hanging for making the mistake of tying in with the likes of the Wonderland boys.

"Maybe if you tell us about the rustlin' operation goin' on out at the Wonderland Ranch, we can keep you from the hangman's noose. Tell us what happened down in Elroy and who all is involved in this rustlin' deal. I wanna know about Jesse Wonderland's part in this," Emmett said.

"Jesse don't know nothin' about the rustlin' his brother's been a doin'. I'm sure of that. Terry always wanted it kept hid from him. He'd tell his brother that he found a good deal and bought the cattle himself. Sometimes he'd say he had won them in a poker game. Jesse never questioned Terry, though I think he was suspicious at times."

"I know there were more involved in this than just you and Terrance," said Emmett. "So come on, let's hear the whole story."

"Sure.., sure there were more involved; but ya killed Burch Wendell and Billy McQueen. I don't know what happened to that half-breed Indian, Turquois. He left the ranch here a while back. I don't know nothin' about before that, because I wasn't around then."

"How'd you get mixed up in this in the first place?" I asked.

"I got all drunked up with Wendell, he's my uncle, McQueen and Terry about six months ago down in Contention. They come in the saloon and bought me a drink and started talkin' to me about makin' some easy money. I was pretty well down on my luck at that time, so I listened as they bought me drinks. They said all I had to do was help them drive a few head of cattle north a ways, and I'd get paid a share of the sale. Sounded easy enough. I hate to admit it, but I pretty well had it figgered these cattle they were tellin' me about were more'n likely stolen."

"So you joined in and been with Terry ever since?" Emmett asked.

"Yeah, that's right, that's pretty much it. But, we never got into no shootin' matches until the other night. I swear to ya, I never fired a shot. I wanted to leave the cattle behind. I wanted out of the whole mess, but Terry was wounded and I wasn't sure what to do. He insisted we bring the cattle into the corral up at Miner's Gulch before I quit. We went ahead and drove them up there. By then, Terry was in pretty bad shape, so I brought him to town to the Doctor. I was afraid he was

257

gonna die. That's the whole story. I can't tell no more, cause I don't know no more."

"You're positive Jesse doesn't know anythin' about this rustlin' that's been goin' on?" asked Emmett firmly.

"As fer as I know, he don't know a thing. Terry always insisted we keep it quiet around his brother."

"Well kid," Emmett explained to Marcus, "I tell you what. I'll see what I can do about lettin' you off easy since you cooperated with us. That is, if you will tell that story in court to a judge."

"Now wait just a minute here. Y'all didn't say nothin' about testifyin' in court."

Emmett said, "You can testify or you can hang. That's the way I see your choices."

"That's the only way I can get out of this? I'm not shore that's fair."

"I'll tell you what's not fair; stealin' someone else's livelihood so you don't have to do the work. So yes, that's the only way you're gonna get out of this without hanging."

"Some choice ya give me."

CHAPTER TWENTY-FOUR
JAIL BREAK

When Terrance came around the next morning, boy was he upset about being shackled to that operating table. Emmett brought him down to the jail in Doc Baker's buckboard. He was too weak to put up much of a fight.

Later in the afternoon, when Terrance had regained some of his strength, I brought in some food. Terrance started running off at the mouth the second I came in. "I don't know what this sod-buster's been a tellin' ya, but it ain't nothin' but a bunch of lies. You'd better let me out of here before my brother gets wind of it, or there's gonna be trouble, big trouble," warned Terrance.

"You tell Terrance that you cooperated with us, did you Marcus?" I asked.

"He wanted to know what I had said to ya. I just told him I wasn't gonna hang for somethin' he did. He said when he gets out of here, he's gonna kill me."

"I wouldn't worry about that too much Marcus, he ain't gonna get away from Emmett and me."

"We'll see about that when my brother gets here McCord."

I cautiously slid supper plates under the cell doors. "You and that stinkin' Marshal are gonna get yers I'm tellin' ya," Terrance shouted as I walked out of room.

It wasn't a half hour later that Jesse came storming into the office madder than a stirred up hornet's nest. "You got my brother locked up here again, Cross?"

"As a matter of fact, I do. And, we got the goods on him this time," Emmett said calmly.

"You got nothin'. What's he supposed to have done this time. Just tell me what it's gonna cost to bail him out, and we'll be on our way."

"It's not gonna be that easy this time Jesse. He's bein' charged with cattle rustlin' and murder down in Elroy."

"You don't say." Jesse was taken back a bit when he heard that. "Just what kind of proof do ya have of this?"

"Got lots of proof." Emmett got up and showed Jesse the branding irons and the mud on Marcus' boots. "That ain't all, besides shootin' a man to death down in Elroy; those hundred head of cattle that were stolen are corralled on your ranch up there where this mud comes from. One of the men that rustled those cattle was shot in the leg just like your brother is. We got him dead to rights this time. The cowboy that was with him told us the whole story. We know you ain't involved in it Jesse; though at first, I figgered you were."

"I wanna talk to him."

"Sure Jesse, I got no problem with lettin' you see him."

Emmett led Jesse back to the jail cells. Terrance was real glad to see his brother. He thought his troubles were over. Jesse had always bailed Terrance out of every scrape he had ever gotten into since their parents had died.

"Damn Terry, you really done it this time. Man, we make out all right without you goin' out and stealin' cattle from other folks. What's wrong with you anyway?"

"I ain't stole nothin' Jesse. That Marshal's just tryin' ta frame me, him and that stinkin' sod-buster kid over there," Terrance pointed at Marcus. "I don't know nothin' about those cattle up at Miner's Gulch," he repudiated.

"Ain't no sense in lyin' Terry. I seen the evidence." Jesse looked over at Marcus. "You with him, was you?"

"Yes sir, Jesse I was."

"You see'm shoot that fella down in Elroy?"

Marcus looked down at the floor and mumbled, "Yeah, I'm sorry to say, I did."

"Ya can't go believin' this bunch Jesse," Terrance moaned. Then he straightened up and shouted, "THEY'RE LYIN' JESSE, they're tryin' to railroad me I'm tellin' ya. Ya ain't gonna believe that lyin' Marshal and that sod-buster over your own brother, are ya?"

"You got yourself in deeper than I can help you with this time Terry. I'll do what I can, but I'm afraid it won't be much." Jesse turned and walked back into the office. All the while, Terrance was screaming he was being framed and railroaded with a bunch of lies, even after we shut the door.

Jesse asked, "What's gonna happen now?"

"There'll be a fair trial down in Elroy; and if found guilty, which the evidence shows he is, he'll more than likely, I'm sorry to say, be sentenced to hang for murder and cattle rustling," Emmett explained to Jesse.

"HANGED?—Wait a damned minute, I ain't gonna let you hang my brother. I know he's done wrong; and maybe he deserves some jail time, but ain't nobody gonna hang him.

"Look here Marshal. I'll tell you what I'll do. I'll have my boys take those cattle back down to the ranch where they were stole from, and fifty head more besides. I'll even give them fair market value for fifty head on top of that. You don't get much more fair than that. Just let my brother go with a few months in jail to teach him a lesson, and everythin' will be square. What do you say?"

"I can't do that Jesse," Emmett said. "Sure your offer's fair as far as the cattle part of this deal is concerned, but the law just don't work like that. We're dealin' with murder here. Besides, it ain't up to me. It's up to the people and the County Court."

Jesse pointed his finger in Emmett's face. "Look here Cross. AIN'T, nobody hangin' my brother. Not you, or any of those yea-hoos down in Elroy. Do you understand that? Do you..?"

Emmett stood up and slapped Jesse's hand out of his face. Jesse reached for his pistol, but Emmett had the barrel of his Peacemaker on Jesse's nose before he even cleared leather.

"Now look Wonderland, I know this ain't no pleasant experience for ya; I understand your feelin's about your brother. I know yer upset, but you just can't buy him out of this one. You ain't done your brother no good by not lettin' him suffer the consequences of his own actions. Now he's went too far. Ain't nothin' you can do this time, so just get on out of here before I have to lock you up with him."

Jesse was boiling mad, but knew he couldn't buffalo Emmett. Jesse turned and headed for the door. He jerked it open and gave Emmett a hard, hateful look. "It ain't over Cross. I ain't lettin' nobody hang my brother..." Jesse made fists with both hands. "Nobody's gonna hang my brother." SLAM went the door and he was gone.

"What do you think he'll do Emmett?" I asked.

"I don't know Deputy, but I'm sure we had better keep our eyes open and keep close watch on those two prisoner's"

Later that night around eight o'clock, I took the Greener shotgun, checked the load, and started for the door on my way out to make a check around town.

"Watch yourself out there Deputy. I'll make the late rounds and let you stay here and keep watch on the prisoners."

"Fair enough, Emmett. I'll be back in about an hour," I said, that is what it usually took to make a good check around town.

"Like I said, watch yourself. Who knows what Jesse might try to get his brother out of jail."

"I know Emmett, I'll be watchful." I certainly ended up eating those words before the night was over.

I stopped in at the boarding house to say hello to my mother. Her and Miss Packard were pretty busy cleaning up after the supper-time crowd. We didn't talk much, since they were so busy; but my mother gave me a whole apple pie to share with Emmett when I got back to the Marshal's Office.

So there I was, carrying the shotgun in one hand and balancing the apple pie in the other as I finished up my rounds. I walked across the alley that ran down alongside the Cantina. I was just going to look in at the Cantina and then cross the street to the Marshal's Office.

I was about to step up on the porch in front of the Cantina when I heard a pistol cock next to my head and felt cold steel on my neck just behind my ear. I stopped dead in my tracks, and the pie plopped on the ground. Someone had stepped out of the shadows from the alley.

"Lose the shotgun, lawman."

"I recognized the voice, it was Jesse. I carefully lowered the shotgun to the ground and said, "You don't want to do this Jesse, it'll just cause you a peck of trouble."

"Shut up Deputy. Jake, get the shotgun."

"Sure Jesse," another voice answered from the darkness of the alley. The other voice belonged to Jesse's foreman Jake, from the ranch. Jake reached down and picked up my shotgun, cocked back both hammers, and pointed it at my back.

"Hey mister, careful with that Greener. Those triggers are pretty sensitive on pull."

"I told you to shut up," Jesse said as he poked my head with the pistol barrel. "Now, get movin', over to the jail."

I walked carefully across the street with Jesse and Jake right in step behind me. Jesse's pistol never left its place behind my ear.

When we were about five yards from the front door of the Marshal's Office, Jesse told me to stop. He yelled, "MARSHAL CROSS, come out here. I got somethin' for you to take a look at."

"Nothing happened. A moment later Jesse repeated, "HEY CROSS. You better come look see what I got out here. I might just put a bullet in him if you don't come out here."

The door opened slowly and Emmett stepped out with the 'Henry' rifle that had belonged to Reese. He had it pointed right at Jesse, who was standing off to the left side of me with his pistol still stuck to my neck.

"You let my brother out of there, Cross; or I'm gonna blow your Deputy's head off," Jesse threatened.

I was shook, but tried to remain as calm as I could. I felt pretty stupid for letting myself get in that predicament.

"I'm sorry Emmett," I said, apologizing for my carelessness.

Jesse shoved the pistol barrel into my neck again. "I told you to shut your mouth."

When Jesse did that, Emmett cocked the rifle. "I'm gonna kill this kid if you don't let my brother out of there. Now, Cross."

"I ain't lettin' no prisoners go. You kill my Deputy and I'll drop you where you stand. Give it up Jesse, and go on home. Your brother's a murderer; and he's gonna have to go to trial and

265

face up to it, and there ain't nothin' you can do to change that."

"Come on Jesse, the Marshal's right," Jake said, trying to persuade Jesse to give in. "You been bailin' Terry out of trouble ever since I can remember. Don't you think he's got to stand on his own on this one? Come on, let's give this up and go home. We got a ranch to run."

"Better listen to him Jesse. You ain't gonna win this one. Jake's making sense" Emmett said.

"You're fired Jake," Jesse snapped. "Ain't nobody gonna hang my brother.

"Let my brother go Cross, or the Deputy dies," Jesse threatened again.

"I told you Jesse. If he dies, you die with him. Now put that gun away and go home. I'm tellin' you, I'm a crack shot with this 'Henry'. And I've got a bead right on your forehead."

Jake lowered my shotgun and uncocked both hammers and pleaded, "Come on Jesse. You don't want to kill that Deputy, and the Marshal ain't gonna let your brother go no-ways. Come on, it ain't worth two good men dyin'."

After a long silence, I felt the pressure of the gun barrel ease from off of my neck; and Jesse uncocked the pistol. Jake handed me the shotgun. "Sorry Deputy, he's just upset about his brother, and I've been with this family a long spell," Jake said.

"I know, thanks," I said, as I took the shotgun.

Jesse stood there with his pistol down to his side staring at Emmett, who hadn't lowered the rifle yet. Finally Jesse put it in his holster as he looked down at the ground. He took a long deep breath and turned to walk away. I noticed a tear running down his cheek.

Jake started walking with Jesse, and put his hand on Jesse's shoulder.

Jesse threw back his elbow and knocked Jake's hand away. "I told you, you're fired. You can come out and collect your gear and I'll pay you what you got comin' and a month's salary. Then you can ride out. You're done workin'for my outfit."

Jake had worked as foreman on the Rocking 'W' Ranch for as long as I could remember, even before old man Wonderland had died. He was a hard-working hand and had always been loyal to the Wonderlands.

"You don't mean that Jesse, you're just upset about all of this."

"Yeah, I'm upset all right. I'm upset that you can side in with that Marshal over my brother. You're fired. I damned well mean what I'm sayin', don't you tell me I don't. You got till mornin' to get your gear and ride off my ranch. If you ain't gone, I'll throw you off."

"I worked for your Pa Jesse," Jake tried to reason. "You can't just up and kick me off the ranch like that. Come on now, you're just upset. You'll get over this."

"You're through Jake. I ain't talkin' about it no more. Remember what I said. If you ain't gone in the mornin', I'll throw you off my ranch."

Jesse headed for his horse tied at the hitching post in front of the King's Palace Saloon.

Emmett kept his aim on Jesse until he mounted his horse. He stood ready as Jesse and Jake rode by, until they disappeared into the darkness on their way out of town.

"I'm terrible sorry about this Emmett," I said. "There ain't no excuse for lettin' myself be taken like that."

"You'll know better next time Deputy. I'm just glad Jesse gave it up. I'da had a hard time explainin' it to Phoebe Ann when she came up."

"Thanks Emmett. I appreciate yer not bein' sore at me. I got to tell you though," I said sheepishly, "about the fresh-baked apple pie from my ma. You see, I dropped it on the ground when Jesse stuck that pistol barrel in my ear."

"WHAT?" "You lost a whole, fresh-baked apple pie?"

"Yeah, but I'm real sorry about it. I mean I wanted my half of it too."

Emmett swatted me on the head with his hat and said, "Now that's UNFORGIVABLE, just plain unforgivable."

The next day Emmett sent a telegram to Sheriff Pickett down in Elroy. The Sheriff answered back, telling us he would send a couple of his Deputies with warrants to pick up our prisoners within the next day or two.

Emmett sat down and wrote a letter to send along with the Deputies to the Judge who served in Elroy area asking leniency for Marcus. He explained in the letter that Marcus had cooperated fully with us in the investigation, and that he felt

Marcus had fallen into bad company due to his young age and inexperience. Emmett told me he 'hoped that the letter would keep Marcus from the hangman's rope and he wouldn't get too stiff a sentence'. I didn't know anything about the people down in Elroy. The town had sprang up almost over-night, and I had never been there.

It was pretty quiet that day except for an occasional shouting bout from Terrance. He would rattle the bars and threaten Emmett or Marcus. He was like a caged mountain lion, pacing back and forth in his jail cell and yelling out obscenities from time to time. For some reason, Terrance never made any threats toward me; maybe because we had grown up together. I was really never sure.

Late that afternoon, Emmett said, "Hey Deputy. What say we have Gonzales come over and watch those two back there and you and me go down to your Ma's place? We'll get us a meal and see if she's got any more of that apple pie."

"Well, if you think things will be all right here. You know me. I'm always ready for some of my ma's cookin'."

"Good. I'll make rounds and bring Gonzales back with me, if he ain't too busy."

Emmett and I made pigs of ourselves eating chicken and dumplings. Then we topped that off with big wedges of fresh hot apple pie with cream.

As we headed back to the Marshal's office, Emmett said, "I'm gonna stop over at the Cantina to see Rosa. I ain't seen much of her lately. I might just have a beer while I'm there too. You don't mind do you Deputy?"

"No, go ahead Emmett. I owe Gonzales a good beatin' in checkers anyway. I'll see if he wants to take his lickin' now or not."

"I don't know Deputy, Gonzales is pretty tough. See you in a while then."

As I pushed on the door of the Marshal's Office, it gave way. Somebody was pulling it open from the other side. I figured it to be Gonzales. I even started saying how I was going to beat his pants off in checkers. I was really taken by surprise when I saw that it was Terrance. I started to raise the Greener, but Terrance laid the side of my head open with a pistol butt before I could. I dropped to the floor right in the middle of the doorway, knocked senseless.

I was in a daze as I felt Terrance pull my pistol from its holster and toss it out the door. Then he picked up the shotgun and did the same with it. Terrance had both of his pistols strapped on, and he stepped over me and headed for the street.

I was seeing everything in a blur. Terrance limped to the middle of the street and screamed, "MARSHAL…You stinkin' lawman, COME OUT here and get yours."

CHAPTER TWENTY-FIVE
DEATH IN THE STREET

I could barely see across the street over to the Cantina. A fuzzy outline of a man that I took to be Emmett, appeared on the porch in front of the door at the Cantina.

I tried to raise myself, but everything just started spinning around and I couldn't get up.

"Step on out here...YOU," Terrance ordered. "You're done. Ya been at me long enough. I told ya I was gonna kill ya. Now's your time lawman."

Emmett answered Terrance's challenge. "If you're sure that's what you wanna do, then I'll shore enough oblige you."

Terrance went for both pistols; a split second before they fired, Emmett's Peacemaker spoke once loud and true. Terrance's two shots, one out of each pistol went wild, one ricocheted and sang as it echoed off into the distance, the other shattered the small front window of the Cantina. Terrance dropped down on his knees in the street, his pistols fell out of his hands as I heard him gasp his brother's name, "Jesse…Jes-s-e. Terrance fell back on his legs in an awkward position, dead in the street.

Everything went black then for me. The next thing I remembered was waking up on the cot in the Marshal's Office with one terrible headache. Doc Baker was there tending to my head. Gonzales was setting in the desk chair with blood running out of his nose, both of his eyes were almost swelled shut, and he had cuts all over his face. Rosa was taking

271

care of her father with a clean wet cloth. Emmett stood watching as Doc Baker stitched the gash across my brow back together.

"Hey," I asked, "What's happened to Marcus?"

"He's dead. Terrance killed him," Emmett told me.

"How in the...OUCH."

"Hold still dog-gone it," Doc Baker scolded. "I'm trying to sew your head back together here, if you haven't noticed."

"I'll tell you the story later," Emmett said.

"You have a concussion young man. I want you to take it easy for the next few days. Do you understand me?" dictated Doc Baker.

Later, Gonzales told the story of what had happened and how Terrance had escaped. It seems he was setting in the office looking over some wanted posters when he heard a commotion back in the jail cells. He got up, stuck a loaded pistol in his belt, and went back to see what was going on.

Terrance had taken a piece of rope webbing out of his bunk and somehow had managed to get it around Marcus' neck through the bars and was choking him. He told Gonzales that he would choke Marcus to death if he didn't open the cell door. Gonzales opened the door, not to let Terrance out, but to try and stop him from choking Marcus.

In the struggle, Terrance got the gun out of Gonzales' belt and still managed to keep a tight grip on the rope with one hand. He held Gonzales back with the pistol until he choked the life out of Marcus. Then he pistol-whipped Gonzales to the floor and kicked him into unconsciousness. He then went into the office, where he strapped on his pistols and met me at the door.

It was a terrible thing, Terrance killing Marcus like that. Terrance deserved what he got. Emmett just saved the county and the people of Elroy the cost of a trail and hanging the way I saw it.

There was an impressive funeral for Terrance Wonderland. Jesse spared no expense. I attended out of respect, mainly due to the fact I had known Terrance and Jesse my whole life, had grown up with them in fact.

Emmett didn't attend because he knew it would most likely cause a ruckus between Jesse and him. Emmett just wanted to let it settle down and be over and done. With his hat off, Emmett stood respectfully in front of the Marshal's Office as the procession passed by. Jesse gave Emmett a cold look of hatred as he passed by. I hoped that somehow, this would be the end of it; but only time would tell.

CHAPTER TWENTY-SIX
A NEW JOB AND A NEW LIFE

I was as nervous and excited as I had ever been in my entire life. It was well after eleven o'clock on Wednesday, and the stage would be bringing Ann and Lucy in at any time now. Emmett had given me the day off and asked Gonzales to work with him for the day. Emmett had said something about the town being big enough that maybe we ought to consider putting on another full-time Deputy.

My mother and I stood in front of the stage line depot waiting in eager anticipation. Finally, at five to the hour, the stage coach came rumbling up the street with a cloud of dust trailing closely behind. The driver shouted a long drawn out 'WHOA' as he reined back the team of powerful horses. Stretched far back in the seat with the reins tight and his foot jammed hard against the brake, he brought the stagecoach to a halt right on the money in front of the depot. The cloud of dust that had been trailing the stage now almost entirely engulfed the whole outfit in a thick fog. As the cloud settled down, it left a considerable film of dust on the whole coach.

Through the clearing haze, two sitting female figures formed inside the coach. When the dust had almost completely settled the stage driver, who had jumped down, opened the coach door to help the ladies out. Lucy stepped down first. "Hey, Johnny boy, how are ya?"

Taking off my hat I said, "Just fine ma'am, now that you two are finally here. How are you?"

She chuckled in her usual bubbly voice, "Ma'am? Ya just gotta love'm, don't ya?" Lucy's eyes were painted and lined, and her lips were a bright ruby red. She wore a revealing, low cut, emerald green dress, matching wide brimmed hat and was holding a parasol that also matched the outfit.

You should have seen the look of relief on my mother's face when I introduced Lucy to her as Ann's sister.

Then, my heart jumped right into my throat as Ann appeared in the doorway of the coach and stepped down before my eyes with the assistance of stagecoach driver.

I just kind of stood there stunned with my mouth open. My attention was so focused on Ann that I couldn't even tell you if there were any other passengers on the stage. Even with a layer of road dust on her, she looked like a dream. Her hair had grown out some; and at that moment, to me, her beauty was incomparable. I really did love her, and I hoped that her love for me was as strong. She was in a not so revealing summer blue dress that accented her shapely figure, topped off with a quaint little paper flowered hat and she had only a light hint of rouge and face paint that let her natural beauty shine through.

I didn't come back to reality until Ann kissed my cheek and spoke up to say, "John, is this your mother?"

"Oh…Yes…yes this is my Ma.., I mean my dear mother, Mrs. McCord. And Ma, this is Ann."

My mother said 'Hello' and took charge by telling Lucy and Ann that she had a room for them at the boarding house. Lucy mentioned that she wanted to look around town and see what Cold Creek had to offer.

Ann noticed my head was bandaged and I had to fill her in on all the recent town events we had been involved in, and then I had to assure her that I was all right and on the mend.

"After we have some lunch, John will be glad to show you ladies around town," my mother told them. My mother and the two women hit it off just perfectly. I hardly got a word in edgeways as we ate our meal. Ann and my mother swapped recipes, while Lucy wanted to know all about the businesses in town.

I helped my mother clear the table when we had finished our meal. I wanted to talk with her about something. "Ma, I really do love Ann," I said when we got into the kitchen. "And I want to ask her to marry me."

"Son, now that I've met her, I understand why. She's very sweet and I think she'll be a good wife. So what's botherin' you?"

"Well, I really like my job as Deputy and I wouldn't wanna leave it for nothin'. The thing is Ma, I don't know if on my salary I'll ever be able to buy a house for her. And she deserves a house Ma."

"John, what am I gonna do with you? You're always a worryin' an' a frettin' over small things that will more'n likely turn out okay anyways."

"Ma, a house is no small thing you know? I love livin' here at the boardin' house, but I want to give Ann a home of her own."

"Well it's gonna spoil the surprise, and you'd better not let Ann in on it."

"What Ma? What surprise?"

"Unbeknownst to you, because I wanted to surprise you on your weddin' day, I settled a deal on the widow Carlton's house a few days ago. I had been savin' the money for quite some time for that very reason."

"Ma, I can't let you go to that kind of expense."

"John, it's already done. You're my only child, so don't you stand there and try an' tell me what I can and can't do," scolded my mother.

"All right Ma, if your heart is set on it, who am I to say anythin'." I hugged her tight and said, "You're the greatest mother that a fella could ever ask for."

"I don't know about that, but I do love you son and I'm certainly proud of you. Now, you do your part and ask Ann the question; and don't you dare let her know about the house. That's my surprise."

"Okay Ma, I will. And I won't say a word about the house."

I showed Ann and Lucy around town, and Lucy took particular interest in an empty shop beside Cahill's General Store. She mentioned to Ann that it would be a great place to open up a hat shop. Ann agreed and told me they hadn't found anything in Tombstone yet.

She said, "If I were to have reason for staying here in Cold Creek, Lucy and I could buy the shop and start that hat shop right here. And, maybe we could get in to a line of women's apparel."

"You never know what might come up," I said.

That evening we had supper at the boarding house, and Mayor Potts and his wife joined us. Miss Packard served us and acted very pleased when I introduced Ann to her. Then she proudly showed us a ring that one of Mort Cahill's nephews had given her the day before. We all congratulated her on the engagement.

Mayor Potts addressed me and said, "You know John, the town is very pleased with the job you and the Marshal are doing. I spoke with Marshal Cross today and he told me that you and him had been talking about the need to put on another full-time deputy. In view of the growth of Cold Creek over the past year, and the railroad building a station here, I had to agree with that. In fact, I told Marshal Cross I figured we could use two more full time deputies.

"Well John, that would make you senior deputy. It would mean more responsibility, so you would be entitled to a substantial raise in pay. So what do you say John, are you willing to take on more responsibility on the job?"

"Shore Mayor," I responded, "I would be proud to take it on. This is my town, my home, and I enjoy watchin' over it and keepin' the peace."

"Good," said the Mayor. "I will bring the matter up at the next town council meeting. I know they pretty much feel the same way as I do."

After supper, Ann and I took a walk down toward the new train depot building site. Earlier in the week, I had bought a ring myself; though it wasn't as flashy as the one Miss Packard had showed off. When we got to the building site, we found a comfortable spot to sit on some lumber and marvel at the stars. We talked about the town and the new job and the responsibilities I would be getting if the town council went along with Mayor Potts' recommendation.

As we were looking at the stars, and the silence of the night made the moment right, I looked into Ann's eyes. They sparkled in the light of the moon. "Ann," I said, "I hope you know that I love you more than anything on this earth."

"And I love you too, John," she replied.

"Well, Ann," I said as I pulled the ring out of my breast pocket and presented it to her. "If you'll have me, I would like you to be my wife and share my life here in Cold Creek."

"Oh John, you know I will be your wife. And I'll stay by your side in whatever you do or wherever you go." The lilac perfume that was always so intoxicating to me filled my nostrils and heightened my senses. I pulled Ann close to me, and as our lips met, I felt strong and sure. I no longer was nervous or felt apprehensive about the moment. I knew I had what I really wanted and I knew it was the best choice I could make. Ann felt good in my arms. She made me feel like a man, strong and confident.

We sat holding hands and talked about our plans for the future. We set the date for two weeks from that night.

When we broke the news to my mother, she insisted we get married right there at the boarding house. Ann could come down the staircase; and if Judge Bryant got back in time, he could perform the ceremony.

Lucy had spent the evening at the boarding house. She had happened to meet the man that owned the empty building next to Cahill's General Store when he came in for supper. After congratulating us and mentioning, 'it was about time', she told us she almost had a deal worked out on the building.

Ann and Lucy made plans to bring their things up from Tombstone. Lucy insisted that Ann stay in Cold Creek while she traveled back and took care of everything. There was a room above the empty building that Lucy said she would live in when she came back.

Ann and I walked down to the Marshal's Office to tell Emmett the news. I wanted to ask him to stand up with me and be my best man.

After we told Emmett, he gave me a firm handshake and hugged and kissed Ann. He gave Ann such a kiss that I almost got jealous.

"I'm real happy for you two, and I'd be honored to stand up with you as your best man, Deputy."

He told us about his conversation with Mayor Potts. He said, "It would make the job a lot less dangerous with four of us to take care of the town." Ann certainly appreciated hearing that.

"You got anybody in mind for the job Emmett?" I asked.

"I talked with Gonzales and he said he was interested. He told me that he owned a business in town and wanted the town to be a clean and safe place for folks to live. He said his wife and daughters pretty well ran the Cantina anyway.

"And believe it or not, Casey March said he would take on the job if it was decided to put on more deputies. He said he was gettin' tired of the gamblin' life and figgered it was time to settle down and earn a respectable livin'."

"We ought to be able to handle just about anything with an outfit like that," I said, and Emmett agreed with me.

TWENTY-SEVEN
A NEW LIVERY STABLES

My mother decided it might be better to go ahead and tell Ann about the house since she was staying in town till the wedding. She knew Ann would want to decorate it to her own taste, so it would feel like home to Ann; and she also wanted the house to be ready for us right after we were married. They hugged and Ann thanked her so appreciatively that I thought my mother was going to break out in tears. I was so glad that Ann and my mother took to each other so well. Who wouldn't like Ann, she was the sweetest person I had ever met. I was as happy as a man could be. I felt on top of the world.

Ann and my mother were busy as bees, buzzing all over town buying material for Ann's wedding dress and things for the house.

It was pretty well business as usual for Emmett and me. On Friday night at the town meeting, the council voted to put on the two extra deputies. So I was kept pretty busy training our two new deputies, Manuel Gonzales and Casey March.

I instructed them on points of law they would need to know and showed them what was to be done during their rounds to check the town. We would work a swing shift so nobody would have to be up at night all the time.

It was Saturday afternoon when a telegram arrived from Saint Louis, Missouri. It was from Judge Bryant. As soon as the telegraph operator handed it to me, I walked out of the telegraph office and read it aloud for everyone. They all were waiting for me; we had just left the boarding house after eating a noon meal. As I read, Emmett, Ann, and my mother looked over my shoulder with eager interest.

The telegram stated that the judge presiding at Ben's trial had turned out to be an old friend of Judge Bryant's. They had attended law school together.

First, Judge Bryant mentioned in the telegram that Ben had been found guilty by the jury; and that the presiding judge, Joseph R. Spencer, had sentenced Ben to ten years hard labor. We all gasped and were taken aback by that bit of news, until we read on. Judge Bryant then told us that Judge Spencer, being a fair man, suspended the sentence. He agreed with what had been said about Ben being a foolish young lad at the time of the robbery and had since proved himself to be a respected citizen of the town of Cold Creek. Judge Bryant said the three of them would be back to town in four days.

Judge Bryant also told us in the telegram that Taylor was furious about Ben being let off; and had made such a scene right there in the courtroom, that Judge Spencer fined him fifty dollars for contempt. Judge Bryant said he told the Pinkerton after the trial that it wouldn't be a good idea for him ever to show his face in Cold Creek again.

In the last part of the telegram, Judge Bryant sent authorization for Emmett to draw eight-hundred dollars out of his account at the bank. He was to take the money and buy materials for the building of a new livery stables. He also asked Emmett to round up volunteers to start construction on the new livery. He said Ben didn't know anything about it. He figured it would be a good welcoming home surprise for him.

The train arrived on Tuesday afternoon, bringing Judge Bryant, Sally Belle, and Ben back from Saint Louis Missouri. Emmett and I were waiting when it pulled into town. A railroad construction crew was busy putting up the new railroad station. At the same time, a lot of the townsfolk were busy with their own project, constructing a new livery stables; and the barn was already near completion.

After a hand-shake from the Judge and a hug from Sally Belle, Emmett and I said hello to Ben and welcomed him home.

"Thanks," he said. "It's good to be back and out of those shackles. Ain't much of a home though, if a fella ain't got a livelihood no more."

As we walked toward the boarding house, Emmett told the Judge the story about Terrance Wonderland and about his attempted escape from the jail. After Emmett had filled the Judge in on the whole thing, he asked Emmett about the message he had sent. "Did you get that matter I wired you about taken care of Emmett?"

"Yes sir Judge, I did. Got one heck of a good start on it anyway. And by the way, Mr. King donated almost all of the lumber, so there's gonna be plenty money left over. Mr. King said as long as it contributed to the town's growth and wasn't at competition with his business, it was the least he could do to help."

"What the heck are you fellas talkin' about anyway?" questioned Ben. "Ya finally buildin' a court house for the town?"

"Not exactly Ben. It's just a little project I put together for the good of the town, something they want and need real bad," Judge Bryant told Ben.

"I'll tell ya what this town needs, a blacksmith shop and livery stables, but that's gone. And somebody with some money will prob'ly come ridin' in here and be buildin' one before ya know it, with the way things are pickin' up around here. Well, at least I got a piece of property to sell them for it anyway," Ben said in a despairing tone.

"Hey, what say we get a drink at the Kings Palace Saloon. I really need one after that long train ride," Ben said.

"Let's hold off on that drink Ben, at least till we show you what's goin' on down by the Marshal's Office," Emmett said.

"I need a drink now. Besides, there's nothin' down there I wanna see. I don't like seein' the remains of what once was my livelihood and future. It just makes me sick."

"Come on now Ben, stop feelin' sorry for yourself," I encouraged. "I think you might even change your mind about that drink if you come and see what's goin' on down there."

"Just what are you fellas up to? I don't wanna go down there, don't ya understand? I hate lookin' at that mess."

Emmett said to Ben, "Well you can either walk down there on your own, or we can carry you. Don't matter, either way you're goin'"

"All right, all right I'll go, but I sure don't know what all the fuss is about," Ben said, finally agreeing. Curiosity had gotten the best of him. He just didn't catch on, though it was getting quite obvious.

As we passed by the Kings Palace Saloon, Ben asked again, "Ya sure ya don't wanna stop in for a drink?"

"Will you come along peacefully and forget about that drink before I hog tie you an' drag you down there?" Emmett told him.

When we got within sight of the construction of the new barn, Ben stopped dead in his tracks; stood and just stared with his mouth open.

"What do you think Ben," asked Judge Bryant.

"It's big, a lot bigger than my old place. Who's buildin' it?" Ben asked.

"The town is," I answered. "It's gonna be your new livery stables and blacksmith shop."

"How can that be? I ain't got no money ta build no new livery."

"You don't need any dad-blame money. The town's doin' it for you," Judge Bryant told Ben. He was starting to get irritated at Ben's negative attitude.

"No sir, I don't need ya all's charity. If I can't do it on my own, then I ain't gonna do it at all," Ben persisted.

"Emmett. Talk to this fool man, before I bust his head open," said Judge Bryant.

"Look here Ben, don't be so dog-gone hard-headed. It ain't charity. The town's growin' and needs a good blacksmith and a livery stable; you said that yerself, so what's wrong with them fillin' that need," Emmett explained, taking his turn reasoning with Ben.

"The way I see it, it's still charity. If a man can't pay his own way, he ain't much of a man. I'm a goin' down an' get me a drink."

Judge Bryant was fed up with Ben and started for him.

"I'll show you charity you ungrateful..." At the same time Ben started for Judge Bryant. Emmett grabbed Ben and held him back, and I grabbed the Judge right as he was ready to take a swing at Ben.

"What's the matter with you anyhow?" Judge Bryant demanded. "I traveled all the way back east to Saint Louie to save your mangy hide, and then I put up money for a new livery for you. And, and you're too dog-gone proud to accept a friend's help. I tell you, if Deputy McCord didn't have hold of me right now, why I'd.., I'd skin you alive an' take you out to the desert to let the buzzards eat you."

"Ya mean ya'd try, ya ol' goat," Ben spit back.

"Who you callin' an' old goat? I'll show you a thing or two," Judge Bryant challenged, struggling to get loose.

Emmett jerked Ben around and said in his face, "Now you shut up and listen, the both of you. If you wanna pay your own way, well that'll be just fine; but you're a darned fool for not acceptin' the help of a friend. A friend doin' somethin' out of the kindness of his heart, well, that ain't never charity.

"I'll tell you what, though, this town needs your skills as a horseman and blacksmith. So listen up, here's what you do Ben. You're gonna make money runnin' the business and that's a fact. So what you do is, consider the Judge's contribution as a loan, you'll pay him back every penny; and as far as the town's concerned, you supply the Marshal's Office with free service for the next two years and I think that will square it for the town's part. Now what do you say about that boys?" Emmett looked over at Judge Bryant and then back at Ben.

"Well, I reckon that would be fair enough. I mean, that wouldn't be charity that way, would it?" Ben said.

"No, it wouldn't Ben," I agreed.

"Hey, I like the deal about not havin' to pay for service. Sally Belle and me been plannin' to get us a carriage anyways. How about makin' that same deal with me?" Judge Bryant asked.

"All right Judge, ya got a deal," Ben answered. "And Judge, I'm sorry I went off at ya like that. I know you're my friend and I do appreciate all ya done for me through this whole mess. Why, if it weren't for you, I'd prob'ly be at the end of a rope about now. I just lost my head over all of this," Ben explained appreciatively.

Emmett and I let Ben and Judge Bryant loose from our grip and they shook hands and renewed their friendship. Then they thanked Emmett and me for helping them iron it all out.

"How about that drink now fellas?" Judge Bryant asked.

Ben replied, "No, not for me, I think I'm gonna lay off that stuff for a while. Let's go on down here and see what the new livery looks like. I gonna go dig my anvel out and figger where I'm gonna set things up."

Ben just needed to think the whole thing was his idea, that's all. He was real impressed with the new building, and everybody on the building site stopped their work to welcome Ben home. It had been a long while since I had seen him smile as big as he did that day as everyone patted him on the back and shook his hand.

CHAPTER TWENTY-EIGHT
A WEDDING TO REMEMBER

On Wednesday, a week before the wedding, Lucy came back to town in a hired freight wagon. The wagon was loaded down with all of her and Ann's belongings from Tombstone. Lucy was all prepared to settle in and make Cold Creek her home.

Emmett and I helped Lucy unload the wagon and set up the upstairs room over the building that she and Ann had purchased for the new hat shop. Lucy said she had already ordered plumed hats for the ladies; and beaver, silk and felt hats for the men. Emmett told her if she wasn't going to have any wide-brimmed Texas cowboy hats, she probably wasn't going to get much business from him. She said she would order one especially for him. The hats would be arriving from San Francisco, coming from all over the world. Lucy told us the hats would start arriving in less than a month.

Judge Bryant had agreed to perform the wedding ceremony for us. My mother had everything set up for the wedding there at the boarding house two days ahead of time. Doc Baker was giving us use of his carriage; and the plan was, that after the wedding party came out on the porch at the boarding house for a picture, it was to be taken by the new photographer in town, 'Dandy' Lance. Of course 'Dandy' wasn't his real first name. That's just what everybody had tagged him with because of the bright colored plaid suits he wore. After the pictures were taken, the carriage would be pulled up in front of the boarding house, then Ann and I would get into the carriage. Our best man, Emmett, and bridesmaid, Lucy, would drive us to our new home at the north edge of town.

On Saturday, the Chambers were throwing a wedding party for us out at their ranch. Their plans were to roast a couple sides of beef, and everyone in town was invited. Ann was so excited about the way everything had turned out that she could hardly contain herself. Me, I wasn't too much excited at all. 'HA'.

Nobody planned to be armed at the wedding. We had decided at least one person would have to be on duty to watch over the town. Deputy Casey March volunteered to be the one since he wanted to stay clear of weddings anyway. He told us he wanted to stay as far away from marriage as he could; wasn't no woman gonna put a ring in his nose. However, Casey was happy to attend a party rather than a wedding; so, Gonzales said he would take care of town while the rest of us attended the party out at the Chambers' Ranch.

Tuesday night, the night before I was to marry, Judge Bryant, Ben, and Casey March took me out on the town. We hit the Silver Stallion Saloon and the Kings Palace and finally ended up at the Cantina. Everybody bought me a beer, including a dozen Mexican cowboys up from Mexico on a cattle drive. I wouldn't drink any hard stuff; still I didn't want to seem ungrateful of everyone's good wishes, so I drank many times more than I ever had. After all, I was just a two-beer man, never any more. That night, however, I must have downed fifteen or twenty mugs of beer, with Ben, Casey, and Judge Bryant cheering me on.

My so-called friends and drinking companions dropped me in front of the Marshal's Office on the porch sometime around two o'clock in the morning. An hour or so later, Emmett found me passed out right there where they had dumped me.

Emmett picked me up and took me out back to the pump where he soaked me with cold water for about a half hour, and then poured black coffee down me until I think I threw up everything I had eaten or drank from two days previous.

It was a good thing the wedding wasn't until that afternoon. I'm telling you, my head was about to come off when I woke up on the cot about ten o'clock at the Marshal's Office. Emmett had just come in. "I thought you were just a two beer man?" he said.

I sat up. "Yeah... Well, from now on that's the way it's gonna stay. In fact, I'm not so sure I'm not gonna be a 'NO' beer man from now on. I thought those fellas were my friends, but I think they're jealous and tried to kill me last night."

"From the looks of you last night, I thought they had," Emmett said.

It was Wednesday afternoon, and I had recovered fully from my hangover. The big day I had been waiting for was here. I'll tell you the truth, I was nervous those times in Tombstone when Ann and I had met before; but they really couldn't hold a candle to my nervousness that day. When I saw Ann coming down those stairs, all adorned and glowing in her wedding dress, all that disappeared.

There wasn't anything else on my mind, except how lovely a bride Ann was and how happy she was making me by becoming my wife. Judge Bryant said all the right words, and when I repeated those vows and heard Ann say she would love me until death we parted; well, I just knew she really meant it and I knew I had everything life had to offer.

Things were going along just smooth as silk. Every person I knew, and a few I didn't know, was there at the wedding. That is, except for Casey March, who was on duty, and one other person I hadn't even given thought to that day.

After the pictures were taken, Emmett and Lucy stepped down off the boarding house porch to bring up the carriage. As if from nowhere, Jesse Wonderland appeared in the middle of the street, his sixgun low, and hatred in his eyes. No one had noticed where he had come from. No doubt he had been drinking that day, but Jesse was the type that could hold his liquor and you would never tell when he was drunk. Jesse was a hard man whether he had liquor in him or not.

He just stood there at first, that is until Emmett just ignored him and headed for the carriage. Everybody was silent. Not even Judge Bryant said anything at this point.

"CROSS," Jesse shouted to get Emmett's full attention. "It's good to see you and the rest of the town are havin' a good time today. That way I won't feel so bad about killin' you."

"Look Jesse, this ain't no time to discuss our differences. Why don't you just wait till we can sit down and talk this thing out like reasonable men."

"Time for talkin's through. I tried to talk to you about my brother, but you wouldn't listen. You just went ahead and murdered him."

"Emmett didn't murder nobody Jesse," I yelled out. "Terrance didn't give him no other choice. Besides that, your brother was the one that committed the murder, two of'm, matter of fact."

"You stay out of this McCord," Jesse said. "You and Terry went to school together. You used to be friends until you pinned on that tin badge and got ta thinkin' you was better'n him."

"That's not true Jesse," I said in my defense. Terrance and I had never really been very close. "I never thought I was better than anybody."

"Oh yeah, it's true all right, but that ain't important right now. My fight's with YOU Cross," Jesse pointed an accusing finger at Emmett. "I've come here ta kill you for shootin' down my brother. So let's get to it," Jesse demanded.

"I'm not armed Jesse. I don't think you're the kind to gun down an unarmed man. Beside why would you want to spoil John's special day with this kind of thing"

"I don't care about none of that. Somebody give him a gun," Jesse ordered.

"Ain't nobody got a gun to give me Jesse," said Emmett.

"Then I'll kill you with my bare hands." Jesse unbuckled his gunbelt and dropped it to the ground.

Emmett said, "Everybody stay out of it. This is between Jesse an' me."

Jesse came at Emmett at a dead run; and when he was about five feet away, he took a flying leap through the air. Emmett caught him and both men hit the ground with a hard thud. A cloud of dust engulfed them as they rolled around with death grips on each other.

When they stopped rolling, Jesse was setting on Emmett's chest choking him. Jesse cursed Emmett while straining to choke the life out of him. Jesse was a strong man, and it wasn't looking good for Emmett. Then Emmett raised his legs high in the air and drove his heels hard into the sides of Jesse's head. Jesse hollered out in pain as Emmett pushed him off to the side. Jesse came right back, though. He was tough.

Jesse jumped to his feet, but Emmett was already up and waiting with a haymaker to Jesse's jaw. SMACK, and Jesse went sprawling to the ground once more. Again, Jesse recovered; and from his position on the ground, he spun around with his leg and kicked Emmett's feet out from under him. Emmett hit the ground hard. Jesse was on top of him pounding away before Emmett could get his senses back. The women were gasping at each blow and brutal move. Once again, Emmett was in a desperate situation with Jesse beating him in the face and on the sides of his head.

Emmett's hand reached out to the side and gathered a handful of dust from the street. He struggled to take careful aim and threw it full force into Jesse's eyes. Jesse's hands went to his face and

Emmett managed to kick his way out from under Jesse once again.

Jesse was on his knees, frantically trying to clear his eyes of the irritation, when Emmett stood up; and with all the strength he had, he kicked Jesse in the face. Jesse flipped backward and lay motionless for a few seconds; but then he staggered to his feet, and as he tried to stand erect, Emmett managed to muster enough strength to put Jesse away cold, with an uppercut to his jaw. Jesse hit the ground with such force that it knocked all the breath out of him and once he caught his breath back he only laid on the ground and moaned. He couldn't even raise his head off the ground.

About that time, Casey March appeared on the scene. He was all apologies for not knowing about Jesse being in town.

"I'll lock him up Emmett," said Casey.

"No, that won't be necessary," Emmett said, as he attempted to brush the dust off himself. "Just unload his pistol and take the cartridges out of his gunbelt and put them in your pocket."

Casey did what Emmett told him. Emmett asked for a bucket as he wiped blood from his nose and mouth with a handkerchief someone had given him. Somebody in the crowd brought him the bucket in short order. When he got it, he staggered over to a nearby horse trough and filled the bucket with water. Then he carried it over to Jesse, sloshing water over the sides as he stumbled along. Emmett dumped the whole thing into Jesse's face.

Jesse spit and sputtered back to life. Both men were a dirty and a bloody mess. Emmett's best outfit was ripped to shreds.

Emmett put it to Jesse in no uncertain terms, "Get up and get out of my town. Next time you come back, if you're wearin' a gun, I'll take it as a threat on my life and I'll have you arrested an' thrown in jail for attempted murder of an officer of the law."

Emmett helped Jesse to his feet, went over and picked his hat up off of the ground, and slammed it down on Jesse's head. "Get on your horse and ride out, now.

Jesse shook his head in acknowledgment and walked off toward his horse. Casey handed him his pistol and gunbelt as he walked by.

Jesse rode out of town and we didn't see any more of him for quite a spell after that. Emmett was a mess, and Rosa was right on the spot with clean towels and water to clean him up as he flopped on the porch step of the boarding house. Doc Baker sent someone over to his office for his medical bag.

After Emmett was patched up, we took up the plans where we had left off. Emmett stopped the carriage in front of our new house, and my new bride and I went inside.

Next day out at the Chambers Ranch we danced and ate our fill. It was a wonderful day.

Later in the afternoon, a number of us fellas were sitting around talking. Mayor Potts explained, as he puffed on a large, long stogie, that the new rail station was going to make Cold Creek grow.

Everyone agreed, already there were a lot of new faces around town.

Judge Bryant told Emmett that now that the rustling had been stopped in the area, there wouldn't be any justification for the special Territorial Marshal's appointment and it would be rescinded. However, he told Emmett that if he would accept it, he was sure he could get a United States Deputy Marshal's appointment for him; so he could have jurisdiction anywhere in Arizona Territory. Emmett said he thought it would be a good idea to have that authority in view of the railroad's increased activity around Cold Creek.

The town was growing and everything was changing. My mother's boarding house was so busy now that she had to hire two full-time people to help. The hat shop went over big. Lucy and my wife Ann were doing quite well. Emmett did get the U.S. Deputy Marshal's appointment; but still remained the town Marshal of Cold Creek, and I remained his Deputy. There was a lot more responsibility for me, being senior deputy, and Emmett having business out of town pretty regular due to his new appointment. Ben's business grew to where there was a need to build on an addition to the new stables.

There were a lot more exploits that Emmett and I experienced through our years together. It wasn't the last we heard of Standing Eagle. Jesse Wonderland didn't make it to town often, but when he did, he came unarmed. It was finally decided to build a courthouse. Yes, Cold Creek was starting to make a real mark on the map.